Over the Wall

John H. Ritter

PUFFIN BOOKS

PUFFIN BOOKS
Published by the Penguin Group
Penguin Putnam Books for Young Readers,
345 Hudson Street, New York, New York 10014, U.S.A.
Penguin Books Ltd, 80 Strand, London WC2R ORL, England
Penguin Books Australia Ltd, Ringwood, Victoria, Australia
Penguin Books Canada Ltd, 10 Alcorn Avenue, Toronto, Ontario, Canada M4V 3B2
Penguin Books (N.Z.) Ltd, 182-190 Wairau Road, Auckland 10, New Zealand

Penguin Books Ltd, Registered Offices: Harmondsworth, Middlesex, England

First published in the United States of America by Philomel Books,
a division of Penguin Putnam Books for Young Readers, 2000
Published by Puffin Books,
a division of Penguin Putnam Books for Young Readers, 2002

5 7 9 10 8 6 4

THE LIBRARY OF CONGRESS HAS CATALOGED THE PHILOMEL EDITION AS FOLLOWS:
Ritter, John H., date
Over the wall / by John H. Ritter.
p. cm.
Summary: Thirteen-year-old Tyler, who has trouble controlling his anger, spends an
important summer with his cousins in New York City, playing baseball and
sorting out how he feels about violence, war, and in particular the
Vietnamese conflict that took his grandfather's life.
[1. Anger—Fiction. 2. Violence—Fiction. 3. Baseball—Fiction. 4. Cousins—Fiction.
5. Vietnamese Conflict, 1961-1975—Fiction. 6. New York (N.Y.)—Fiction.]
I. Title.
PZ7.R5148 Ov 2000 [Fic]—dc21 99-049911
ISBN 0-399-23489-6

Puffin Books 0-698-11931-2

Printed in the United States of America

To my Sky Pilot,

Ch. (Col.) Edwin Christian Gomke,

United States Army (retired),

for your many acts of loyalty and courage

above and beyond the call.

You teach and touch us all.

This book, like most, is indeed the end result of the efforts of many. I wish to thank all of those who shared with me their eyewitness accounts, offered feedback, or otherwise had a hand in its creation, including my father and mentor, Carl W. Ritter, my wife and teacher, Cheryl B. Ritter, Vietnam War scholars Dr. Ralph K. Beebe, Dr. James Reckner, and Prof. Lawrence Tritle, as well as James Wingfield, Samantha Churchill, Benjamin Ritter, Brian Ritter, Bill Ethridge, Mike O'Sullivan, Amy Granite, Beth Wagner Brust, Jayne Haines, Maria Biard, Liz and Scott Wing, and the real sharpshooter of this whole dang outfit, my editor, Michael Green.

With love—JHR.

"IF YOU HAVE AN OPPORTUNITY TO MAKE THINGS BETTER, AND YOU DON'T DO THAT, YOU ARE WASTING YOUR TIME ON THIS EARTH."

—ROBERTO CLEMENTE,
PITTSBURGH PIRATES, 1971

chapter 1

PEOPLE SAY TIME HEALS ALL WOUNDS. I USED TO think so. Now I know better.

Time won't heal anything.

Time is nothing but a stack of yesterdays. Nothing but a stack of full moons waiting for a new one. Or a stack of memories waiting for a better one.

I've always known there was a pull to the moon. Standing on the edge of the Pacific Ocean, my mom once told me that's what makes the tides roll in and out. But I never knew how much one or two memories could tug at your brain. Or that a single yesterday could pull down all of your tomorrows.

You see, back when I was four years old, my dad did something that shook our family like an earthquake. Like one side of the earth just took and shook loose from the other, shook down California, the mountains, the oak trees and boulders, and rattled every inch of that rickety old ranch house we lived in, too.

And it's pretty much been like that ever since.

I'll never forget the date. August 12, 1990.

I was in the side yard that dry, windy day, under a huge pepper tree. The Santa Ana breezes lifted the long, feathery branches that usually broomed the ground, lifted them like leafy banners that flickered and tickled my arms and face.

Mom and Dad were in the house. My six-year-old sister, Alyssa, was hiding next to a cracked, gray-granite boulder alongside the garage.

I took a step toward her, but she shooshed me away, shaking her head and putting a finger to her lips. So I froze.

Dad pushed open the front screen door, jangling his keys.

All set with his clipboard and map book to go check out a landscaping job, he crossed the wood plank porch and hopped into his work truck with its fat, old camper shell.

"Tyler's out here!" he shouted back at the house. "He's all by himself."

But, no, I wasn't. My big sister, Alyssa, who I called Lissie, was right with me. Only now she'd crept up near the red rock wall along the concrete driveway. To hide from Dad. To play a trick on Dad.

Couldn't he hear her giggle? It was contagious. I put my hand over my mouth and I giggled, too.

When Mom looked out the front door, I watched her eyes find me, then search for Lissie.

But I was the only one on earth who knew where she was. I saw her crawl beneath the coyote brush that grew along the red rock wall. Right in front of me. Saw her waddling on all fours with her daylily sundress bottom stuck up in the air, like a pesky skunk sneaking up on a cat food dish.

Sneaking around the back of the truck to the camper shell door, Lissie raised up over the bumper, her hand reaching for the silver door handle.

Going to climb inside, I could see. Like we always did. To hide among the tools in the thick, black air of gasoline engines and motor oil and sacked-up grass clippings rotting into sweet mounds of mulch.

And I remember jumping up and down as she swung the camper door open—clamping my mouth so I wouldn't give away our joke on Dad.

Then, *clunk*.

The big truck's gearbox clanked, metal into metal. Before Lissie could step up, the truck started rolling backwards, down the concrete drive.

Lissie screamed as it knocked her over.

Knocked her over and kept on coming until I ran up yelling and banging on the door.

"Daddy, stop, *stop!* You runned over Lissie!"

Even going so slow, his tires screeched to a concrete skid. He bolted out of the cab and sprinted to the back of the truck.

Mom came running, too, and helped Dad drag Lissie out from under the bumper, and she was bawling, screaming through the blood of a busted lip. But she wasn't crushed. No wheels had rolled over her daylily dress. No sign of big damage anyplace.

No outward sign at least. By looking, you couldn't tell that a blood vessel had burst somewhere in her brain.

From then on, my memory gets foggy. I don't

remember how or when exactly, but I know that night she died.

And I know that from then on our house grew dark and quiet.

Over the next few days a line of people came to our door. People came to tell my father that it wasn't his fault. That of course he'd been careful, that of course he'd thought Alyssa was safe and sound inside the house. That it was an honest mistake.

They let him know that they knew how he must feel. And they let him have his dark days, his dark thoughts, and his dark face.

No one bothered to say much to me, though. I was too young.

But, see, I not only lost my sister that day, I lost my father, too.

No, worse than that.

I had an empty shell of a father. This part-time, odd-jobbing, tree-trimming ghost of a father. A walking weed-whacker is what I had. And people said, over and over, "Just give him time." But weeks and months had turned into years, and all that time didn't change a thing.

At church Mom had been telling people, "Now, you'll have to forgive Lyle. He's been a little preoccupied lately with getting his business back on track." Then she'd whisper through gentle lips, "Since the *accident*. He's trying, though. Bless his heart, he's trying."

Dad's business was mowing lawns. And he'd been

trying now for nine years. Ever since that summer day back in 1990.

Meanwhile, Mom and I walked around on eggshells. Lived our lives on cracked eggshells. Talking neutral, talking easy, not doing anything that might upset Dad. Of course, Mom was better at that than me.

Me, I'd bust an eggshell every once in a while. Smash my boot down and shatter it all over everywhere sometimes. I'd slam out of the house, grab some rocks, and blast away at an old pile of broken statues and stuff leaning up against the toolshed wall.

I mean, Mom had her sad days, too. I knew she did. But at least she had her garden.

Grew big, green, jalapeño peppers, huge red tomatoes, and silky tasseled ears of white corn sweet as watermelon. She could bury herself in those vegetable beds for hours.

I'd pray that Mom would always have her garden.

And I'd pray that one day Dad would see what he was doing to us. How he was making us outsiders in our own home. That he'd see and he'd change. But it was like he was facing a big stone wall. And he couldn't see a thing.

In our house, Dad got all the sadness.

And we got all the grief.

And after nine years I was tired of it. Tired of watching him get all teary-eyed over some little girl in a hamburger commercial. Clamming up. Drifting off. I couldn't take it. I wanted my dad back.

Because, you see, there'd be other days when he

seemed okay. Almost normal. Watching baseball games on TV. Talking to the hitters, telling them which pitch was coming next.

There'd be days when Dad and I would walk outside with our baseball caps and gloves, past the rope clothesline and eucalyptus trees, and down into the black clay meadow. And we'd play catch over the yellow tops of the wild mustard plants.

He'd even rattle off old-time baseball stories about guys like Bob Gibson and Don Drysdale, Roberto Clemente and Carl Yastrzemski.

I loved when he did that. Because I loved baseball.

And Dad did, too.

"Ol' Yaz," he'd tell me, "had the quickest hands I ever saw. Gibson and Drysdale were the meanest pitchers. Crowd the plate on them, and they'd knock you down. But Roberto—he had all the tools. Great hitter, great fielder. Man, he was fun to watch." Then after a moment, he'd softly add, "Too bad he died at the top of his game."

Once we'd warmed up, Dad would throw batting practice and have me guess which pitch was coming. Curve ball? Sinker? Fastball? Change?

"I'm mixing 'em up like ol' Bob Gibson," he'd say.

"And I'm hitting 'em out like Roberto Clemente," I'd shout back.

But that would only last for so long. After a while, one of my fly balls would go unchased. Dad would stare off, acting like he was watching where it landed. But he was seeing other stuff.

And pretty soon he'd wander up toward the toolshed, get out his wrenches, and work on his lawn mowers. Or head off downslope toward the empty horse corral, into the shadows of the eucalyptus trees, and sit and stare till the moon came up.

And everyone understood. Everyone knew it wasn't his fault.

But in school, I had learned about earthquakes. And I had learned about faults. And every earthquake has one. A fault, that is. Sometimes it runs right along the surface. Sometimes it's just too deep to see

So when Aunt Chrissy and Uncle Phil called from New York City to invite me for the second year in a row to spend the summer hitting, chasing, and throwing baseballs on the old-fashioned, tree-bordered ball fields of Central Park, I didn't hesitate.

I took one look out the torn screen door, into the searing May-day heat of the chaparral mountainside, past the goats and dogs fighting in the trash over empty cans of refried beans, past a long line of upside-down lawn mower carcasses strewn across the oily front yard, and I said, "Yeah, I'll come."

See, baseball was my life. To me, baseball was dream-come-true territory, but it was set in a world you could count on. A world that was umpired, where everything was either fair or foul, ball or strike. It was a place where you couldn't just sit and stare and be an empty shell.

"Good for you, Tyler," said Uncle Phil, who had a loud, salesman way of talking. "But it's going to be a lot tougher this year. Older boys, you know. Thirteen and fourteen. Some tough city kids on those teams. And you'll be one of the youngest."

I nodded, even though I was on the phone. Then I said, "Yeah, that's all right."

I mean, I might've been just thirteen and I might've been small for my age, but I played baseball like I was going to battle. To me, nothing else was worth fighting for. Nothing else really mattered.

So bring it on, I felt like saying. *Bring it on.*

After all, how many of them city boys'd ever been through an earthquake?

chapter 2

"THE NUMBER ONE THING A PRO SCOUT LOOKS for," our New York coach told us, "is a guy who's head and shoulders above the rest. Not just an All-Star. They're looking for the guy who thrives on pressure. The *star* of the All-Stars."

It was two and a half weeks later, at the end of my first practice. I glanced at my cousin Louie, who seemed bigger than ever in his catcher's chest pad and shin guards. And I winked.

He just shook his head, half grinning. As if to say, "No chance."

But he knew better. The way cousins know cousins.

He already knew what I was thinking. That I'd decided right then, I was going to be that star.

Three days later, I was smack in the middle of my first game in Central Park's North Meadow. And though I'd played Little League here last year, these guys were older, bigger, and stronger. Even so, I figured it was time to show this coach—Coach Trioli—what I could do.

So when I stood in the batter's box in the final inning of that game—score tied, 2–2—I was focused and I was ready to do a little earth shaking of my own.

Squinting out across the ball diamond, some 250 feet away, I eyed the flimsy outfield fence made of skinny redwood slats wired together.

Well, at least this field had a fence, I thought. Most of them here didn't.

Farther out, a line of huge oaks, walnut trees, and sycamores flickered in the afternoon breeze. The sticky, muggy East Coast air had cooled some, leaving the sweat in my green-sleeved Munibank uniform caked-up and stiff as it rode against my skin.

The third baseman turned to the outfielders. "Move in!" he shouted. "Little guy. No power."

No power? I thought. Yeah, you watch.

I snugged my helmet against my skull, my eyes fixed on the pitcher's right shoulder. Never his face. Never his eyes. I wouldn't play that stupid stare-down game.

The only image in my brain was a deep fly ball. Real deep.

Every day I did a hundred push-ups. Building my upper body strength. Hoping to do one thing I'd never done before. This season I was determined to hit one over the wall.

"Tyler!" Coach Trioli called from the third base coach's box, trying to get my attention so he could flash me a sign. He clapped his hands, iron hands that clanged more than clapped, sending tremors rippling through his thick biceps. I stepped out and gave him a quick glance.

Skin, buckle, skin. Two claps.

Bunt sign! No way, I thought. C'mon, Coach.

I glanced down, then out at the left-field fence. Acting. Pretending like maybe I missed the sign. I mean, I knew what he was thinking. He wanted me to bunt my way on, then use my speed to steal second, and let someone like Louie come up and drive me in.

Well, "Fuh-get about it," as Louie would say. This pitcher had a fastball that would fly off my bat. I had to swing away. Besides, I had talents Coach Trioli needed to know about. And this was the perfect time to show him.

"Hey, Orange Head," the first baseman yelled at me. "What'd you do? Shampoo with carrot juice?"

I ignored the jerk. He wasn't going to rattle me over my hair color.

The tall, chunky kid on the pitcher's mound glared in at the catcher, taking his sign.

I calculated the odds of the first pitch being a curve. I knew the guy had a blazing fastball, but I figured he'd show me his slow curve first to mess up my timing. Then he'd try to rifle a few inside fastballs past me.

And sure enough. A big, fat curve floated past my gut.

I didn't move.

"Stee-rike," the umpire called.

"Tyler!" Coach yelled again. "Come on, now. Pay attention."

He went through the signs once more. Skin, buckle, skin.

I wrinkled my forehead—acting confused—then shuffled back into the batter's box and got set.

Coach, you gotta understand, I thought. I have a feeling.

It's like that feeling I'd get sometimes when my dad was pitching, and I felt firm and focused. Felt like I could hit one over the waxy, dark green laurel sumac bushes and into the scraggly branches of the flattop buckwheat.

Please, I prayed. This pitch. A fastball. Inside. Belt high.

The instant I saw the pitcher bring his arm forward, I lifted my front foot, cocked my hands back, then set my shoe down just the way Tony Gwynn taught. "So soft, you wouldn't hurt an ant."

And the pitch started out right where I imagined it. No, better! Not inside, but over the heart of the plate.

I crushed it.

For a split second I just wanted to stand there and watch. The ball shot off the bat, arcing through the sky like a missile into the right-center gap.

Was it? I wondered. Was it my first real home run?

Rounding first, I caught a better angle and realized it would come up short. Like a dying bird, it plopped against the base of the fence and bounced off.

I dug for second. Triple, I was figuring. With my speed, I could make third easy and be only one base away from scoring the winning run! I pumped with my arms, digging the dirt with my cleats, leaning hard into the turn at second.

Everyone yelled. My team, their team, the fans. But

I didn't hear a word. Just the jet wash of wind past the ear holes in my helmet.

As I approached second, the center fielder ran down the ball. He made a strong throw to the shortstop, but I never broke stride, hoping I could beat the shortstop's relay to third.

I didn't. But as the ball entered my vision I could tell it would airmail the third baseman and skip into the chain-link fence behind him.

At third, Coach gave me the stop sign, two hands held high.

No! I thought. Why stop now? I knew I could beat the throw home. It'd have to be perfect to get me. Besides, I had to show these guys. I had to make a statement.

Halfway to home plate, I realized that all I'd made was a stupid move.

The pitcher had backed up third. His throw shot past me toward home.

Oh, great, I thought. I'm dead.

But the throw short-hopped the catcher and bounced into his gut. He fell forward smothering the ball while hard, shin-guard plastic scraped against the dirt.

I had one chance.

Before he could gather up the ball, I started my lunge. Headfirst. Like some sneak-attack dive-bomber on a do-or-die mission, I aimed way off the baseline, on the pitcher's side of home plate.

Then, stretching out with all my four feet ten and a

half inches, I reached around the catcher's knees and tagged the scuffed, white plate with my right hand.

In the same instant, he pounded my head with his mitt. Hard. He swung like a hammer driver busting up a stone wall. *Wham!* A cracking thunk against my helmet that sent it flipping off my head toward the pitcher's mound and sent me twisting backwards like a shot dog.

But, so what? He was too late.

I'd just *won the game!*

In the powdery dust of the infield, I rolled once more, onto my stomach, taking in the boom of the crowd's roar, and knowing that what I'd just done was the type of thing that got you noticed. The type of thing an All-Star star would do. Under pressure.

Yes! I thought. Perfect.

"You're out!" screamed the umpire.

"Yo!" said the catcher, showing me the ball. "You're out cold, sucker." He jumped over me and scampered off. I felt the ball drop on my ribs and bounce away.

chapter 3

A FRESH RUSH OF ADRENALINE SURGED THROUGH me.

Pushing myself up, I yelled, "What do you mean, *out?* No way! I was in there."

The umpire—some thick-necked, teenage dropout from car-jack school—pointed at the plate. "You missed the base."

"No stinking way!" I walked over, crouched down near home plate. "Right here! I got my hand in."

He gazed at my paw print like it was a new scientific discovery. "Too late," he said. "After the tag."

By then my coach was on the scene. Coach Trioli and Louie, then practically the whole team, came rolling up, roaring. They'd seen it. They knew.

"He was in there!" said Louie.

"Who *you* tellin'?" said Eugene, our second baseman. "He was safe as a baby in lace!"

"All the way," said our pitcher, Tony. "He beat the tag!"

I shot to my feet. "The guy didn't even have the ball!" I shouted. "He was juggling it."

Coach Trioli grabbed my shoulders from behind and

steered me aside. "It's all right, Tyler," he said. "I'll handle this."

But no way. As big as Coach was, I shrugged him off. There was a principle involved here. I was safe. They called me out. And that was wrong.

"I had him dead!" the catcher called from his on-deck circle, still in his shin guards. He pointed. "You never got close, you little clown boy!"

I ran right over to him. Those guys'd been dissing me all game, making fun of my height, my curly orange hair, whatever they could pick on. And I'd had enough.

"You lying sack of dog diarrhea." I gave him an elbow across the chest, trying to shove him backwards, but he wouldn't budge.

Coach Trioli was there in a flash. He jammed his forearm under my chin and spun me around. "Tyler, knock it off! Whata ya, nuts?" He dragged me toward the dugout, then raised his voice. "Everyone, just go back. Now! Let me handle this."

I froze. Somewhere in the back of my brain, a little common sense started ticking. My first game here, I couldn't go completely ballistic. Besides, Mr. Trioli wasn't just this team's coach, he also coached the All-Star team at the end of the season.

So, out of respect, I backed off.

All I did was lean under Coach's elbow and jab my finger at that fat catcher. "You missed me and you know it."

"You're full of California duck squat," he shot back. "Somebody oughtta hose you off. You're drawing flies."

"Yeah, and I'll be drawing blood in about two seconds," I promised.

"Tyler!" Coach Trioli pushed me away. "Back off! Now!"

By then, the fans were aiming their shots at me, too.

"Sit down, you little Bozo Head!" one man yelled.

"Watch your mouth, little boy!" screamed someone's mom.

I looked into the green-board bleachers, full of old yuppie parents, mean-eyeing me over mountain bikes and stroller handles.

"You wanna be next?" I shouted at the closest one. "Come on down here, you ignorant—"

Now Louie grabbed me, pushing hard. "Shut *up*, Tyler. You're an idiot! Just cool it. Let Coach handle this. You're gonna get thrown out, man."

I snatched at my cousin's fists as they squeezed my shirt, twisting me close. Louie was bigger, stronger, and a year older, so all I could really do was slap away at him. Which only boiled my blood more. "Let go of me!"

He ran me backwards, all the way past our dugout, his breath blasting against my face. "Stop it, Tyler!" he said. "Right now. And don't move. Or *I'll* kick your butt."

I knew Louie was not a fist fighter. Strong, yes. A tough talker, sure. And he could blast you out of the sky in any computer game there was. But he never fought anybody for real and he wasn't going to fight me here.

But no way was he going to hold me back, either. Especially not with everybody watching. I flung my body sideways with all my might.

Then, white! A white flash came. Boiling white.

I knew that might happen. And I let it come.

I twisted, burst free, felt my shirt rip.

"Tyler!" someone screamed. Louie?

I swung away. At something, at anything. That's all I can remember.

"Tyler!" Louie's hot breath poured over me.

That's when I realized that Louie and two other guys were holding me back, shoving me against the chain-link fence way up the third-base line.

That's when I saw the blood in Louie's mouth. Saw him turn and spit a string of red into the dirt.

"You jerk," he said. "Why'd you go and do that?" He shoved me once more, this time in disgust, then let me go.

The other guys turned to Louie. "You okay?" asked Tony.

Louie spit again, touching his finger to his mouth, and slowly they all walked off to meet Coach Trioli coming back from home plate.

And, man, I felt like a world-class jerk. I'd slugged my own cousin. How stupid was that? I stood there leaning against that fence, feeling lower than the worst traitor in history.

In a gray fog, I realized that the game was resuming. Guys were taking the field. Coach was coaching, barking. Maybe he didn't even know what I'd done.

I wandered into the dugout, grabbed my glove, and straggled off.

Just outside, Coach took my arm.

"Hold on, Tyler," he said. "Where you going?"

"Out there." I pointed to shortstop.

"No, you don't. Didn't you hear the man? You're tossed."

"I'm what?" I spun around. "What for?"

"Look, hotshot. There's a rule against fighting. You shoved that guy and you're out of the game."

I stood, mouth open, glaring at the field. "I barely pushed him."

He squeezed my arm, staring straight into my face. "Hey, what's your problem anyway? You hear me? I mean, yeah, okay, you're only in New York for the summer, so maybe all this doesn't mean jack to you. And believe me, we got no shortage of hotheads and loudmouths out here ready to run around and act like idiots. But on my team, no one acts like that. Other coaches might put up with it—look the other way because you've got a little talent—but not me. You got that?"

I hung my head, studying my toes as his words rained down on me. Then I nodded, turned, and headed back to the dugout.

"And one more thing," he said, following me to the bench. "Skin, buckle, skin."

Oh, no, I thought. Here it comes. He was busting me for swinging through the bunt sign.

I raised my eyebrows, making my face the most

innocent I could. "Yeah," I said. "That's hit-and-run. But there was nobody on base, so I was confused."

"It was the *bunt* sign. Hit-and-run is skin, hat, skin. Hat for *hit*, buckle for *bunt*."

He didn't say it like he was teaching me, but with disgust, like he knew I was lying. "Been here long enough," he said. "No excuse not knowing our signs."

I could've crawled under the bench like a horse-kicked coyote. Now I'd lied to him.

Coach Trioli turned and called to our pitcher. "Benny, top of the order. You know what to do. Tight defense, everyone!"

But by the next inning, we'd lost. Tony took over for me at short, booted a ball with a guy on second, and they beat us, 3–2.

A game we should've won, sure, but that wasn't what bothered me. Lying to the coach—so automatically, without a thought—that bothered me. Losing control and hitting my cousin—that bothered me.

On the long walk home, Louie asked, "What were you doing out there, anyways? Jumping that guy like that."

He gave my shoulder a playful shove, causing my sports bag to slip off. I didn't respond. I learned that's the best way to handle it when you screw up. Pretend like you're still mad and blame someone else. "The guy's a jerk."

"Oh, yeah?" he said. "That why you hit me? Because *he's* a jerk?"

"You should've let me go."

"Dude, you were nutso. I never saw you like that. You blew it, too, man. Because Coach likes you. Don't ask me why. You're a real pain in the *buttocks*. But he does." Louie stopped, looking at me to see if I'd match his grin. I didn't. I just couldn't let myself smile.

Louie grunted. "Good thing you hit like a girl," he said, then walked on ahead.

And I let him. I focused in on the grime-stained sidewalk, the row of green, plastic trash barrels, overflowing into the street, the chained-up bicycles lining the black iron rails that ran in front of all the old-time apartment buildings, anything to ignore the fact that, bottom line, he was right. I had blown it big time.

Out of everything that was wrong with me—and believe me, I had a list—the one thing I hated most was my stupid, white-hot anger. Going "nutso."

I mean, I'd always had a bit of a hot temper. Why not? I played with a ton of emotion. That's how I was. But these past few months, I'd noticed something else. That it was getting stronger. And hotter.

And I knew what it could do. Today showed me that. Not only did I hurt Louie, but I also hurt myself, hurt my chance to make a good impression on Coach Trioli for All-Stars.

And as I shuffled down this tree-lined street, dodging dogs on leashes and little old people dressed in big, long coats, I promised myself that I wouldn't let it hurt anyone else.

chapter 4

BY THE TIME LOUIE AND I'D REACHED THE CORNER of 96th and Columbus, he was ready to turn back around and start joking with me. That's how he liked to make peace. He made jokes.

And I welcomed it, though I never said so.

"Yo, I was just wondering," he asked, thumb-tapping the side of his gear bag. "What were you gonna do if Coach hadn't pulled you off that guy? Were you gonna jump on his back and ride him like a surfboard?"

"Yeah, right, Goofy Foot." I gave Louie a quick kick in the back country as he dodged away. "That's about all you New York City guys know about California. You think the whole state's full of surfers and beach babes."

"Yeah, well, that," said Louie, "and orange-colored airheads."

"Shut up," I said, whipping off my cap, fluffing my curly mop, and feeling a bit better now that we were teasing each other.

And my hair actually was a pretty good target. It was naturally curly, which was goofy enough, but last month I dyed it stop-sign red. Then the principal at my church school got all hissy and said it was disruptive.

But when I tried to bleach it back to blond, it came out orange. So I left it. I mean, big deal, these days.

Anyway, as soon as The Carpenter's Son Lutheran School let out in late May, I packed my glove, my cleats, and my camera and hopped on a jet plane east to stay with my dad's sister, Aunt Chrissy, and Uncle Phil, and my two cousins, Breena and Louie. They went to a private school, too, though it was ten times bigger and more ritzy than mine.

But this year we timed it so that after I finished up the first half of my baseball season back home, I got here just a few weeks before the second half of the Uptown Riverside Baseball League. That was important. To be able to play in both leagues. Because, you see, I had a plan.

Once I got my height—soon, Mom thought, now that I'd turned thirteen—I planned to bulk up and shoot for the big leagues. That's why I did a hundred push-ups a day. And that's why I didn't mind leaving my little town out east of San Diego and flying way back here to play on these bombed-out, bad-hop ball fields in Central Park. I mean, me and baseball—hey, we belonged together like peanut butter and jelly or beans and tortillas.

Besides, the way I saw it, if I could make a name for myself in Manhattan *and* get a good reputation going for me as a high school freshman next year in San Diego County, that would double my chances of being noticed.

Which is what I was shooting for. Making a baseball scout's report.

And Mom liked me coming here. She worked as a physical therapist for a sports doctor, and someone in her office told her it'd be a good idea if I got away for a while. That way, she and Dad could have some time alone to "try to work through some things."

Well, good luck, I figured. Dad go to counseling? I mean, he seemed so wrapped up in himself, I doubted he'd ever see anybody else's side of things.

He sure never saw mine.

Without baseball, we'd have nothing in common. At least he liked to watch the games. Especially the big games, like the play-offs and World Series. That's what was so cool about the '98 season. When our team, the San Diego Padres, went to the play-offs and beat the Astros and the Braves, and then faced the New York Yankees in the World Series, I'd never seen my dad look so alive.

Even after the Padres lost—got swept in four games—the sparkle stayed for a while. Stayed in his eyes the way all those San Diego fans stayed in the stadium and gave the Padres a *twenty-minute* standing ovation just for having a great season.

That's what you do in a town that loves baseball.

And that's what you see in a guy who loves the game, too.

So that was another reason, I guess, why I tried so hard in baseball. Crazy as it sounds, after I saw the effect those games had on Dad, I figured maybe if I did good in baseball, if I could really shine in some big, important games, then maybe I could put that spark back into his eyes again.

Even for twenty minutes.

"Hey, Louie," called Ali, outside his little market on Broadway. "Tell your mama, tangelos!" The dark-skinned, bald man pointed to four green and white boxes propped up on a plywood tabletop set over two rusty filing cabinets. "Fresh, ripe tangelos all this week." He polished one against his dark green apron until the fruit glistened.

"They gotta be sweet," said Louie as he secretly nudged my arm. "Not just shiny. I can't send my mother down here for sour fruit."

Ali must've seen the nudge. "They plenty sweet," he said, then tapped his fingertips into the palm of his hand. "Sweet as the money it takes to buy them." He waved us off. "No free samples."

"Okay, okay," said Louie as we rambled by. "I'll give her the big news." He rapped his knuckles on the makeshift fruit stand.

Two steps later we heard Ali yell, "Hey, you boys!"

We turned just in time to snag two bright orange tangelos floating our way and to catch a glimpse of Ali's smooth bald head as he disappeared into his shop.

And stuff like that was just one reason why—contrary to what you might guess—I liked it here in the Big Apple Sauce.

See, I was from a small town. And New York City's got a real small town feel to it—I mean, if you don't look up.

They've got a corner grocery, corner drugstore, doughnut shop, whatever, on practically every block. You pass people on the street who get to know you, people who remember your face. There's local gossip going on, all of that.

And pretty soon you realize that people in New York really don't think that anything very important ever happens anywhere else, which is, of course, real small-town thinking.

But I liked the people, even though at first they seemed to have this automatic hatred of anyone from anyplace else. Especially California. Then I realized, it wasn't hatred. They just liked to make fun of other people. For laughs. Part of their culture. After I learned that, it didn't seem so bad.

There were people who did that to newcomers in our little town, too. Which only proved what Uncle Phil— who's a native New Yorker—always said. "New York is just your basic small town piled higher and deeper."

But, of course, there were some big differences. Like having this hard sidewalk under my shoes all the time, instead of a powdery dirt path.

And the noise. Screech-clanging trash trucks at the break of dawn. Jackhammers all day, music blaring all night. Not to mention the horn-honking street traffic screeching and roaring anytime at all.

And people, people, people. Everywhere you go. You're never alone. Swarms of people, all in dark, bulky clothes, looking slightly worried and very important as they scamp and scramble the streets like cattle.

On the other hand, there's tons of good stuff, too. Something's always happening. And I mean *always*. Sometimes Aunt Chrissy would take us out for ice cream at midnight, and you'd think it was the middle of the day. People cruising the sidewalks, having dinner, shooting hoops, playing tunes.

Streets are safe, too. I mean, if you don't do something stupid. Cops are everywhere. Walking in pairs or groups. Or in cars. Or on bikes. Which bugs us because they hassle bike riders for, like, nothing. One day I almost got a summons—that's a ticket—for riding on the sidewalk. Ten minutes later, I *got* one for riding on the grass! They got rules here against every little thing.

But one of the biggest differences for me was Sunday. At home I'd just finished my Lutheran confirmation classes and I was an acolyte, which meant I had to show up early for church, put on a silky white robe, light the candles, and set out the wine chalice and wafers if it was Communion.

Here, we didn't even go to church. It was like, once my plane touched down, my whole routine went on vacation. And I was free in ways I'd never been free before.

Most of all, I was free to play baseball and try to squeeze my scrawny self onto the Uptown Riverside All-Star team.

"So what do you wanna do tonight?" Louie asked as we kicked plastic water bottles down Broadway, past ancient, narrow storefronts slapped one upside the other, all sitting under three or four layers of dog-dreary apartments. Some days we rode our bikes to the games, sometimes we walked. Today, we'd had lots of time, so we hoofed it. "Wanna rent some videos?"

I jumped up on a blue mailbox bolted to the sidewalk, leaped off the top of it, and slapped the droopy wings of a red canopy covering the entrance to a Pakistani restaurant.

"Whatever's clever," I said, after I landed and noticed two girls staring at me. Then I added, "Tony Gwynn's supposed to have a new video out. On hitting. We oughtta get that."

"Yo," said Louie, "I was thinking more like *Playboy Bunnies on Parade*. You know, something educational."

I spoke a little louder for the benefit of the girls. "Yeah, well, learning how to hit four hundred in the majors is educational enough for me." Then, as we crossed the street, I added, "You know, maybe we could get 'em both."

We turned down 91st to our place near Riverside Drive.

Uncle Phil was some kind of wholesale, international merchandiser or something—a glorified traveling salesman, as far as I could tell—but lately he'd been making huge commissions, cranking the big bank, so he'd moved his family into this deluxe, three-bedroom apartment up on the twelfth floor of some ancient-looking, stone-stacked building with thick shoots of ivy jungling up the wall.

It had everything you could dream of, too. From cable TV and Internet hookups in all the rooms to skateboards, blades, and mountain bikes in the front closet. Plus a treetop view of Riverside Park and the Hudson River beyond.

"Not bad for a former Air Force flyboy," Uncle Phil liked to say.

But he was never home, it seemed like. Or even in the country. And Aunt Chrissy was out a lot, too. That is, she was off. Constantly "going off." If she wasn't out fixing herself up, she was out fixing the world, volunteering at the thrift store for Louie and Breena's private school or at some sort of "function" for, say, The Metropolitan Museum of Art.

We'd be doing something, watching BET in our room, playing twitch games on the PlayStation, whatever, and she'd shoot down the dark, oak-paneled hallway heading for the door.

"I'm off," she'd say. And next time we'd see her would be around 9:00 or 10:00 at night. Which meant, of course, that we ate dinners late and, most of the time, the three of us cousins had total free run of a pretty cool place.

"Hello, Pedro," Louie said, greeting the elevator attendant, as we entered the building. "Mom home yet?"

From the elevator platform, Pedro shook his head. "Not yet. How'd you boys do today?"

"We lost," said Louie as we jumped inside for the ride.

"We *won*," I corrected. "Pedro, we got robbed. I hit a home run—well, sort of—on errors. Then I slid home—you should've seen me"—I slapped my hands together—

"headfirst! But the umpire got blinded by the catcher or something, so he called me out."

Pedro hit the button and the door closed. "Too bad," he said. He shook his head and squinted. The elevator rose.

Pedro tilted his head like he was checking for cobwebs. That was the basic code of elevator men, Louie had explained to me. After the general greeting, it was always, don't ask, don't tell. And don't see, don't smell—in the case of boozers.

On the twelfth floor, the door opened and we stepped out. "Thanks, Pedro," we both said.

"You're welcome, boys."

Louie and I clanked down the hallway, lugging our gear. He pushed open the door and—oh, wow. I mean, I'd already been in town almost a week now, but I still couldn't get over the surprise I kept getting every time we came home.

That is, Sabrina, my other cousin. Or Breena, as everyone called her. But to me, she was Wonder Girl.

She sat lounging in an overstuffed chair, painting her toenails and talking on the phone, looking cool in short blue shorts and a tank top.

See, that was all different to me. Not her clothes. *Her.* She'd always been my "little" cousin, a few months younger than me—and a year behind me in school—but now she was almost two inches taller. And full of *wonder.*

This year, when I showed up, I expected to see the same skin-and-bonesy, metal-mouthed kid I'd left behind last summer. My little buddy, Breena. But, no. I came back and she'd *exploded.* All over the place.

Made you wonder, was all I could say.

"How was your game?" she asked, lowering the phone.

Louie shrugged. "We lost."

"We *won,*" I said again. "The ump was blind."

Louie trudged through the room, calling over his shoulder from the hall. "Mr. Big Mouth here got tossed out for jumping a guy. And I had to rush in and save his life. Save him from being stomped into California duck squat. And for that, he hauls off and slugs me."

"What?" Breena closed her eyes and moaned. "Kelly, can I call you back?" She paused, holding the phone close. "No, no, that doesn't mean she wants breast implants! It could mean lots of things. Okay? Yeah, bye." She beeped the phone off, leaned forward and stared at me. Waiting.

chapter 5

BREAST IMPLANTS? I JUST STARED BACK AT Breena, wondering what she'd been talking to Kelly about. But I didn't say a thing.

For one reason, even on a bad day, Breena was pretty. There were models on magazines who weren't as hot as she was. Or as athletic. Or as nice. That was the strange part. She was pretty *and* nice.

As far as I was concerned, her only real flaw was that she played soccer, of all sports. Baseball, she claimed, was like slow dental work.

"Well?" she finally asked.

"Nothing," I finally said. "It was no big deal." I flopped into the leather couch across the room, untying my shoes. "I scored the winning run. I was safe by a mile, but the umpire couldn't see around the big, fat catcher, so he called me out."

"And so you hit Louie?" She narrowed her eyes and shook her head like she couldn't understand, which made the curled ends of her light brown hair dance along her bare shoulders. Very distracting.

"It was an accident. All these guys grabbed me, and I was just trying to get free." I had to watch what I said here. I knew Breena hated fighting. She was on some "peer arbitration" committee at school and she had no patience for guys who would not settle their differences peaceably.

Besides, unlike me, she was the more sensitive type. She collected these little ceramic birds from this ceramic arts cafe on Amsterdam Avenue that she painted in exact, precise, natural colors. Took days. She even mixed her own paints to get the right shades. After all that, she took them back to the cafe to get them glazed and fired.

Louie thought they were dumb, but I didn't. They were just Breena. Quiet and kind of strange, but so neat to look at.

"Oh, yeah, that's right," said Louie, reentering the room, stripped down to his padded sliding shorts and socks. "He jumps that guy by accident. So Coach pulls him off, and then Mr. Carrot Top here goes playground on me!"

"Tyler Waltern!" said Breena. "I can't believe you did that. You got into a *fight?*"

"No, wait," I said. "I didn't *fight* that stupid Snorlax. Just shoved him around a little. Big deal."

"But you hit Louie!"

"On accident! C'mon." I stood up and walked over to Louie and took a boxer's stance, then slapped him lightly on the cheek. "You gotta learn how to duck, dude."

Louie pressed his lips together. "I gotta learn to smack you cross-eyed. Or from now on, let the other guy do it for me."

"Okay," said Breena, waving her purple nail polish at me. "That settles it. I'm coming to every one of your games from now on."

"What for?" Louie and I both said, almost together.

"Because I can't believe my sweet, curly-haired cousin from La La Land could suddenly turn into some goon from the World Wrestling Federation. So I'm going to be the embarrassment factor."

"Oh," I said, "like I won't fight in front of you?"

"You better not. Or I'll walk straight out onto that field."

I stopped right there. No use arguing. I knew Breena was using all that peer arbitration stuff she'd learned in school. "Peace Patrol," they called it. She had training and everything, which gave her all these dumb ideas and slogans like, "It takes a lot more courage to step back from a fight than to step into one."

Totally backwards, of course. As anyone who'd been in a fight could tell you.

"Well," I said, standing, gathering my things. "Maybe next time I'll just go off and paint my toenails bright purple. That seems to be a much more mature way to act."

With a quick twist, she recapped the bottle and held it up. "Here. Don't let me stop you." She flipped it to me. "Listen, it would take more courage for you to paint your toenails than to hit someone."

Her eyes grew wide, challenging me.

I stared down at the bottle. My cue to exit, I figured. Pronto. I gathered my shoes with one hand, while setting the nail polish down on the teakwood coffee table. No way was she going to trick me into slopping purple goop all over my toenails like I was one of her delicate little birds.

"Hey," said Louie. "Where're you going, tough guy? What're you scared of? I wouldn't be afraid to paint mine. If I felt like it."

"Go ahead, man. I won't stop you." At that point, I knew it was time to leave.

I mean, Louie was a good guy, but his needling could be annoying. And it could push me too far. Besides, I liked him on my side. I thought it was cool that even though he wasn't much of an athlete, he was playing one more year of baseball in the thirteen-and fourteen-year-old division just so we could finally be on the same team together.

Because, to be honest, I was sure he'd rather be on his computer than on a baseball diamond. To put his aviator sunglasses and pilot's cap on, and sink down into his shoot-'em-up war games while bobbing to hard-throbbing hip-hop on his headphones.

He claimed it was good practice for the Air Force.

I thought it was nutso. But we didn't argue about it. And I liked that.

"I'm gonna shower up," I said. "How do you guys stand this muggy air, anyway?" I struck my boxer's pose again and flicked Louie on the other cheek, then left.

And as I walked past the little alcove at the rear of the living room—the "war memorial" I called it—with dark wooden shelves full of dusty old books and pictures of Waltern men in uniform, I paused a moment and peeked in.

First I snuck a quick glance at the five-by-seven color photo of our toolshed with two toilets and a headless Greek god stacked against it. I'd brought the photo last year, along with a bunch of others, after I'd spent all of seventh grade taking tons of pictures. Aunt Chrissy immediately hung it up. She said it had "stark honesty." I said it had rats.

I mean, I only took that picture for a joke.

But next to it hung an old photo that was not a joke. Our grandfather. He'd been a pilot in Vietnam, shot down on New Year's Eve, 1972, during a bombing mission over a place called Haiphong.

"Someday," I said, loud enough for Breena to hear, "my picture'll be on this wall, too. In full uniform." I stood there a moment, long enough to catch her disgusted sigh. Breena's idea of conflict resolution was not exactly in line with the military's.

Then I added, "In a San Diego *Padres* uniform."

This time the sneer came from Louie. "Ha! That's about the only team you'd have a chance for. The Padres are like the U.S. Marines. They're still looking for a few good men."

We both laughed at that—unfair as it was. But ours was an Air Force family through and through, ever since the Army Air Corps days of the First World War.

"Oh, hey, man," said Louie, slipping past me and down the hall. "I just remembered. Did Mom tell you?

This summer she wants to take you to D.C. All of us. To see Grandad's name."

"His what?"

Louie paused at our bedroom door. "On the Vietnam War Memorial. Grandad Waltern's name is on that wall. You've never seen it, right?"

I shook my head.

"Well, Mom wants us all to go. It is *so* awesome."

"What's so awesome?" I asked.

"Nothing," Breena called, as she cleared a spot on the coffee table. She unwrapped a piece of paper that held still another white ceramic bird with a long tail. "It's more depressing than awesome."

"Yo, trip," said Louie, "that monument shows every single person that *died* in the Vietnam War. I'm saying, name after name after name. Like one big, long tombstone. Hero after hero. It is so killer. You gotta see that wall, man. I'm serious. You won't believe it."

Behind me, I heard the clink of ceramic on the teakwood tabletop.

"Yeah," said Breena, slowly, softly. "That's one killer monument."

chapter 6

A FEW DAYS LATER, JUST AS LOUIE AND I WERE
getting ready to leave for our next game, Aunt Chrissy
asked me to come into the kitchen.

"I just got a call from your baseball coach," she said.
"Have a seat, Tyler. We need to discuss a few things."

I slumped into a wooden chair, dropping my sports
bag at my feet, all without looking at her.

Aunt Chrissy struck me as an older version of
Breena. Only with bigger hair and thicker makeup. She
talked like one of those serious ladies on the Shopping
Channel who really wants you to believe everything
she says, but instead you just sat there and wondered
how come her face didn't crack.

"You know what this is about, don't you?"

I shrugged.

"Well, it was nice of Mr. Trioli to call." She emptied
a bag of big, brown mushrooms into a strainer in the
sink. "Judging by what he had to say, he must think a
lot of your talent."

She turned to read my reaction. I lifted my eyebrows
for her.

"You know, my brother—your father—was a bit like
that at your age. High-strung. Impulsive."

"He was? He got angry and stuff?"

"Well, at times. He had his moments. Mostly, Lyle was fun and upbeat. A real creative kid. Always seemed to have some project he was working on. Something artistic."

I huffed out a laugh. "Well, maybe that's how he used to be," I said, remembering the vacant, silent guy he'd become.

Aunt Chrissy leaned low to look at me, placing her hands on the table. "And how *is* Lyle doing now?" she asked.

I glanced up at her. In this apartment the plaster ceilings rose ten feet high and the windows nine. Aunt Chrissy stood framed, like some cut-glass saint, by a huge, bright windowpane trimmed in fancy dark wood.

From that angle, I decided, she'd make an interesting photograph.

"Fine, I guess."

"Is he? Really? Tyler, that means so much." She stepped out of the light, back to the sink. Her hopeful tone made me want to give her something to be hopeful about. "Your dad was always a battler. In his own way, he was a real fighter for what he believed in."

A fighter? I thought. Maybe back when he played baseball. That was probably the last time he really cared about anything. Now I couldn't even get him to come see my games.

"Mom's got some counseling lined up," I said, "but who knows? She's tried that before."

Aunt Chrissy nodded as she ran hot water over the

pile of mushrooms. "Counseling! Yes, your mother mentioned that. Did you know that Sabrina was a peer group counselor for the seventh grade? She reports all kinds of success." She paused. "Might even have a few suggestions for you."

I glanced over at one of Breena's birds—a California quail, complete with a finely speckled neck and a droopy feathered crown—sitting in a three-tiered spice rack. "Yeah, well, she already has." I picked the bird up, then added, "Look, I'm—I just play hard, Aunt Chrissy. That's why they call it hardball. I go all out. And I don't like to get cheated, that's all."

"Well, I wasn't there to see, so I can't comment on that. But this anger business is something you're going to have to get control of, Tyler, or you're never going to get along in life. Never going to be happy."

"I'm happy." I flashed a two-second smile at her.

"I'm sure you're *capable* of happiness." She laid down a white cutting board and placed a few mushrooms on it. "But in the long run, you'll have to learn to deal with problems and setbacks without screaming and threatening people. And without fighting."

"What's so wrong with fighting?" I asked, amazed at Breena's delicate work. I touched the bird's feathery crown. "You're never supposed to fight?"

"I didn't say that. Of course there are times when you have to stand up and defend yourself."

"Okay, that's just what I did. I stood up for myself."

She started slicing. "Is that why you went out and attacked that boy?"

I replaced the speckled bird on the rack. "I didn't *attack* anybody. Besides, the guy was bigger and older than me."

Aunt Chrissy stopped cutting and waited until I looked back at her.

"Maybe *you* should tell me what happened, then," she said.

"Well, I don't know," I said. "I just get, you know, *involved* in the game, that's all. And if they're gonna call me a buncha names and cheat and everything, I'm not just gonna sit there and say, 'Hey, that's cool.' No way."

She set the knife on the counter and turned to face me.

"You will," she said, "if you expect to keep playing baseball with Mr. Trioli. That's exactly what you'll do. Because he won't tolerate—and I won't tolerate—fighting or swearing or poor sportsmanship of any kind. On that field or any place else. Is that clear?"

Okay, I thought, that's enough. I mean, I liked Aunt Chrissy. Even though we lived so far apart, I felt a closeness with her. Closer even than with my parents.

But, see, that's also what I didn't like about her. I wasn't used to letting anyone get too close to me.

I rose, shaking my head.

"Aunt Chrissy, I don't know what Coach told you, but what happened wasn't that bad." I glanced at the clock on the microwave. "Oh, wow, Louie and I better get going. We don't wanna be late. Coach hates that."

"That's right," said Louie, appearing in the kitchen doorway with the clang of his bat bag. "We gotta jet."

Aunt Chrissy eyed Louie, then aimed her glare back at me.

"As long as I've gotten through to you," she said. "You know I trust you boys. I really trust you to behave out there and do the right thing." She took a loud breath. "Do you have your phones?"

"Yeah," Louie answered as he grabbed his bike from the front closet.

"In my bag," I said, slipping into the closet myself. And since I fit right under the shelf, I rolled back out again quicker than Louie.

But not quick enough.

"One last thing, Tyler," said Aunt Chrissy. "Mr. Trioli made it very clear that he wanted to see a whole new level of maturity from you. And soon. Or, as he put it, you could find yourself another way to spend your summer."

chapter 7

BEFORE THE GAME STARTED THAT DAY, COACH Trioli took our team aside. Apparently the guys we were playing had a little reputation.

"Look," he said, "this team's gonna ride you guys, okay? You gotta figure that good players draw that stuff. But if something happens out there, things start getting personal, just back off and keep doing your job. You let me take care of it, okay?"

I nodded, along with everybody else. But I wondered, how could I promise him that?

True to her word, Breena showed up, but had to leave about halfway through the third inning. We were winning 5–2 by then, but the coolest thing was, I'd already had a couple of nice hits. One was an RBI double that I crushed—and she jumped up and screamed like crazy for me.

I wished she could've stayed, but her soccer season was going full blast, so she had to get to practice. Left me standing at shortstop pounding my glove. But feeling pretty good. And pretty much in control.

And Coach'd been right. This team with the yellow caps could talk some trash. And more. When our pitcher, Tony Suarez, started having trouble, one of their guys started yipping and making weird noises.

After Tony walked the next two guys in a row, I decided to do what I could to settle him down.

"Just lob it over, Tony," I called. "They can't hit. This guy won't even swing."

Another ball.

Tony stomped around, then gave the mound a big kick. He was a little guy, short as me, who spoke Spanish a lot when he got angry. But he was a fireballer. Hard, robotlike, straight over the top delivery.

And often in the dirt.

All game long, Louie, our catcher, had a problem stopping the balls and keeping the runners from stealing. And now it was getting worse.

After the last pitch, Louie called time and took a step toward the mound.

"Stay there!" Tony yelled. "I don't need no one talking to me." He wagged his glove, asking for the ball.

Louie stopped in his tracks and threw. "Just take a longer stride," he said, before turning back around. "You wanna bring the ball up."

Little Tony mumbled something in Spanish and stomped around again.

He slid his hat brim over his ear, whomped the ball into his glove, and toed the pitcher's rubber. The runner on second took a big lead.

I fake lunged toward the base, trying to hold the runner close. As I crept back to my position, Tony spun around in a pickoff move and threw me the ball.

At shortstop.

I stood flat-footed and caught it.

"Balk!" said the umpire, raising his arms. "Both runners move up one base."

"What'd I do wrong?" Tony asked. "Why's that a balk?"

"Tony," I said, "on a pickoff, you have to throw to a base." I slammed my glove against my leg for emphasis. "You can't throw to shortstop."

"Then cover the base, *idiota*." He whomped the ball into his glove again. *"El estupido vaquero de California."*

"Hey!" I shot back. "I happen to *hablo español!* And I'm on *your* team, remember? So get a clue. Just throw strikes and shut up. Okay?" I spit on the ground and stared over my shoulder, away from him. Man, I thought, like I need this.

The next pitch hit the front edge of the plate and bounced so high toward the backstop, the runner on third practically walked in.

"Oh, come on!" I shouted. "You can't give the game away!"

Coach called time and came out to the mound. I stood back and waited, but whatever he had to say, it didn't work.

Tony walked the batter in three more pitches. But that wasn't the worst part. The guy ran to first base, and when Louie lobbed the ball back to Tony, the runner kept on going and stole second.

I was screaming like crazy and Tony never even

turned around. Seemed like he was giving up. And in the other dugout I kept hearing that irritating jerk yipping like a little dog.

"C'mon!" I yelled again. "You guys gotta pay attention."

"Tyler," Coach Trioli called from the dugout. "Take a breath. Relax."

I took a breath, all right. You can't shout without one.

Cupping my hand, I turned to the outfield. "Nobody out! Hit the cutoff man! Let's go, now. Everybody wake up!"

Yeah, my blood was starting to bubble. But it wasn't my fault. "C'mon, Tony, throw strikes. Let's get these clowns out."

Well, for once, he listened. He threw the most beautiful, most perfect strike I'd ever seen. Right down the middle, belt high.

The batter whacked it, sent it sailing right between the outfielders. And it rolled forever, into some game on the next field over. Home run.

Coach Trioli called time again and once more headed for the mound. Since Benny Navarro, our other pitcher, was on vacation, I wondered what Coach would do since he couldn't do the smart thing and yank Tony. I stayed put while Louie and the other players ran to the mound. I figured, why bother? Our team needed more than a pep talk.

Then disaster struck.

"Tyler," said Coach. "Come in and pitch."

"Me? I'm not a pitcher."

He flipped me the ball. "You are now."

Tony and I switched positions. The only time I ever pitched was during practice. For fun. Not in a game like this that really meant something.

As I took my warm-up pitches, Coach Trioli stood by silently. When I finished, he had only one thing to say before he left. "Just throw strikes."

Yeah, right. If I could throw the ball exactly where I wanted to, I'd be a pitcher, wouldn't I? I was lucky to get it in the general vicinity.

It took me only two pitches to hit the first guy. Four more to walk the second. What am I doing out here? I wondered. I stink.

Coach never said another word the whole time. No pitching hints, no encouragement, no complaints, nothing.

After I walked the third guy, I turned to our dugout, my hands opened wide. Help me, I thought. Something. I knew my mechanics were ridiculous. Maybe a little clue?

Nothing. Except that annoying "Yip, yip, yip!" from the other team.

"Put the first pitcher back in," some guy yelled. "At least he was good for our batting averages!" Their whole dugout yipped.

I pretended to ignore them, but under my cap brim, I glanced over to spot the loudmouth, a guy whose whole face was one big nose. He forgot I had a ball in my hand. He'd have to face me sooner or later. My memory was long and my arm was strong.

But Tony was not so patient. From shortstop, he sent them a little sign language. They got the message.

"Whooa," they all called, then laughed.

"Tough guy. I'm so scared. *Yip, yip!*"

"Yeah," came a squeaky voice. "Pretty tough for a midget."

More howls.

I marked Squeaky's number, too. Inside fastball for that jerk. Way inside.

"Shake it off, Tony," I said. "No big deal. And everybody, get ready. I'm just gonna put it over. Let's get some outs."

I could tell by Tony's far-off, mad-dog glare that he wasn't even listening.

I shifted into half-go. Batting practice mode.

That was all it took. A single to left. Double into the gap. Four more runs in. The game turned into a real laugher.

Not only that, but when the loudmouth got up, I couldn't even plunk him. Missed his fat head and big, hose-nose four straight times, which proves how wild I was.

On first base, he pulled off his helmet to readjust it. One look at his satellite-dish ears, and I knew why. Looked like Dumbo, the flying elephant.

But after Dumbo flew down to second on the next

pitch, Tony paid me a visit. "Gimme the ball," he said. "But secret. Don't let nobody see."

We talked a while, Louie joined us, and I made the secret transfer while I waved my glove at the outfielders.

I knew what Tony had planned. The hidden-ball trick. He'd stand near second base, wait for the runner to take his lead, then step over and tag him out.

And it worked. Perfectly. Except for one thing.

The umpire didn't see it.

"We got him. We got him," Tony shouted, showing the ball. "He's out."

By the time the field umpire looked over, the base runner was back on second, as safe as ever.

"No," said the ump. "He's in there."

"Oh, come on!" I yelled. "He was totally out."

Tony was steamed. "You gotta watch the game, Blue!" he said. "Gotta pay attention here."

"Just play ball," said the umpire. He pointed at me. "Let's go."

"That stinks," Tony shouted. He fired the ball back to me.

I shook my head. In a closer game, I would've cared. But now, I just wanted to get things over with.

From my stretch, I looked back at Dumbo and heard him say, "You two midgets need to come up with a better play'n that, if you wanna get me out."

What a jerk, I thought. I spun and faked a pickoff toss to second just to watch him dive back.

Two pitches later, Tony ran to the mound and waved

Eugene Jespers in from second. "Let's pick him off," Tony whispered. "But this time, Eugene, you go to the base as a decoy. Then when you leave, I'll sneak around behind him."

Tony's plan was hokey, but I admit, I liked his spirit. Reminded me of me. So as he and Eugene hustled back to their spots, I took off my hat, wiped my forehead, and pretended to concentrate on the batter.

Then I started my stretch.

Dumbo stood right next to the base, aware that Eugene was close by. But as Eugene retreated, Dumbo must've smelled a rat. He barely moved.

Tony broke for second. It was useless, because Dumbo had only taken a small lead.

"Now!" he yelled. "Now!"

That's when I realized Tony's real plan. Yeah, I thought.

I spun around and threw the ball as hard as I could, like I was trying to pick the guy off. But Tony didn't catch it. He let it hit the guy square in the back.

That *thud* was as loud as a bass drum.

Man, I thought, that had to hurt.

The next few seconds were weird, I'm telling you. Dead silence.

Dumbo knelt there, motionless, bent in half. Then all of a sudden, he turned and sprinted right at me. He had wide-open, cold-blooded murder in his eyes. I heard both teams come thundering toward the fight. My guys first, then a swarm of yellow hats, screaming and shouting.

Dumbo shoved an elbow into my throat, knocking me backwards and into the dirt. Tony was right on top of us, kicking and scratching. Other guys latched on, trying to tear us apart.

By the time the dust had settled, I had a sore neck, a numb lip, and Tony was nursing a bloody nose. Who knows what Dumbo felt? But all three of us got kicked out of the game.

And without me and Tony, our team had to forfeit.

To the end, we protested our innocence.

"I was just trying to pick the guy off," I said, totally not believing I could've gotten tossed for that. "It's not fair. It's cheating!"

"It was all his fault," said Tony, pointing at Dumbo. "All he can do is yip and squeal like a little dog. *Perrita, perrita, perrita.*"

"Cork it," said Coach Trioli as he ran us off the field. "I thought I taught you two better'n that." He turned to me. "They let you get away with this stuff in California?"

I could tell he was going to use this as an opportunity to launch into one more of his speeches. And I was not in the mood for it.

"They don't have as many jerks in California!"

"Tyler," he said. "You're gonna be lucky if this league lets you play again."

"Oh, yeah, right!" I slammed my glove on the dugout bench. "Hey, I don't care if they do or not. This league is stupid. I quit."

"Oh, is that what you are?" Coach asked. "A quitter?

You just gonna quit when things don't go your way? Well, hotshot, maybe you should. You gonna be a poor sport, then why don't you just give up on baseball altogether? Maybe it's more'n you can handle."

"Shut up," I said, trying to gather my stuff and leave, and fully wishing I hadn't said what I'd just said. "I can handle anything that comes my way."

Coach Trioli waited a moment. Then he answered softly.

"All right," he said, "handle this. Turn in your uniform. You're off the team."

chapter 8

LOUIE TRIED TO TALK TO ME, BUT I WOULDN'T listen. I got all my gear together, grabbed my bike, and rode off.

In the opposite direction.

Instead of heading home, I rode deeper into Central Park. Past all the gray-haired guys kicking soccer balls between gym bag goals. Past all the younger kids flinging Frisbees in the late afternoon sun. Past a few other baseball games and way out to the last set of ball diamonds where I knew that older Puerto Rican boys played serious baseball with serious faces.

I couldn't believe it. I couldn't believe what I'd just done! No baseball, no All-Stars, no nothing.

I pedaled my bike like crazy up the incline overlooking the ball field and dropped it and my baseball bag in the grass. Under the shady branches of a sprawling tree, I crawled up on top of a black granite boulder. The whistle blast of my breath filled my ears. And I just sat there and wondered, now what?

Okay, you stupid, idiot genius. You got yourself kicked off the baseball team, the one thing in life that you have to have, have to do, or else you'll die, and you had to say something dumb, act like a jerk, and get *kicked off the team.* Kill all chance of a great season. Kill all chance of All-Stars. Maybe even killed your whole future. So, now what?

I didn't know.

I blinked away the sweat from my eyes. Mostly sweat.

At least I'd found a cool, soothing place to be. Something about sitting in the middle of a huge-o park, full of thick grass and shady trees, sitting up high on a boulder, just like one I might find at home, and gazing down at a ball field, with two serious teams going at it, a couple hundred fans picnicking in groups and milling around—something about this whole scene tended to soothe me. A little bit. Let me catch my breath.

Below me, I noticed a group of guys watching the game, dishing out rag talk to the players, jibbing and jiving, reacting to each pitch. Behind them, older men straddled low benches, drinking from bagged-up beer cans, backslapping each other after a joke and a laugh.

For a moment, I thought about getting out my camera, my little Minolta that I took almost everywhere I went, and snapping off a few.

Be some interesting shots, for sure. Ever since seventh grade, taking pictures had become a part of me. It was one way, I guess, that I could step back, step away from my crummy life, and focus on something different. Maybe even capture something good and keep it for the future.

But today I left my camera in the bag. I couldn't pull

back from the world this time. This time, I had to figure out what I was going to do.

Near some trees, younger guys with sculpted, brown arms bursting from their white undershirts stood watching for girls, dart-eyed, alert, cigarettes burning.

Farther back from the field, families camped on bright red-and-blue blankets, spread out where moms and girlfriends and little kids watching the game and each other could lay out, kick it, sip sodas in the sun.

Musica blared. Loud, brassy Puerto Rican songs with hard dancing rhythms boom-boxed my thoughts and lifted them like a high fly ball. Lifted them over my problems, over the uncertainties of my next move, and made me soar, made me slap my hands against my legs, slapping in rhythm to the bam-diddy-bam-bam, bam-bam beat.

Then, *crack!*

A deep line drive between left and center fields woke me up. Brought me into the game as the hard-charging, bull-chested batter raced around first, then strolled into second base with a stand-up double.

Something about the sound of the hit made me look back to see what kind of bat he'd used. And I saw.

Wow, I thought. He laced a shot like that with a wooden bat! That's incredible!

But it also explained the sweet sound I'd heard.

Then I spotted the next guy using wood, too. In fact, the whole bat rack was full of wooden bats. Not a metal one in sight.

I wondered if they had a bat my size. I'd used one once in practice. The ball didn't go as far, but you could *feel* the hit, the vibration in your hands. And when you kissed a fastball on a wooden bat's sweet spot, man, you didn't feel a thing. That ball just flew off like a scrub jay darting through the summer sky.

Then I remembered. I'd have no use for a wooden bat. Or any bat.

My spirits sank like a diving jayhawk. My stomach tightened up again. What would I tell Aunt Chrissy? What would I tell my parents when they called? And what about Breena, who thought I was doing so great?

"Yo! Omar!" the catcher yelled to the runner on the other team. "Go easy. The ball wants to *live*. Has to last all game, *'mano*."

"Hey, I barely tapped it. *Lo siento mucho*."

The shortstop slapped Omar on the butt and said something with a big grin. They both laughed at that.

Happy scene, I thought. Not much like the one I'd just left. What kind of game was this? I wondered.

I scanned the teams. Their uniforms didn't exactly match. Red caps on a black-cap team, gray pants on a white-pants team. High socks, long pants, bare calves, whatever.

But something bugged me. Something down there didn't add up. I mean, these guys were in their teens and twenties, hard charging, tough ballplayers. But they jibbed and jabbered back and forth like old friends from the neighborhood. Lifelong friends. Which they probably were. And, I guessed, that's the way New York was.

Guys grew up close to each other and stayed that way. Well, why not? They did that in small towns, too.

But seeing how they treated each other only made me feel worse.

I was the outsider, the intruder, blowing into town thinking I was God's gift to baseball. Well, I blew it, all right. They didn't need me. No one in this park needed me. Just remembering that got me super depressed.

It was times like these when I really missed Lissie. Missed my older, smarter sister who always knew what to say and what to do to make me feel better. Who hugged me—I could still feel her strong arms around me now—and taught me new words and how to write my own name and taught me a song about Christopher Robin who went to a palace with a girl named Alice.

And I sat there hoping you could hug in Heaven. I mean, I know how everyone's supposed to be a spirit when you die and stuff, how all the movies show angels and ghosts walking through walls and everything.

But right then I just hoped that you could, even if you were a spirit. I hoped you could still hug in Heaven.

I stood up, stretched. My thinking time was done. What else could I do but go home and face *la musica*? Louie'd be there by now. The story told. Decisions made.

I slung my bag over my shoulder and rolled my bike downhill to the path behind the backstop. One last pitch, I told myself.

Through the fence, I watched the hitter grip the wood with bare hands. Gobs of dark pine tar oiled the bat handle. I saw his fingers squeeze, loosen, and resqueeze as he stood waiting for the pitch. And then, *crack!*

Another long fly. Center field. Catchable, but the runner would tag up and go to third. That was teamwork. It was pure textbook baseball. And with the wooden bats, it was almost like I was getting a close-up, real-live look at the Padres or some other professional team, because only amateurs used aluminum.

I turned to a kid nearby, about my age, leaning on his own bike. "Don't any of these guys use metal bats?"

"Nah, they don't let 'em. Too dangerous. These guys hit too hard."

I nodded. I gave his bike a quick glance. Tricked out and lowered down to the max. A big, balloon-tired Schwinn with chrome everything. Handlebars, chain guard, spokes, and fenders. Out of the black, spongy handle grips flared bushy, brown foxtails. Behind the wheels hung black rubber mud flaps spangled with orange-and-red dime-sized reflectors.

"Nice bike," I said. "Took some time to do all that."

He grinned. "Yo, tell me about it. Like two years. And I'm not done yet." He touched the frame. "All this gets repainted this summer. Cherry red metallic lacquer."

"Cool," I said. "Be sweet."

He bobbed his head in agreement as we both turned our attention to the hiss and sizzle of someone sliding up the walkway on Rollerblades. A girl.

"Hi, Hector," she said to the boy with me. Her head

was covered with a blue-and-white Puerto Rican flag-scarf tied flat across her forehead, pirate style.

He lifted his chin at her. "Angelina."

The tall girl skated by, her feet floating on pink neon. And I decided to follow.

Now, that was something new for me. Not girls. Following them. See, there was something extra mysterious about girls lately—New York girls, I figured—that'd caught my eye, that'd stirred up the energy in me somehow, and I was just starting to realize that.

So I followed her. James Bond style. Secret-agenty. One eye looking, one eye scoping the baseball game, but always pretending to be bored—just in case she glanced back and saw me. At an overstuffed trash can near third base, I stopped while she joined a circle of friends.

Her skates slid in place to the bam-bam radio song, while she joked and laughed, but each time the downbeat came, she juked her hips to the side. She looked about my age, or maybe older, like fifteen or sixteen. With girls, who could tell? So I studied her.

I wished I could take her picture, but she'd see me. So I did the next best thing. I clicked on her face in my mind, memorizing something, anything, like the dark freckle below her eye on her left cheek. *Click.*

She wore a white, cartoony T-shirt tucked into belted blue jeans. Tight blue designer jeans. But what I liked was her face. Little, baby-acorn dimples. And what dark, dark mysterious eyes! Eyes that kept half flash-looking my way.

Girls, I thought. They were full of wonder.

And I wondered. For four full heartbeats, I wondered what she'd look like close-up. In the dark of a ballpark night.

Then, *crack* again. Only this hit sounded different. A foul ball squibbed toward third. The batter looked at the bat, shook his head, then flipped the stick around. He tapped the handle against home plate. *Click, click.*

Broken. Even I could tell that.

He tossed it toward the dugout and someone brought him another. Two guys took the rosy-red, cracked bat and examined it. I rolled my bike closer to see what I could.

"Ay," said one. "Right on the hands."

"Had to be a fastball," said the other. "That's too solid a bat." He tapped it on the concrete, then sent it skipping up against the chain-link fence near me.

"What're you gonna do with it?" I asked.

The guy looked over his shoulder, gave me an up-and-down glance and shrugged. "Nothing."

I inched forward. "Could I, um, see it?"

He grinned. "Yeah, sure." He shoved it under a gap in the fence bottom.

I picked it up and couldn't believe the feel. Heavy, solid wood, warm to the touch. Only a jagged crack along the handle disturbed the fine lines of parallel grain. Gripping the handle, I felt the sticky residue of pine-tar paste and smelled its sweet, tree-bark scent.

I took a slow-motion swing. "Wow."

"That's a fifty dollar bat," the guy said. "Pro stock.

I don't know how Mario broke it. This is the same bat, same wood and everything, that they use in the pros."

"Wow," I repeated. I could already see myself squirting glue into the crack, taping it up and trying to reuse it. Choking way up on the handle. Waiting for a fastball.

Just once.

Yeah, but when? I thought. I was off the team. Aunt Chrissy would have a long, sincere, kitchen-table lecture ready for me. Not to mention what Louie and Breena would have to say.

"Can I keep it?"

The guy grinned. "Knock yourself out. Otherwise, it's just gonna end up over there." He pointed back at the trash can, where near the bottom, stuck in the grass among the spilled-over trash, I spied the barrel end of another bat. A black one.

I laid the red bat across my handlebars and headed back to the trash can for a closer look. The black bat was busted all right, and someone had stuck the jagged end into the ground so it stood there angled out like a cannon barrel.

Worthless to me, I thought. Beyond repair.

Still, something made me touch it, made me reach over and pull it out of the ground to feel the wood, the shiny black enamel.

I read the signature. "Tony Gwynn."

Somehow, just that name comforted me. My favorite baseball player of all time. I set the black bat across my handlebars, on top of the other one, and rolled away.

Might as well go home, I decided. Get it over with. Repair what I can.

Pumping slow, wobbling my bike, I rolled past the Puerto Rican girl, past her friends, past the game. Away from the sweet music, the Saturday afternoon picnics, the safe haven of the baseball fields. From sweet dream to nightmare.

And into the battle of my crummy life.

chapter **9**

I SLID MY KEY INTO THE FRONT DOOR LOCK, TOOK a big breath, and twisted the knob.

They're all gonna jump on me, I thought. The poor sport. The fighter. The hothead. Yeah, well? So what? I can live my life any way I want. Besides, they're not my "real" family. My real family sent me here, so they could take care of other problems. So, I'm on my own, I figured. I can do what I want. And everyone else can just shut up.

"Hi, honey," Aunt Chrissy called out from the kitchen. "Just in time. We're ordering out. Key West Diner, Tyler. Your favorite. What would you like?" She grinned but didn't wait for my answer. "I heard you had an exciting game today. You got to pitch." Her smile was my only clue. And it told me she was clueless.

"So how was it?" she asked.

"Fine." I rolled my bike inside, then turned sideways and gave her a cheek to smoosh with candy-apple lipstick.

"And did you get some good nature pictures of the park?"

What'd she mean by that? Now *I* was clueless. But something told me to play along.

"Um, well, we'll see," I said. "And, uh, I'll have a cheeseburger, I guess. Please. With fries."

"Okay, that makes three." She picked up the phone. "I'm running off in a few minutes, so I'll call it in right now."

I shoved the bike into the closet, dumped the bat and gear, then hustled through the living room and down the hall. I shouldered open the bedroom door and kicked it shut behind me. Louie sat staring at his computer through aviator shades, mouth open, headphones poking out from under his USAF cap, while his rap music thudded loud enough for me to hear over his Blood Hawk fighter bomber blasting away at cyberspace villains.

He was so intense, when he completed a mission, he liked to jump up, drop his controls, play a little air guitar, then sit back down in time to start the next level.

I flung my cap against his F/A-18 Hornet wall poster to get his attention. But my cap just bounced off and fell onto his model F-16 fighter jet below. So I tore off my shirt and beaned him with it.

"Hey," he said. "Knock it off." He pulled down the 'phones. "Where'd you go, man? I had to make something up."

"Yeah, you did, didn't you?" I said. "About taking some stupid nature pictures? I don't take pictures of *nature*. I shoot interesting stuff."

Louie leaned back. "Yeah, well, I didn't have to say anything at all."

"You got that right. Why should I care who knows what happened?"

He rolled his head in a little circle. "You better care. You've done some dumb things before, but this ranks right up there with Tyson biting off that dude's ear."

"It's no biggie."

He blew out a blast of air. "Yeah? So what're you gonna do now?"

"Nothing," I said with a shrug. One thing I hated worse than doing something stupid was admitting I'd done something stupid. "I'm gonna take the summer off, man. Take it easy. Scope the sights of the big cit-*tay*."

As soon as I said it, the image of that girl on skates filled my mind. I leaned down and slapped him lightly on both cheeks. "I'm gonna be James Bond. *Undercover*. In real life." I stepped back and fell into the cool, blue vinyl beanbag chair in the corner.

"Oh, that's real life, all right," said Louie. "Well, first thing you better uncover is, what ever happened to your brain. Better call the CIA on that one."

I slid both hands behind my neck. "What for? Look, I'm an emotional ballplayer, all right? Everybody should know that by now. Besides, I was just standing up for my teammates. No one else was."

"No one else was because Tony was acting like an idiot. You don't stand up for a guy acting like a moron."

Now I saw my angle and jumped on it. "Of course you do! I mean, if he's on your team, you do. Right or wrong. You always stand up and fight for your own side." I pulled my fake stirrups off and threw them against the closet door. "I mean, you're my cousin. You should've stood up for *me*. Where were you?"

"Tell you where I was. I hung around after the game to talk to Coach Trioli for you, you jerk. And I told him how much baseball means to you and how you got this short fuse and how sometimes you go and do stuff that you feel bad about later."

"That's so much bull. Who told you to say that?"

"And," Louie continued, "I told him that you'd come back later and apologize. To everybody."

That made me groan like a dying dog. "Oh, man!" I flicked a hand in his direction and rolled over toward the broken 51-disk CD player. "You wanna do something for me, get this thing fixed. Thought you guys were rich. I wanna hear music out *loud*. I'm sick of wearing those sorry headphones."

He stood, ignoring what I'd said, and raised his voice. "*And*—and I told him that if you did apologize, could he possibly, maybe, give you one more chance?"

I rolled back, crunching the filling in the chair, and folded my arms against my chest. Glaring straight ahead, I kicked my legs out, then slowly turned and looked his way.

"You actually said that?" I asked.

Louie stuck the headphones back on and sat down.

"So, what'd he say?" I asked.

Louie answered without looking up. "Said, how many chances do you think you get?"

Someone knocked on the door. Aunt Chrissy called out, "Boys, I'm off now. Can you open up?"

I rose to get the door. Louie tickled his keyboard.

"Honey," said Aunt Chrissy, waving a fistful of money at me. "Take this for the food. And Tyler, did Louis tell you about our little trip?"

Louis? It always threw me when she called him that. But she always did. Louis and Sabrina.

I shook my head, eyeing a book she carried under her arm.

"Oh," she said, "well, I've been wanting to do this for a long time. Sometime next month, I want us to ride the train to Washington, D.C. Just you three kids and me. We'll visit the sights and stay overnight. Sound like fun?"

"Yeah, I guess so." I tried to show some enthusiasm. I nodded.

"Good." She held out the book. "And I thought that you and Louis might like to read up on some of the historical points of interest before we go. The trip'll mean so much more that way." She gave me a smile.

"Yeah, okay," I said. Fat chance was more like it.

"We have other books in the alcove, but I especially like this one." She handed me a book on the Vietnam War. "It's a profound, thoughtful study of that war. With lots of pictures."

"Oh, yeah, okay." I took the book, even though Vietnam had always seemed so boring when we talked about it in school.

Then Aunt Chrissy lowered her voice and tightened

an eyebrow. "Especially since your grandfather's name is on that wall."

"Oh, yeah," I said. "Yeah, I know that."

Grandad Waltern. He was my dad's dad. Aunt Chrissy's dad, too. And I was named after him.

"Louis and Sabrina have seen it," said Aunt Chrissy. "And I think it's time I took you to see it, too."

I glanced at the book. "Yeah, fine with me."

"Oh, and next week, your uncle Phil will be home from Japan." She slipped on a light suit jacket as she walked away. "He's so excited about finally seeing one of your games. Okay, I'm off!"

I closed the door and tossed the book on my bed. Oh, just great, I thought. Now here comes Uncle Phil with all his questions. Well, at least I had a little time to get ready.

I grabbed a plastic bag full of birdseed, walked to the tall, double-hung window, and slid the bottom half up. Outside on the fire escape balcony, I spotted the two little gray doves—Babe and Ruth, I called them—that lived in a clay pot planter on our balcony. Well, Aunt Chrissy's balcony, really—her room had the only door to it. But I used to jump from our window to the balcony rail. And tossing birdseed into the planter from here was easy.

Louie pulled back his headphones. "She's got an ulterior motive," he said. "Going to the wall, I mean."

"Oh, yeah? Like what?" The birds fluttered up as I spread the seed.

"She called your mom this afternoon."

"Oh, man." Babe made cooing sounds that I took as a thank-you.

"They think—after what Coach said—that seeing the wall and those war monuments'll make you stop and think—"

"About what? Not fighting? Seeing all that death and destruction? Yeah, right. Man, I *wanna* see that stuff. Be cool. But it won't affect me. Besides, I'm not gonna be the big warrior. You are, Blood Hawk."

Louie shrugged and went back to his joystick. I could hear the sound track to his Blood Hawk Bombers video game start up again.

"Told her," he said, "it was worthless."

I tossed one more handful of seeds, then lowered the window. Grabbing my jeans and some underwear, I said, "Well, I'm gonna shower up. Yell at me when the food gets here."

Later that evening, after we ate, I wandered into the wood-paneled alcove. The small, three-sided den was actually one of my favorite spots in the whole apartment. I think it used to be a walk-in closet. Set off from the living room and hall, dark and quiet, a guy could go in there, sit at the desk, and no one'd bother him. In this town, unlike the open hills where I came from, you really needed to find yourself a quiet spot. I mean, besides the bathroom.

So I laid out a few books. Big, old black-and-white photo books on the world wars and stuff. They were great. I wished I could've been a photographer back then and shot the stuff they shot.

Then I pulled out one on the Civil War. My favorite. It was the easiest war to understand and, also, the hardest. For example, what could get a country to fight against itself? I mean, I knew. Slavery and states' rights and all that. But, still. It just seemed like it'd be a lot harder to kill your own people.

And I looked at the flagged page—at Great-Great-Great-Grandfather Waltern's picture in his Confederate army uniform. I could see my dad in his face. That is, a trace of him in the high, broad cheekbones.

But not as much as I saw in Grandad Waltern's face.

That picture haunted me. Not from anything in the photo—it was one of those posed, studio head shots with a phony, sky blue background. But it was taken right before his last tour in Vietnam. He was about Dad's age, a smear of gray at his temples. But what always grabbed me were his eyes. Dad said he had steely, armor-piercing eyes, but I didn't see that. I saw sad eyes. Worried eyes. And I sat back, wondering if he knew he'd passed those sad, worried eyes onto my dad.

Then, right then, something caught my attention. On the wall to the left, next to some smaller books and pictures, I saw my name in a golden frame.

Tyler Waltern.

What was that doing there? I wondered.

I leaned sideways to see clearer. No, it wasn't my name. Not exactly. Part of it had been hidden. It was Grandad's. John Tyler Waltern. In pencil. Like someone had rubbed his name on a piece of paper and framed it.

And immediately I knew what it was. A rubbing from the Vietnam War Memorial. I'd heard about that. Someone had taken the paper and rubbed a pencil over his name that was carved on that wall.

I sat back in my original position, to where I could only see my name. And I felt an eerie chill.

Like I was sitting in a graveyard, and someone had just run a fingernail up my spine.

chapter 10

I SPENT OVER AN HOUR IN THE ALCOVE THAT night. Picture after picture. Reading about the wars and the people who died. And on Sunday morning, right after my push-ups, I went in and read even more.

This was crazy, I tell you, because I was not a big reader. But some of those photos were amazing. They put me right into the action.

And some of them were sickening. The headless corpses, the dead children. There were kids who fought and died in the Civil War who were only twelve years old.

And I'd never realized that the Civil War was our worst. In those four years, we lost more men than in World Wars I and II combined. Almost ten times as many as in Vietnam, which was a civil war, too, I found out. Except, not for us.

The Vietnam book had little personal stories under the photo captions. But it wasn't the typical stuff.

Like the American nurse who told how she'd always refused to treat any wounded Vietnamese. But then one day, they made her help a wounded baby they'd brought in. At first she said no. Then she just looked at it and broke down crying. "How," she wrote in her diary, "could I have ever come to believe that a baby was the enemy?"

Then I saw the grainy snapshot of a soldier sitting cross-legged on a stack of supplies, grinning up at the camera, holding a human ear in the palm of his hand. A war momento, the caption said. I could see a slice of cheek skin dangling from the bottom of the ear.

Flipping from picture to picture, I didn't even notice Breena come up behind me.

"What are you doing hanging in here on a Sunday morning?" she asked.

"Nothing." I slowly shut the book. "Louie's down at Ryan's, and I—well, your mom thinks I should study up on war before we go to D.C."

"She does? She said that?"

"No, not exactly. She said history. But I could tell."

Breena scanned the bookshelves above the desk. "I'll show you the best book in here," she said, running her fingers along the spines.

I wondered what book could be better than the ones I had. She pulled out a skinny little kids' book with a cover full of colored swirls and plopped it on the desk-top.

Oh, the Places You'll Go! by Dr. Seuss.

I grinned, thinking, what's that book doing in here? "Um, I already read that one," I told her. "About five years ago."

"It's my favorite book in the whole wide world," she said. "I *love* it. Last year, they read it to us on the first day of seventh grade. Of course, they also read it on the last day of sixth grade. Not to mention, a bunch of times before that."

"I don't remember it that much," I said. "Just a baby book, isn't it?"

"Well, I don't know. Doesn't seem like you've outgrown it." She ended that sentence by sticking out her tongue.

"Oh, and I can see you have." I pushed my chair back to leave.

Didn't faze her. "No, listen to this," she said, throwing her arms wide. " 'Congratulations! Today is your day. You're off to Great Places! You're off and away!' " She stopped and grinned like a dork. "That fits so many things."

"Yeah, that's right," I said. "Like war and death and—and—"

"And getting kicked off the baseball team," she finished.

I closed my eyes a second. Now I understood.

"So Loudmouth Louie ratted on me," I said. "Nice guy."

Breena hopped onto the wooden desk, hugging the book against her, watching me the whole time with eyes the color of the blue flame in a log fire. And she could burn right through you with those eyes if she wanted to.

"He was really upset," she said. "You probably don't know it, but you're kind of a hero to him. The whole time before you got here, he was telling all the guys on the team, 'The All-Star shortstop is coming. The All-Star shortstop is coming.' "

"Oh, sure."

"Serious. He was worse than Daddy about it. And this morning he was so bummed. I guess he just had to tell somebody. I mean, he really looked forward to playing baseball with you this year. And now you spoiled that."

I leaned back in the chair, folding my arms. Hating myself. Wishing I was somebody else. "Whatever."

Breena thumbed through the book. "Listen," she said. "This is you. 'You're on your own. And you know what you know. And YOU are the guy who'll decide where to go.' "

"That's right," I said. "Exactly right. I'm my own guy. If I discovered one thing while I was sitting here, it's that I come from a long line of men who were their own guys."

"I know. It's such a macho thing. You're Mr. Self-Important. Mr. Courageous." She raised the book like a sword. "Mr. Warrior."

"So what if I am?"

"Oh, you think you are? Okay, then." She stabbed at my heart. "Do something courageous."

I pushed the book away. "Maybe I will."

"No, I don't mean sitting here and acting like nothing bothers you. I mean, do something for Louie. For the team. You know where your coach lives, right? Why don't you go and apologize? See if he'll take you back."

"Because he won't. Believe me. You didn't hear what I said."

"Who cares what you said? Oh, Tyler, it's such an *ego* thing. You're such a boy." Breena cracked the book open again and flipped through the pages, searching. "Like it says in here. Your head's full of brains, isn't it? And your shoes are full of feet. Well—" She brought the book toward me, pointing to the next line, tapping her finger. "Read it."

I glanced at the line. Seemed okay, so I did. " 'You're too smart to go down any not so good street.' " I looked up. "That's true. So don't worry, okay?"

She stood, gathered up a chunk of my hair, tugged on it, and growled. "Who says I'm worried?" she asked.

I brushed her hand back and stood up to face her. "Who says I'm gonna go down the wrong street?"

Breena closed the book with a *whap!* "Hate to tell you, Mr. Macho. But you already did."

Chapter 11

FOR THE REST OF THE DAY, I THOUGHT ABOUT Breena's words, about how I'd gone down the wrong street. And about war.

When Mom called Monday morning—Memorial Day—I leaped from topic to topic to keep her from asking too much about baseball.

That turned out to be no problem. As usual, mostly what I got from Mom was the Farm Report.

"Your dad just picked a basketful of Big Boy tomatoes, Tyler. The plump kind that you love. We'll have to start canning them. And the zucchini are over a foot long. We can't keep up. We had squash and corn with our eggs this morning, too! With," she added softly, "homemade salsa."

Hearing the word "salsa" kicked up the juices in my mouth. One thing I really missed was my dad's homemade salsa.

"No fair," I said. Then I laughed, mostly for her benefit.

Because, you see, underneath all she said, I got the message Mom wanted me to hear. In Mom-code, I called it.

Memorial Day was always an especially tough day

for Dad. Not just because of Grandad, but the memories of Alyssa, too. So if Dad had been out in the garden harvesting Big Boys and jalapeños, then he was doing okay, Mom was happy, and all was right with the world.

She sure didn't need to hear my problems.

So I answered back in Mom-code, too.

"Don't forget about my sweet corn," I said. "I could sure use some now. Will you have another crop ready for me in September?"

"I promise," she answered. "It's in the ground. Don't worry."

"All right." Man, I missed Mom. I really did. I just couldn't say so. See, this was pretty much the way we talked about ourselves and the future. If crops were planted and harvests planned, then everything was under control.

And in my family, control was very important. And I knew it was phony. She did, too. But, so what? When you had our reality, phony wasn't so bad.

"Tell Dad, I miss his salsa, too."

Mom read that line perfectly. "I will," she said. "I'll have him send some along, how's that?"

"Yeah, good." And on that note, we hung up.

I reached for a tangelo and sat on the bed a little longer, thinking.

Louie was two floors down, at Ryan's, his best friend's place. So after I peeled the fruit, I opened up the bedroom window and sat on the windowsill to eat it.

It was the coolest feeling, sitting up there like on a canyonside boulder, dangling my legs out the window, a hundred feet off the ground, feeling the breeze whip up the side of the building.

Last year, I used to jump from there to the fire escape rail a few feet away and climb on. That was totally cool and not as dangerous as it looked. But they made me stop after Breena saw me one time and almost had a heart attack, and Louie told Aunt Chrissy.

But the window ledge was still a good place to be, so today I just sat there wondering what the heck I was going to do, while I tossed birdseed to Babe and Ruth and spit out tiny tangelo seeds on the taxis cruising by twelve stories below.

I was kicking around an idea when Aunt Chrissy knocked on the door. Quick as I could, I hopped back inside and opened it for her.

"Clean uniforms," she said, handing me a bunch of laundry stuck in cleaners' bags. "Your shirt was ripped. They mended that."

"Oh, yeah. Thanks."

And as I took the clothes, the idea came clearer.

It was a long shot, I knew. But the more I thought about no baseball for the rest of the summer, the more I realized I had to do something.

Coach'd told me to turn in my uniform, right? Okay, I figured, that'll give me the chance I need. I threw everything on the bed and stuffed the uniform in my backpack.

Out in the front closet, I grabbed my bike. "I'm going down to Riverside Park," I announced. "My coach has a game. Be back in a little while."

"Take your phone, honey," said Aunt Chrissy. "I'm not sure where I'll be later. Do you have money?"

"Yeah, I'm okay."

"Well, Sabrina's at soccer. Not sure exactly when she'll be done. And Louis is supposed to help me drop off the CD player. Then we'll go shopping. So I'll check in, and maybe we'll meet up for dinner."

"Yeah, okay." I rolled the bike out the door.

I knew where I could find Coach Trioli. Five o'clock Mondays, he played in a men's slo-pitch softball game in Riverside Park.

Once I was outside the building, I raced north up Riverside, whipping straight through the Joan of Arc park, ducking tree branches over the dirt path, popping out into the 95th Street intersection, timing the light just right so I could zip across Riverside, roll down to 97th, blast past the hot dog cart, drop into the park's lower level, and shoot under the jungle of treetops past the red, yellow, and blue blur of Dinosaur Playground.

As I rode farther north, I tried to imagine what I was going to say to him. I guessed it depended on what he said first. By now he probably hated my guts.

Down below, on my left, stood the old ball fields by the river where I'd played last summer. As I sailed by, I got so caught up watching the younger teams playing down there, I plowed right through a big pile of leaves, scaring up two black crows who went cawing off.

I barely caught my balance, zig-zagging past the quiet army of dog sitters and owners standing inside the Dog Run rink watching all the sniffing while sipping their coffee from the Hudson Beach Cafe.

In a minute, I bounced down a long row of white stone steps that led to the lower level softball fields set against the West Side Highway. On the far diamond, two men's teams stretched out, warming up and tossing balls beneath a row of leafy, long-branched trees.

Coach spotted me as soon as I spotted him and he greeted me with a flat voice. "Tyler," he said, dropping my name like a weak bunt. "What's up?" He tossed the ball to another guy, then took a few steps my way.

"Not much," I said, opening my pack, feeling embarrassed, feeling like everyone else knew exactly why I was there. "Um, I brought my uniform. It's washed and everything."

He nodded. I pulled it out.

But I didn't hand it to him. Because, first, there was another street my feet chose to go down.

"Coach," I said, directly into his chest. "I wanna say I'm sorry for how I acted and what I did and all." I gave his face a quick check glance.

Stern. Solemn. Angry?

"And I know this is a lot to ask, but—" Suddenly my chest filled with pounding. My breath felt locked up inside me. "But, um, if there's any way—if I could make it up to you—" I stumbled around for the right words, hoping no one else was listening. "If—if you'd give me another chance, I promise I'll do better. I won't—"

"Hold it, Tyler." He nodded his head, motioning me over to the concrete walk between the ball field and Skate Park. "Let me tell you something."

I followed, happy to be away from the eyes of the other men.

"Look," he said, "I don't know what you were trying to accomplish out there the other day, but when you treat other players the way you did, you treat this whole game with disrespect. And I'm not gonna stand for that. Baseball's a game of integrity. Of dignity. And what you did, essentially, was turn it into a gang fight."

I gripped my forearm and kept my eyes lowered as he continued.

"And so I gotta ask you, what're you so scared of?"

That caught me off guard. "I'm not scared of anything."

"Oh, yeah? Well, you know, when I played high school ball, I used to think the same thing. I'd be going along fine, then all of a sudden somebody'd say something, or something'd go wrong, and I'd blow up just the way you did. Over the littlest thing. And you know what it all came down to? Years later, when I sat down and figured it all out, I saw that it came down to one thing. I was scared. Scared of what people'd think. That if I struck out, then I wasn't a very good ballplayer. Or if I made a wrong decision, they'd think I was stupid. And I couldn't take that. So I figured, if I was angry all the time, people'd have to back off, leave me alone."

"I ain't scared."

"Okay, but let me put it to you this way. You'll never

see a self-confident guy running around getting angry all the time or getting into fights or quitting his team."

I couldn't move. My whole face heated up. In the park next to us, I could hear the constant rattle and clack of skate wheels skimming over the curled ramps and jumps.

"Now, look at me," he said.

Slowly, I did. Into gray-green, wall-piercing eyes.

"If you were to somehow get picked for All-Stars—which after Saturday, your chances of that are just about zilch—your teammates would be the same kids you think are scum right now. But you'd think they were terrific, because they'd be on your side. But you know what? They'd be the same good-hearted, hard-playing guys they've always been. The only thing that'd change would be your attitude toward them. You hearing me?"

"Yes, sir."

"They're no different than you, Tyler. Full of the same doubts and the same hot air. But get your confidence up, man, and all that stuff'll fall away. You won't feel so scared. You understand?"

"Yeah, I guess. But I'm not scared. That's not what gets me all angry."

"Yeah, okay," he said. "Maybe you're right. Maybe I'm wrong. In that case, prove it. Because, so far, I'm seeing something else."

I really, really wanted to let him know that I was different. Different from those other guys *and* different from how I'd been. That he wasn't seeing the real me.

But all I could say was, "Yes, sir." Quietly, sadly, lowering my gaze back down to my toes.

On the inside, though, I was jumping. My brain was flipping. Because didn't he just say, "Prove it"? So didn't that mean he was gonna let me back on the team? That I could play baseball again!

"Well," he went on, "it ain't up to me, hotshot. You need to talk to that man right over there in the warm-up suit."

He nodded toward a gray-haired guy in jogging sweats, holding a clipboard and talking to two other men.

"Who's he?" I asked.

"That's Fred Steinmetz, the Uptown Riverside Baseball League president. And he's my coach on this team. Whatever he says, goes. You need to tell him what you told me, and see what he thinks."

Oh, no, I thought. I can't do that. I can't go up to some stranger—in front of everybody—and say what I just said. Why was Coach making me do this?

"Um, right now?" I asked. "He looks busy."

Coach Trioli shrugged, then stepped away. "I guess it all depends on how much you wanna play."

I wanted to play *mountains*. With all my heart, I wanted to play. I always did.

Okay, okay, I told myself. No problem. I'll just walk up, tell him—um, tell him that I—tell him *what?* How do I start? He doesn't even know me. And what about all those other guys standing around watching?

No, no, I told myself, don't worry. You can do this.

I tried to walk, just to wander over in his direction, but I could barely even pick up my foot.

And for the first time, I realized how afraid I was of being embarrassed. How much I worried about what other people thought.

I watched Coach walk away and onto the ball field, taking his position. Other guys called out to him. The game was about to begin.

Finally, I crept close enough to catch the old man's eye.

"Um, Mr. Steinmetz?" The rumbling roar of the river of traffic on the West Side Highway nearly drowned my voice.

With a sharp turn, he sent me a glare. "Yes?"

No words. No breath. No brains.

I just stood there, squeezing my green Munibank uniform.

And I could not do it. I hated myself and the spot I'd gotten myself into more than anything in the world.

My lips trembled like a 6.0 on the Richter. I bit down hard.

And I started to cry.

chapter 12

I CAME HOME CRUSHED FLATTER THAN A SKUNK on the road. Crushed by two jerks. Coach was a jerk, I decided. And that old guy, Steinmetz, was a bigger one.

All the way home I wondered, what right do either of them have to make me come crawling back? I *am* a self-confident guy. I have my dignity. I have my *pride*. I pushed my bike into the dark apartment and swung open the entry closet door.

It'd taken tons of courage just to talk to Coach Trioli. Couldn't he see that? So why'd he have to dish me off to the old guy with the cold eyes?

After shoving the bike beneath the shelf, I closed the door, and in the low afternoon light, made my way through the living room to the alcove and slumped down into the velvety, high-backed reading chair.

And slump was the word for it.

Man, I hate this, I thought. What am I gonna do now?

Somewhere in the building water ran. Above us, below, to the side? Couldn't tell. The hiss of the water ran through the pipes like the air leaking out of the giant balloon of my life.

I hid myself in the chair, feeling the cozy warmth of

its arms in the emptiness of the lonely apartment, my lonely life.

Then the thought I'd been avoiding all afternoon hit me like a truck. Why was I such a stupid coward? Man, I hated myself! Just because I didn't know the guy, why was I so scared to talk to him?

I kicked the desk in front of me so hard I hurt my toe. Then I just sat and stared blankly for a while at the bookshelf. Stared until I decided to pull out a Vietnam War book—the one with all the pictures—flicked on the green-shaded desk lamp, and starting thumbing through it.

I had run away. I admitted it. Run like a coward. Not from a fight, but from a simple request to apologize to some stranger and tell him I was wrong. Compared to that, fighting was easy.

But why did I *cry?* Why did I let him see me start to cry?

I scanned the book for bloody shots, mortar blasts, stuff like that. After all, you know what misery loves.

And I found enough of them. Enough shots of blown-up dead guys and walking war zombies to make me realize my life could sure be a lot worse.

Then I came across a giant picture. One that'll stay with me for a long, long time. Not half-dead soldiers, not bomb blasts, not bloody, mangled bodies in the jungle brush.

It was a picture of children. Running right at me.

In the middle was a naked girl. Screaming.

Her face. It tore into me. Mouth twisted in pain, crying eyes shut into slits. I had to stop and read about the photo, to know what was going on.

A skinny, little nine-year-old girl who lived in a tiny Vietnamese village ran for her life, her arm on fire, her clothes burned off by napalm.

By our napalm, it said. Our side had done that to her.

The caption said that the picture had won a Pulitzer Prize, that in 1967 it was published all over the world. But all I could think of was, how could this happen?

In war, I always thought that you're supposed to kill soldiers. Not regular people. Not kids.

I finally pulled my eyes away and stared off into the twilight gray of the room. I heard the pipes in the wall shudder as someone turned the water off. I shut the book and clicked off the lamp.

In the dim light, I stared down at my hands, roughened now, scraped and scabbed over from playing hardball. And I did the only thing I could think to do.

I folded them together and started to pray.

And it occurred to me that I hadn't even prayed once since I'd come to New York.

I closed my eyes. Please, dear God, I started, help me out of this mess. Please tell me what I need to know and help me do what I need to do. Amen.

And in the next instant, I knew it had already happened.

That I already knew what I needed to know. No pain I felt was worse than that little girl's burning arm. No fear could be worse than what I saw in her face. If she could go through that, then I could go through this.

If I could only make myself get up and do it.

Turning sideways in the chair, I stared off into the cave of the hall, with its dark wooden floor and walnut-paneled walls.

Click.

The miniature electric candles that lined the hallway lit up, shining into the alcove.

I froze. Who was home? I wondered. I thought I'd been alone. I leaned forward to get a better angle.

At first I didn't know what I was looking at. I mean, I knew, but for a second, nothing registered.

It was Breena. She stepped right into the hall, looking as if she'd come straight from the shower. Her hair was wrapped in a white towel. And that's all she had on.

Going to the kitchen? I didn't know, but she had no idea she was heading right past me.

Instantly, I lifted my head up, turning it toward the high plaster ceiling, and rested my neck on the top of the chair back. I hoped that if she noticed me, she wouldn't think I'd actually seen her.

"*Tyler!*" she squealed. I heard her bare feet slam to a foot-bone stop.

I didn't move. Kept my head straight up, my eyes narrowed like I was deep in thought.

She retreated, her feet scampering against the wooden floor.

My eyes held the swirls of creamy white ceiling

plaster above me. But her image—that strange, wondrous image—filled my brain. At first, I wished I hadn't seen what I just saw. Too much, I thought. It was like an overload.

Then again, I felt lucky.

Instantly, I felt like I was years older than my age. Wiser. All-knowing. By sheer luck, I was sure I had shot ahead of every guy in my class. By sheer luck, I was sure I'd seen something no one else had ever seen.

My heart was surging, adrenaline flowing, and my mind was on fire. I couldn't have felt more fired up if I was batting in the World Series with the game on the line. And I felt confident. Fearless.

Right then I realized, just like in baseball, life sometimes throws you a curve. Or a fastball. Whatever. Mixes 'em up. You never know what's coming your way.

Could even be a girl with no clothes heading right at you. Like a knockdown pitch.

But you gotta decide what you're gonna do. Sometimes you take a look and let it go by. And sometimes you use the adrenaline to step up and swing with all your heart.

I sprang out of that chair. I knew what I had to do and I knew I'd better hurry. I had to make it to the park before the end of that slo-pitch softball game.

"EXCUSE ME, MR. STEINMETZ?" I SAID. "MY NAME is Tyler Waltern. And Coach Trioli told me I should speak to you."

I said all that while holding my breath.

The skinny, old guy peered at me through cut-in-half reading glasses, then moved his head down to look again. The game had just ended, and he was clutching a score book and a brown clipboard. Near his feet was a blue mesh bag full of giant softballs.

Coach Trioli sat on the grass nearby, starting to pull his sweatpants on over his shoes and trying to catch my eye.

I didn't let him. I let out my breath.

"Tyler Waltern," Mr. Steinmetz repeated, slowly, as if some hand in his brain was dusting off an old picture.

Did he remember me at all? That I'd just been there, looking stupid, eyes brimming, before I'd run away?

In a few seconds, though, his puzzled face grew into a military-style stare, like he was bracing himself for a tough job and needed to look tough to do it.

"Oh, yes," he said, placing his foot up on the bench. He crossed both arms over his knee and gunned me with a "what's-wrong-with-you?" look in his eyes.

"You, huh?" he said. "A little lad such as you is be-hind all this ruckus?"

How could I answer that? What? Did he think I was too small to cause a problem?

I shrugged. "Yeah, I guess." Then I remembered my mission. I stood straight and stiff. Another breath. "And, um, I wanna apologize for that fight on Saturday. I was hoping maybe I might get another chance."

He stared silently for a moment—his face could've been a photo in Aunt Chrissy's alcove—then he nar-rowed his eyes.

"Son, give me one good reason why we should do that."

For a flash second, I stood there thinking about how much I loved baseball, the challenges, the surprises. About Louie—how much he wanted me on the team. Then I saw my dad and the lawn mowers and his spark-less eyes.

And I remembered how I figured that someday, if I became a top ballplayer, Dad might come see a game, watch me hit, and shout great stuff at me like what pitch he thought was coming next.

But in the end, all I said was, "I treated the game with disrespect. And I hoped I could get the chance to show I have respect for baseball. I really do."

He gave a cough that rattled something in his throat.

"Yes, well," he said. "It's not going to be quite as simple as that. Mr. Trioli and I have discussed this mat-ter in some detail." He gave me another long look, like he still couldn't believe I was such a dink.

"Young man, we hate to lose you, I have to say that. You would've been an asset to the league. But at the same time, we can't put up with someone who loses his temper, whose actions can injure another player."

"No, sir," I said, my heart sinking like a slow curve.

"In the navy, we'd call you a loose cannon. Because when you get to rolling around on deck, you're not as dangerous to the enemy as you are to your own men. Including yourself."

"Yes, sir."

"So why in the name of Jack Cheese should we let a loose cannon back on board?"

My heart kept sinking. Like that cannon dropping to the bottom of the sea.

I didn't know what to say. Just said the first thing I could think of. "Because I'll strap myself down. Buckle down—you know, so I'm not so loose and everything. I can do it. I can do better."

His eyes blasted into mine. Armor-piercing eyes.

"Well," he said, letting the word just hang there like a flag over the ocean. "Since you decided to straggle on back here and stand up like a man, I figure we can take a chance. On two conditions." He rose up straight, breathing in, then out, through his nose. "Number one. For the rest of the season, son, you'll be on probation. One slip-up, one mistake, and you'll be packed up and shipped out in a hurry. You got that?"

"Yes, sir." Whoa, I thought, that didn't seem so bad.

"But keeping your nose clean won't be enough."

Oh, no, I figured. Here it comes.

"Number two," he continued. "What we want to see is a *demonstration* of good sportsmanship on your part. And I don't mean this 'Yes, sir, no, sir' malarkey you're handing me now. And I don't mean going around kissing someone's *derriere*, either." His eyes shot again.

"I mean a real, honest-to-goodness demonstration—in front of God, country, and everybody—that you know how to conduct yourself with maturity and restraint. On the ball field, in the heat of battle, wherever. And that you can treat everyone—even your opponent—with respect and dignity and still get the job done."

I tried to picture it. "Like how?" I asked. "I mean, what should I do exactly?"

"That's for you to work out. Could be as simple as speaking up and getting your teammates to tone down their name-calling against the other team. Or, might be something larger than that. But what we want to see is consistency. A new pattern of behavior. We're going to be looking for an indication that you have the maturity to play at the All-Star level. Because, if not—well, we don't have time to fool with you, now, do we? Am I clear?"

"Yes, sir," I said, then quickly corrected. "That is, yes, Mr. Steinmetz, I understand."

Finally, I glanced over at Coach Trioli, who was still hovering nearby. He pointed at me, as if to say, "It's up to you now, kid. Don't blow it."

I raised thumbs up to Coach, then turned to the president to shake his hand. "Thanks," I told him. "Thanks a lot. I really—I won't let you down."

He shook once and kind of "humphed," then went

back to his clipboard. But I just ran over, hopped on my bike, and raced out of there.

With a wave to Coach, I flew off along the big stone wall that skirted the outfield. Up the steps, past the park-path joggers and stroller-pushing moms, breezing by the volleyball courts and the 101 Street Soccer Field. Then I dodged a shirtless homeless guy who was white-washing a big, craggy plank of plywood with a rolled-up sock.

Racing like mad, I headed back down south, block after block, leaving the asphalt roadway once to spin a few doughnuts in the grass, then I popped a wheelie and kept on going.

There was a charge flying through me. It was like I'd climbed to the top of a faraway mountain, and I could see forever. See something I'd never seen before.

And I couldn't wait to get into the next ball game. To face some flame-throwing fourteen-year-old and look him in the eye.

Hey, forget about it, I thought. I pity the poor guy. I'd pity anybody who had to face me in the mood I was in.

Except Breena. Instantly, Breena's image filled my brain.

I mean, speaking of seeing things I'd never seen before. What would happen the next time I saw her?

Nothing, I decided. Nothing. I'd play it fully cool. Like I never even saw what I saw.

Through the park, past the Hippo Playground I sped, past pushcarts with their ice cream bars, hot dogs, and ice chests full of fruit juice teas.

Down around 88th, I saw the tall Soldiers and Sailors Monument shoot up and I realized I'd gone too far. I pedaled back up the hill until I reached the park that was built around that Civil War monument with its checkerboard tabletops and three black cannons set on blocks of stone.

I slalomed past the cannons, jumped the steps to the monument's flagstone plaza, then skidded around the flagpole as I reached out with my foot to kick an empty booze bottle that spun, but didn't break.

Then I tore off again. Nothing was going to slow me down as I headed back to 91st, back to home, certain that I was destined to be the star of the All-Stars. I mean, why else would they make it so I could be back on the team?

With a final burst, I shot toward the same cluster of trees that we could see from our apartment window. Then, with a hard brake, I laid a big rubber patch down the center of the path.

Yes!

Well, yo! as Louie would say.

Because the next time I saw Breena was right then. Ten feet away. Sitting in one of those trees, looking out at the sunset over the river.

"What're you doing up there?" I asked.

Her eyes shot through me. Glaring, icy, don't-bother-me eyes.

Oh, no, I thought. She hates me!

Breena sat parked in the crook of a little tree with a

hollow trunk, on top of a thick branch about five feet high that grew straight out.

Her long, black-jeaned legs stretched out over the branch. Around her neck, resting on her collarbone, a set of headphones hung like black jewelry. As I straddled my bike, trying to catch my breath, I could hear slow bass notes and the clink of a guitar melody. Her backpack sat in a hole in the trunk with two ceramic birds nestled on top.

"Well," she said, "that's pretty obvious, isn't it?" She held up a book, something called *Weetzie Bat*. "I'm just hanging in my favorite tree, reading and thinking and hoping no one comes along and pesters me." She raised her eyebrows and squinched a crooked grin.

"Oh. Sorry."

"Question is," she said, "what are you doing, screeching through the park like a dirt-bike terrorist?"

For some reason—hearing her say that, knowing that she'd seen me go so wild and knowing I was bothering her and knowing everything else I knew—I couldn't even look at her. I spoke to the tree trunk.

"Oh, nothing." My voice squeaked like bad brakes. I coughed to cover it up. "What were you thinking about?"

Breena waited a moment, then said, "My friend Kelly. Her parents' divorce just got final. Then her mom gets the brainy idea to go and make an appointment with some plastic surgeon. For, you know, whatever. And Kelly's freaked. And I should be there, but—" She let the word just sort of flutter down to the little golden hippos in the playground below.

Whoa, I thought, what could I say here? People get divorced all the time, but I couldn't say that. "Oh, wow, that's too bad. That's, um, sad."

She looked at me like, oh, just be quiet—what could *you* possibly know?

We stared in silence while I scanned my brain for a subject changer.

"Oh, guess what?" I finally said. "They let me back on the team. They said it was okay."

"Really?" For a second she seemed almost happy. "They did? What'd you have to do, apologize, or pay them money?"

"I apologized. Twice."

"Is that all?"

"Yeah."

"They must like you. You must be really good or something."

I shrugged.

Was she making fun of me? I wondered. Did she despise me?

"Well," she said, "*I* would've made you earn your way back. If it were me, I would've made you promise to walk over and shake the hand of every single player on the other team before every game you play from now on."

"*Before* the game?"

She gave a nod. "Otherwise, it's like you can just get

in a fight, say you're sorry, and then everything's la-di-da until you go and do it again."

"I won't do it again, believe me. I don't wanna blow my chance. I wanna make All-Stars."

She shrugged. "That'd be nice. All-Stars. But still. If you just act all goody-goody because of that, it's kind of phony, isn't it?"

"No, it's not."

"Oh, really?" She plopped her hand over her mouth in mock astonishment. "Oh! You mean you're doing it because you've *changed?* Because now you know how the other boy felt? Oh. I see."

"Breena! I do. I know all that." Then I remembered the peer counseling stuff she'd learned and I knew what she was doing now. "I know exactly how that guy felt," I added for emphasis.

For a second, I glanced up into her eyes. But only for a second. It felt totally strange—I mean, knowing what she looked like with just a towel on her head. And feeling dressed just like that myself right then.

I rolled backwards on my bike. Time to make my exit. "Well, I better go tell Louie," I said. "You coming up soon?"

She smiled directly at me. Not shy. Not angry. Her best smile of the day, actually. "In a little while," she said. "I wanna finish this chapter."

"Oh, okay." I rolled a few more feet. "What's it about?"

She gave a short laugh. "So far, it's about these crazy,

silly, imperfect human beings with hearts full of love who can't stop hurting each other."

She smiled again.

"Uhh," I said as intelligently as I could. "See you later, then." And I tore away.

And as the wind hit my face, I suddenly realized what that strange energy inside of me was. At least, I thought I did. That is, in a crazy, silly, imperfect sort of way, I thought I did.

I mean—can you fall in love with your own cousin?

chapter 14

"THERE AIN'T NO BIG LAW AGAINST IT," SAID Louie, as he zigzagged his bike north along Amsterdam Avenue.

It was the next week, the second week of a warm June. The season's first half was over, and we'd finished fourth out of six teams, and now Louie and I were on our way to the first game of the season's last half.

We'd just been talking about guys in the big leagues, how sometimes, like during batting practice before the game, they'd laugh and joke around with players on the opposite team.

"It's called fraternization," said Louie. "And it's no big deal for us. We're not in the pros or anything."

I wished he would've said something like, "Oh, no, don't do it. You'd be a traitor." Because after my last two games had gone so well—no blowups or anything and lots of rah-rah teamwork and stuff—it got me to thinking.

Uncle Phil was even in town for one of them. He'd popped in for a few days and drove us to practice one afternoon so he could drop off some brand-new catcher's gear for Louie. Well, for promotion, really.

"It's the latest," he told Coach Trioli, knocking on

the helmet and mask. "Lightweight, high-tech plastic. Bulletproof. Major-league quality. Keep it for All-Stars," he said, winking.

Just watching him work got me to thinking that maybe I should promote myself a little, too. So today I was kicking around the idea Breena had mentioned last week—fraternization—trying to imagine what would happen if I really tried it.

"But the coaches hate it," I said. "They think it makes their guys lose their edge against the other team and not go all out and try and clobber them."

"Some coaches," said Louie. "Others don't care."

At this point, I figured, it wasn't like I had to worry about making All-Stars. Coach had already moved me from leadoff to third in the batting order, the spot for the team's best hitter. So I knew I was back in good with him.

But, still. I remembered what Mr. Steinmetz had said about looking for a *demonstration*. So I was just thinking. Just in case.

"Okay, then," I said to Louie. "What if I walked up to some of the guys on the other team today and shook their hands?"

"Big deal. We always do that."

"No, I mean *before* the game, not after."

"Why would you wanna do that? So they'd go easy on you? And not call you 'Carrot Top'? Or 'Shorty, the shorty-short shortstop'? "

"Nah, not that. Who cares about that stuff?" I said it just like I believed it. But I *was* trying. "Just, you know, for sportsmanship. Might show Coach Trioli how much I'm changing."

"You? Change? Yeah, right. Dude, I'm dreading the next close play that goes against you. I'll probably have to run out and tackle you before you go postal. Wanna chomp some guy's ear off."

"Oh, like you gotta take care of me."

"Like I don't." He cut down 95th toward Central Park, pedaling off ahead as if he wanted me to think that over.

So I let him. What a dumb thing to say, anyway, I thought. I was no time bomb, waiting to go off. I was one cool dude, wiser now, and I could prove it.

Down the block, as I passed a bunch of those narrow brownstone apartment buildings, I saw some plasterers with their heads wrapped in white cloth working on a busted wall lining a front stoop. I listened to the sounds of their foreign language as they flowed the gray plaster out with their tools, smoothing the mud over the old cracked and cratered surfaces, while they laughed in loud bursts.

I stopped my bike and watched for a minute under a huge Siberian elm. I knew the kind of tree because this was the block where Louie's class—as he often pointed out—had stuck name tags on all the trees as a community service project.

Can't say why, but something about standing under that shady canopy of trees and seeing the work those guys were doing made me feel good.

On the inside.

I whipped out my camera, took a couple of pictures, and left.

All the way to the field I held that feeling. I even imagined warming up, taking infield and everything, then—right before the game—running over to the other bench and shaking hands with every player on the team.

"Have a good game," I'd tell them, smooth as rain. "Good luck."

I mean, hey! That would take some *real* courage, right?

But it never happened. And not because I didn't actually consider it. But you don't know how hard it would be doing something like that. What if they all laughed at me?

There was one instant, one flicker of a moment right before we took the field, that I really could've done it. Could've easily gotten up, slipped into their dugout, shook any hand I could've reached, then walked out the other end.

But no way.

I couldn't do it. My body wouldn't let me. Like on the day Coach told me to go talk to Steinmetz. My legs froze. My hands trembled at the thought like some toothless guy on the corner holding out his cup.

So shoot me, but I did the expected thing. The normal thing. Shouted a few tough words at the guys on our bench and clapped my hands together hard. "Heads-up defense out there today! C'mon, tight *D*. Let's shut 'em down!"

And I sprinted out to shortstop with another little piece of knowledge about myself that I didn't like.

Lucky for me, though, that was just an imaginary test. The real one came about an hour later.

They started in on me early. And it was either my hair or my height.

"Hey, Orange Blossom!" some guy called. "I know you! Aren't you a big star on MTV? Yeah, yeah. Not Beavis, but, you know—the other one!"

Later on, the "short" jokes came. As I took my spot in the field, one guy yelled, "Wait a minute! Time out! Somebody dropped their hat at shortstop."

Then right away he added, "Oh, no. Never mind. There's a guy standing under it."

It went on and on.

Nothing I couldn't handle, though. And I actually kind of enjoyed being Mr. Cool about it, walking around with a smug little smile on my face, ignoring those idiots, showing them I was above it all. Burned them good just to see it, I was sure.

And I felt good about it. Not only was I proving myself to Louie, but it's what Coach wanted to see, too. I hoped he was impressed.

But sooner or later something had to happen. It wasn't on the field, though. It was behind the backstop. Around the fifth inning, right after Louie blooped a fastball down the line and knocked me in, about five guys showed up. They were from the team we'd played the day I got tossed. All wearing their yellow caps, like they'd just come from practice.

And it wasn't that they were calling me names as I stood at shortstop. I could've taken that. And they weren't laughing and joking among themselves, either. What bugged me were the long, cold stares.

And their silence.

So two innings later, when I got called out at first on a bang-bang play—and I swear I thought I was safe—I was cool and liquid.

Flowed back to the dugout like water through a gorge. Not a peep out of me. Not a face. Not a foot stomp. I didn't even break my stride. *No problema.*

It helped that Breena was there. Helped that she shouted, "Nice try, Tyler!" in her high-pitched voice as I jogged back.

But what helped most was Coach's reaction.

"Good hustle down the line, kid," he said. "And that was a good at bat. Showed a lot of patience. That's what we want."

He didn't say anything else, but it was the easy, casual jostle of his hand on my shoulder that told me everything. Told me he'd noticed.

And I wish that would've been enough, wish that could've given me the strength I needed.

But I needed more than that.

Not then. Later. After the final out. After we'd snuffed a seventh-inning rally to win the game. After we'd walked up, slapped hands with the other team, and exchanged our "Good game" grunts. After Louie and I'd loaded our gear and lost track of those guys with the cold, hard stares.

"You two want an ice cream sandwich?" Breena asked, pointing to a cart about a hundred yards away. She was always a sucker for an ice cream sandwich.

"You buying?" I said.

"Of course." She slung her black-and-neon-pink blades over my handlebars. "Carry these, okay? I'll catch up to you. I'm fast."

"All right," I said, hoping no one'd see what I was carrying. "Hurry."

"We'll go slow," said Louie as he stood on his pedals to start off.

We coasted on our bikes, walking them really, as we relived the game and Louie's RBI single that eventually won it for us.

"I was looking fastball all the way!" he said, as if that explained his lucky looper.

As we entered an open, grassy clearing, I heard a shout. That was our only warning. Within seconds they'd surrounded us. The yellow hats swooped up on their bikes likc hornets from out of the trees.

"Hope you guys ain't in no hurry."

The big kid with the nosc and the soup-spoon cars—the one who looked like Dumbo, the elephant—straddled his bike sideways across our path. Two other guys flanked him. Over my shoulder, I spotted Eugene Jespers, our second baseman, as he ran back the other way, past two more guys in yellow caps riding up.

No sign of Breena, but all I could think was, Yeah, right, Eugene. Thanks for the help.

"You can go," the big kid told Louie. "We got a little business with Stump Boy here."

"Oh, yeah, sure," said Louie. "I think I'm gonna leave my cousin all alone so you guys can jump and stomp on him. Yeah, five against one. That's real fair. You're real tough dudes."

Dumbo ignored him. "We ain't gonna beat nobody up." He dropped his bike and stepped over it. "We're just gonna pick him off."

My heart swelled and boomed in my chest, adrenaline burned in my gut.

In a flash, two guys grabbed Louie, and Dumbo shoved his foot into my stomach, kicking me to the ground.

Barely able to breathe, I glanced up to see Dumbo pull a baseball out of his sweatshirt pocket. A sick wave surged through me.

He glared at me a moment, cocked his arm, and fired.

I pulled my arms up around my head, saw the white missile flare down at me as I tried to twist out of the way and into my tumbled bike.

Thunk. Rib cage. Man, that hurt. Like a hammer.

"Whata ya, nuts?" Louie shouted. He started to swing and kick at the guys holding him. "Lemme go!"

Dumbo reared back again. "And here's one to grow on, Stump Boy!"

I spun again as this ball skipped off my hipbone.

I looked up to see Dumbo cock his head at the guys holding Louie. "Let the fat boy go," he said. "We're done here."

That's what he thought. On the grass, lodged underneath the rear wheel of my bike, was a baseball.

While Louie and the two other guys had a little shoving match, I spidered my hand over to the ball and elbowed myself up to my knees.

"Hey, cabbage head," I called. "Forget something?"

Dumbo glanced back at my cocked arm, swung a leg over his bike, and slowly pushed off.

I stood. I had a perfect shot. He was barely moving.

"Don't do it," said Louie. "Let the jerk go."

Another guy lunged for me, but I dodged him. "Don't mess with me or you're next," I said. "I'll split your face open."

Dumbo stopped and looked back. "You guys coming or not?"

His teammates scrambled to their bikes and rolled off, pumping to catch up.

"Let him go," Louie repeated. "He ain't worth it."

I still had a clear shot. I reared back again and heard a high-pitched voice scream at me.

"Tyler! Stop!"

I fired anyway. I had to.

The ball shot past Dumbo's head, missing it by inches. Missing everybody and skidding along the grass in the far distance.

I turned to the scream. To the eyes. Wide and frightened.

Breena running. Right at me. Her face twisted.

Behind her, Coach Trioli came hustling up, with Eugene Jespers at his side.

chapter 15

"TYLER," BREENA SAID, NO LOUDER THAN A BIRD. "You could've killed him. He had his back to you. You lied to me. You—"

Before she could finish, Louie jumped in.

"No, no," he said. "You didn't see everything. Those guys—"

"I saw enough," she answered, coming closer, eyes firing.

I felt her eyes on me, felt her trying to get me to look at her, but I wouldn't. All I did was pick up my bike and untangle my bag from her blades.

By then Coach and Eugene had joined us. Behind them, Tony Suarez came coasting up.

But since Coach had only seen the end of the fight, he listened while Louie backed me up big time. Told Coach everything, how those guys jumped us, how they pushed me down, threw a couple of balls at me, the whole enchilada and a couple of tacos on the side.

By the time he finished laying it on, I came out smelling like a level-headed hero. Or so I thought.

Coach took in a breath, let it out, then calmly asked me, "You okay? How's your side?"

"It's all right." I rubbed it with my palm. "Kinda numb."

Coach sharpened his glare. "Kinda dumb, don't you mean?"

"Coach—"

"Hey," he said, "you're not making any points here, pal. And you're lucky you had the good sense to throw that ball over his head. Because if you'd hit him . . ." He didn't finish. Just pointed that finger at me, like it was a pistol, and lowered his thumb.

I got the message.

"But, Coach, it wasn't my fault. They attacked *me*."

"Maybe, but your actions set this whole thing up. And you should've seen it coming."

"No way. It was a sneak attack! They hid in the trees."

"That's not what I'm talking about. There were plenty of warning signs. And you gotta see 'em. And Louie, you gotta help him see 'em."

Louie gawked, mouth open, ready to protest.

But Coach charged ahead. "Because, Tyler, you're in a revolving door with this guy now. And you'll go 'round and 'round with him until one of you has the guts to step away."

Now he was getting to me, and I hated having him say that in front of everyone, especially Eugene and Tony. What, I had no guts? Was he blind?

"Hey!" I slammed my bag to the ground. "If they're gonna do it to me, I'm gonna do it to them. Because, man, for two weeks I've been trying it *your* way out there. Holding back. Not causing any trouble."

Coach raised his chin. "Yeah, like a drunk avoiding a drink. How long's that gonna last?"

That threw me off stride. "What're you talking about? I'm in control."

He lowered his voice. "Look, here's what I'm saying." He glanced up. "And Tony, this goes for you, too."

"Me?" said Tony. "What'd I do?"

"Both of you," said Coach. "It's time to cut the Angry Man routine. No one's impressed. It's the easiest and the laziest reaction there is. And on my team, I expect my guys to work hard. At everything they do."

For a second, I was speechless. What was he, crazy? Lots of guys in pro sports got angry all the time. Helped them bear down and get focused.

I was about ready to tell him what he could do with his stupid ideas on anger, when I realized he'd nailed me.

If I blew up any hotter, I'd just prove his point.

Because anger *was* easy. I mean, for me it was. And it was hard not to get sucked into it. So I didn't. But, man, that was work.

In the most even voice I could manage, I said, "Okay, Coach, but what am I supposed to do when all of a sudden some guy comes up and he wants to fight? Just out of the blue."

"It's never out of the blue," he said. "You can always see it coming. There's name-calling. Stare-downs." He glanced over at Tony. "Agitation. And you can feel it.

You tense up, your stomach gets cheesy, and something in your brain gnaws at you."

With a wiggle of his fingers, he motioned us closer while he squatted down near my front wheel. "Come here you guys."

The three of us shuffled toward him. I glanced around for Breena, since I hadn't seen her leave, but all I saw were three ice cream sandwiches dumped and melting on the grass.

Coach paused a moment. "I know what I'm talking about." He lifted his right hand, angling the back of it toward us. A long, jagged scar ran across his knuckles and over a bony bump.

"I broke a kid's jaw with this hand," he said. "Busted out four of his teeth. Then I blackened both his eyes. And it took thirty-one stitches to piece my hand back together again. But, see, I didn't care. Because I was going to Vietnam, and he looked at me wrong."

I lifted my eyes from his hand to his face. "What?"

"La Guardia Airport in the sixties. Three weeks before I shipped out."

"You were in Vietnam?"

He rolled past my question. "What I'm saying is, I know what's going on here. And I can see where you guys are headed, Tyler. And it ain't All-Stars. And it ain't the major leagues."

That was hard to take. "Coach," I said, "you don't know squat about me. Or how hard I been trying."

"Tyler, shut up," said Louie.

"No, you shut up."

Coach just sat there, rubbing that scar. Then he pushed himself up to his feet and said, "Naw, it's okay. Relax." He balled his fist up and held it in front of us. "Look, I nearly went to jail over this. And it burned me up every time I thought about it. Later on, things just got worse. I don't need to get into details, but when I got out of the service, I turned into one of those guys you didn't even wanna look at, much less talk to. You know what I'm saying? Like I had this big roll of razor wire all around me that said, stay away. And the thing was, it was like I actually had been sent to jail."

"I ain't going to jail," I said.

"Maybe not, but you're on that road."

I wanted to shout in his face. To force him to hear me, to hear my side. It was like, *nobody* ever heard my side! But, instead, I leaned forward and spoke again in that low, even voice. "Then what am I supposed to do? Those guys jumped me."

"See it coming," he said.

I sent him my best sneer. "Yeah, right."

Louie cut in again. "Tyler, just shut up and listen."

"No, Louie, it's okay," said Coach. "I'm done here. But Tyler, look, kid. Prancing around like you were doing out there today and stuffing down your anger ain't gonna cut it. What you gotta do is get to the root of that anger. And here's a clue. It usually has to do with saving face. With pride. Being worried about how you look or that somebody just showed you up. And that's why the worst time to try to avoid a fight is right before it breaks out. Because by then there's too much at stake. Your pride's on the line."

I stood back, feeling the throbbing in my ribs start up, and dropped my head toward three ice cream-dripping lumps of foil.

"Forget it!" I said. "I *hate* this." I straightened my bike, rolled it backwards, ready to shove off. "Why should I even try when people don't give me credit for it? You think you know me, but you don't."

Coach lifted his hat and ran a hand over his thick hair, scouting something in the distance. Now he softened his voice, softened his whole face, looking weary.

"You're right, kid. I don't. But I've coached in this league for eight years now and I've seen a lot of players come through. And I don't remember any in the past few years with the patience you have at the plate, the speed and the instincts you have on the bases, the range you have at shortstop." He glared right at me. "Anybody ever tell you what a pro scout is looking for?"

I spit the answer out. I couldn't help it. He was buttering up the wrong guy at the wrong time. "The big, bad star of the All-Stars."

"Right," he said. "But there's five things he judges that on. He wants a player who has a strong arm, good leg speed, good fielding ability, who hits for average, and hits for power. A five-tool player, we call that. Now if you get to where you're popping a few over the wall, you'll be top rated in all five categories. You realize that?"

I shrugged. No way would I let on that I was completely blown away by what he'd just said.

"That's all I'm trying to do here, Tyler. Save you some grief."

I stood there, shaking, hugging my ribs while Coach started back the way he came.

Louie picked up his bike, loaded his bag across the handlebars, ready to head out. Eugene and Tony were already shuffling off through the park, though I could tell they weren't leaving.

Twenty feet away, Coach stopped and turned. "Tyler," he said. "You got any plans for tomorrow morning? Sunday morning?"

I thought a moment, then shook my head.

"You know that pink and white doughnut shop near my place on Columbus?"

"Yeah."

"How about you meet me there tomorrow around ten? Something I wanna show you."

chapter 16

JUST BEFORE LOUIE AND I REACHED CENTRAL Park's jogging loop, Tony rode up and cut us off. Eugene trailed behind him, rushing up on foot.

"What'd Coach say to you at the end?" asked Tony.

Louie answered. "He wants to see Tyler tomorrow morning. Wants to show him something."

Eugene finally caught up. "Show you what?" he asked.

"Who knows?" I said. "Maybe his medals from Vietnam."

"I didn't even know he was in Vietnam," said Louie, circling back and hopping off his bike so Eugene could keep up. "That's cool."

Tony and I straddled our bikes, too.

"My uncles were in Vietnam," said Tony. "One of them's always showing me his scars."

"Yeah," said Eugene. "Maybe Coach has another scar to show you, Tyler. A secret scar!"

"You're an idiot," I said. "He just wants to—I don't know." Whatever it was, I knew I had to meet him. Or just kiss off All-Stars. "Probably wants to talk about today. How those guys jumped me and everything."

"Yeah," said Tony. "We oughtta kick their butts. We should go to their next game and mess 'em all up."

"Word," said Eugene. "We'll bring Benny and Jarren, too."

"Don't worry," I said, seeing where the talk was going. "Next time I see them guys, I'm gonna take care of business."

Louie laughed at that. "Yeah, you and what air force?"

But it didn't stop him from telling all about the ambush, all over again, stopping on the corner of 96th Street to yell out, "Hey, cabbage head!" and then act out my throw.

He slapped his hands and made a whistling noise.

"Missed his head by half an *inch!*" he exaggerated. "That laser ball would've split his skull wide open."

That got "whoas" of approval from Tony and Eugene as we hustled across Central Park West.

"Next time," Tony kept saying. "We take care of business."

Suddenly Louie stopped, and it had nothing to do with the story. I was sure he smelled what I smelled. "Hey," he said. "Let's eat!"

And I did not object. Because I can tell you right now the best thing there is about New York City in three little words.

Hot dog carts.

And the next best thing. They're everywhere. They make the whole town seem friendly and human, make it seem to care for stragglers and strangers, and best of all, just the smell alone makes you feel like you're always near a baseball park.

We all ordered sloppy, goopy dogs, some with sauerkraut, some with pickle relish or ketchup or mustard or any combo of any of it.

As we started off again, I noticed the muggy afternoon had turned overcast. Glancing up, I asked, "Is it gonna rain?"

"Could," said Louie. "Humid enough."

"Wow," I said. "I can't believe you guys get rain in the summer."

Eugene leaned over and took a big, juicy bite, then paused with his cheek full to ask Louie, "Hey, why was your sister crying?"

"She was?" I said. All of a sudden my hot dog went bland.

Louie mounted his bike, straddle-walking it now, steering with his elbows, eating. "Who knows?" he said. "She's weird. Besides, girls cry all the time. They don't have to have a reason."

"We gotta make a plan," said Tony. "We gotta decide what we're gonna do the next time we see those *perros*."

"Yo, trip," said Eugene, nodding hard. "Next time's gonna be huge."

I blanked out all the talk. Didn't get into their hyper strategic planning session on how they'd bomb those guys with pocketfuls of baseballs or kick them just right so they'd all turn into ballerinas.

Instead, I thought about Breena. Crying. How I'd let her down. How I'd have to make it up to her somehow.

Five blocks later, Louie was still hungry, and since no one wanted to go home, we stopped at a Broadway diner near Tony's place on 89th. We left with a big bag of onion rings, cheeseburgers, and drinks, then headed over to the Soldiers and Sailors Monument park to eat.

By now the talk had gone from mutilating those guys to highlights of the game, and I felt a little better.

"Dude," said Tony, "I was stealing their signs. All game long. I knew every play. That's how I picked that guy off."

"Oh, yeah?" said Eugene. "They never had no problem scoring."

"On errors! None of those runs were earned."

I laughed. "Well, one of them was."

Everyone laughed. We all remembered the towering home run in the fourth inning.

"Here's Tony." I ran ahead for emphasis. "He pitches the ball, the guy murders it, and he's all yelling, 'Back! Back!' And I'm, like, looking at Jarren in center field, thinking, *'Back?'* Dude—" I threw an onion ring at Tony. "To catch that ball, he'd have to go back to *yesterday.*"

"Shut up, Orange Head," said Tony, ignoring all the hoots and trading butt kicks. "How come your hair's so weird, anyway?"

"What's it to you?" I answered, laughing out the words. I double slapped his cheeks, then dodged his foot.

"Better watch out," said Louie. "Tyler's sensitive

about his 'do. He thinks girls like it. He doesn't know it makes him look like a furry pumpkin."

More hoots.

"Yeah," said Eugene, "from now on, we should call him Jack. You know, Jack O'Lantern!"

"Fine with me," I said. "Soon as I jack a few out of the park, everybody'll be calling me that."

We all laughed some more at that one. Even me. Felt good. Felt fun. For a while. Then silence.

Under the low, gray clouds, we crossed Riverside Drive to the park, passed a few homeless guys playing cards, and set up camp near the monument's flagpole. Tony and I took the white stone wall, Louie and Eugene sat on the steps.

"He's the only Vietnam vet I know," said Eugene. "Coach."

"You don't wanna know any," said Tony. "My uncles are crazy."

"They were probably born crazy," said Louie.

Tony grinned, nodding. "Yeah, but now they're better at it."

We all laughed again. Then Tony added, "But they knew Roberto Clemente." He paused, just long enough, then went on. "When they were little, they watched him play down in Puerto Rico. In a town called Santurce."

"They did?" I asked. Then I offered the only real fact I knew about Clemente. "He was a five-tool player, like Coach talked about. Good hitter, base stealer, incredible arm." Not to mention, my dad's favorite ballplayer.

"Yo," said Tony. "He could throw the ball from right field to third base in the air on the line. Perfect throw every time."

"How do you know?" asked Louie. "I never even heard of him."

"Oh, dude," said Tony. "I can't help it if you're ignorant. But, hey, that's probably because he died so young. Still, you should know. Roberto Clemente's in the Hall of Fame. He got exactly three thousand hits in his career and that very same year, he died."

"How'd he die?" asked Eugene.

I wondered, too, since Dad never said, and I'd never wanted to ask.

"Plane crash," Tony answered, eyebrows arched, obviously very pleased to be the source of all this knowledge. "On New Year's Eve, 1972."

"Whoa," said Louie. "No way! That's when our grandfather died. Exact same day. Was Clemente in the Vietnam War?"

"No, no, man," said Tony. "No war. Peace. His plane went down in a storm. He was flying in supplies and stuff down to Nicaragua. For a bunch of earthquake victims."

"For what?" I asked, though I'd heard him perfectly.

"He was helping people," said Tony, "who'd been through an earthquake."

Whoa, I thought. That was my territory, and I could've added something here, but I kept quiet.

"Well, our grandfather died in Vietnam," said Louie.

"He was a fighter pilot. His name's on that big wall in Washington. Right, Tyler?"

I nodded.

"Yo," said Louie. "Our family's got fighters in every war there ever was. Including the next one." He made his fists like they were holding a machine gun, spraying bullets out the back of a jet.

"Including *this* one," I said, pointing up.

"What war was this?" Eugene asked, snaking his head to look up at the towering monument.

Louie answered. "The Civil War, dummy. Can't you read?"

Eugene rose, head tilted way back at the tall, cylindrical monument. He began to walk slowly up to the bronze plaque set in the flagstone and marble plaza.

" 'To commemorate,' " he called out, " 'the valor of the soldiers and sailors who in the Civil War fought in defense of the Union.' "

"The *Union?*" I asked. "Wait a minute. Is that what it says?" I hopped up to read it myself. "What about our side? What about the South?"

"This don't say the South," said Eugene.

"Yeah," said Tony. "The South was losers."

"No way," I countered. "Louie, what's up with this?"

Louie shrugged. "You read it yourself, didn't you? This monument's only for the North."

"That is total bull." I wandered down the steps toward the cannons. "That's not fair. Look at these stones where it says, 'Port Hudson, Gettysburg, Vicksburg.'

Our great-great-great-grandfather, Henry Jacob Waltern, died at Gettysburg. He was, like, a tobacco farmer or something from down South."

Eugene and Tony thought this was funny. "A farmer?" said Tony.

Louie only shrugged and finished off his cheeseburger. "Hey, New York was a Union state. It's a New York monument. What can you do?"

"I don't know," I said. "But it ain't fair. Seems like— I don't know—seems like a Civil War monument should honor everybody. Not just one side. Otherwise, it's like, you know, they're not showing respect. Like they're still fighting the war."

"Dude," said Louie. "Down South, they still are. Believe me, go down there and you won't find no monuments to the Union soldiers. Up here's the same. I mean, that's just how people are."

Tony slurped the end of his double chocolate shake, then stood up and burped louder than a foghorn.

I walked back over and sat down on the bench. Raindrops started falling. Warm and gentle.

"I gotta get going," said Eugene, looking skyward. "I'm getting wet."

"Wait," said Tony. "We don't have a plan. We never decided what we're gonna do to those guys."

Louie grinned. "I think we should just tie 'em down and have Tony burp on 'em."

Eugene tap-danced down the steps. "No, that's illegal. Chemical warfare."

"Yeah," I said. "Nerve gas."

"Shut up, you little girls," said Tony. "At least I wanna stand up for my own. Get even with those guys."

"Forget about it," said Louie. "Besides, we're even now. They got Tyler back."

Tony thought about that a moment. "Twice!" he said. "They got him twice. So now, they're ahead. Now we gotta stand up and show them what we're made of." He jumped up and off the bench, almost dancing now, spinning around, hands waving, hotdogging it. "Show them we're not no girly dogs. Show them we're gonna stand up for Orange Blossom!" He raised a fist, then ran over and bopped Eugene's fist in midair.

"Hey," I called to everybody. "It's nobody's fight but mine, okay? And I told you guys, I'll take care of it. Wait till next time. You'll see."

Louie gathered up the loose trash and bagged it, while Tony argued it was everybody's fight because we were all on the same team.

I sat there watching Tony, his dark face, dark eyes, so intent on getting justice for me, hammerhead fist pumping, emphasizing every point.

I never thought I'd have a friend like him. He was so hyper and off-the-wall. But I noticed I was really starting to like the guy.

Then, like a wobbly, three-wheeled, all-terrain vehicle, they started off for home, talking loud, in full-on jabber mode.

I didn't go. I sat on the pink-and-black marble bench and let the rain trickle over my cap brim.

"Hey, Tyler!" Louie shouted back. "You coming?"

"Little while," I said, enjoying the shower. He waved me off.

Felt good, the rain. Good to let the hot, gray day moist up and wring out cool drops of water to splash against my skin. And weird.

I mean, to get rained on in the summer was not normal for me. Back home we had real summers. There it pretty much droughts up from June to November. That's when the sagebrush drops its leaves and goes all scraggly brown and dormant. Which is, of course, the opposite of here, where plants lose their leaves in winter.

But I was discovering lots of things back home were the opposite of here. And maybe, even me.

In a minute, I was all alone. The rain came harder and louder now, and even the homeless guys by the cannons had better benches to go to.

I walked to the base of the monument and read the plaque once more. It set my mind to wandering, darting over a bunch of images.

Breena crying, Coach whispering over his scar, guys screaming out in ambush. And nothing seemed fair. Not in my life, it didn't.

Except the rain. The rain, I realized, treats everybody the same.

On both sides of an old metal door that led inside the tower, I spotted big stone scrolls. Above them was an indentation in the tower wall. A tiny ledge, set back, hidden. And I decided to do something.

I looked around for sticks or cardboard or even a nice rock. Anything.

In the bushes below me, I spotted a broken length of gray shoestring. I went down, grabbed it, picked some blue and yellow wild flowers, and tied them together with the string. Walking back and hopping up on one of the stone scrolls, I set the flowers up in that little indentation. Then I decided to break open some cigarette butts lying nearby and scatter the tobacco over the petals.

For the farmer.

Out of my sports bag, I took a pencil stub and a scrap of paper. Leaning over to keep the paper dry, I scratched out, "Col. Henry Jacob Waltern."

"There," I said, setting the paper under the wild flower bouquet. "To the other side." I took out my camera, shielded the lens, and snapped a few shots.

Well, Tony was right after all, I thought, as I zipped my bag closed. We gotta stand up for ourselves.

chapter 17

THE NEXT MORNING COACH HAD A LITTLE WHITE bag ready by the time I met him outside a shop called "Kitchen Donuts."

Dressed in his usual sweatpants, T-shirt, ball cap, and star-covered windbreaker, he offered me something glazed and gooey, deep inside the oil-stained bag. "Breakfast?"

"Yeah, thanks!"

"This'll hold us," he said, looking past me, down Broadway. "Then later on, I thought we'd grab a little lunch at a cafe I know downtown. You got your camera?"

"Yeah," I said, tapping my backpack. But I wondered how he knew about me and my pictures.

"Good," he said. "This'll be something like taking a ride back in time. Okay with you?"

I shrugged agreement, not sure what to make of that. How far back? I wondered. But after blowing up at Coach yesterday, I was just happy to be going anywhere with him today. Happy that he'd even want me along.

As we hit the steps to the subway tunnel, he said, "You and Louie are missing our game next weekend your aunt tells me."

Oh, so he talked to *her*. "Yeah, we're going to Washington, D.C."

Down we bounced into an underground world of sticky concrete, thick, hot air, and that faint sour smell you get in old bathrooms.

Coach swiped a card at the turnstile, went through, then passed the card back to me. I swiped and entered, too.

As we approached the train track, Coach said, "She says your grandfather's on that wall."

Oh, I thought. So that's what this is. Another lesson. Well, okay, fine. As long as I still make points for going along.

I handed back his card. "Yeah, I guess. I've never seen it."

"Neither have I," said Coach.

We descended again, then hustled over to catch the number one train, already waiting. And I noticed that, for an old guy, Coach could still move.

Inside, we found seats easy, since the train wasn't too crowded on a Sunday morning. Mostly tourists, I figured, though some people looked dressed for church.

Made me think about Allan Jeffreys, my friend back home, and whether he was getting ready to acolyte at our church. Seven-thirty in the morning, back in California. He'd be there by now for the early service, slipping on his white robe, uncovering the wine chalice, breaking out the little round wafers.

I wondered if, after church, he'd take the sculpted

silver chalice back to the kitchen sink, then sip some wine before he dumped it, like I used to do.

Didn't matter to me what he did, I figured. As I bounced along in this steel subway car with its orange-and-red plastic seats, its word-scratched, shatterproof windows, and stainless steel walls, I felt like I was a million miles away from all that.

Taking a ride back in time. Only wished I really could.

Rattling along, Coach and I talked about the usual stuff. School, what I liked to do, my pictures, where I lived. That took about a minute.

Then I found out he had two grown daughters and had been divorced for twelve years, and that he was a finish carpenter. That he ran his own cabinet shop on the Upper West Side. Two more minutes.

Then we sat in silence, which is the normal thing you do on subways, where you either stand up holding a slimy pole or you sit against the car wall facing other riders whose eyes flicker up at you when they see you aren't looking, then dart away when you do.

Louie'll only sit if two seats are open and would rather stand than squish into a seat between people. That decision, he told me, was based on smell.

In about twenty minutes, we passed the World Trade Center station, and Coach bumped my arm. "Next stop," he said.

Finally, outside, we popped up on a street called Greenwich, crossed it going east, melting into a herd of people dodging double-decker buses full of noisy tourists with cameras noosed around their necks.

A couple of blocks up, Coach stopped, standing with his back to an old brown church made of stone.

"Well, here we are," he said.

"Where are we?" I asked, trying to follow his gaze across Broadway.

"Wall Street." He pointed at a green street sign with those exact words on it. "Long time ago, the Dutch had a fort at the bottom of Manhattan and they built a big wall here to protect themselves from Indians. The wall fell down, but it's been called Wall Street ever since."

"Should've had a guy like you build that wall. It'd still be up."

He barely smiled. "I've done some building around here," he said.

For a second, I thought he was lost the way he first squinted down Wall Street, then took a sharp glance down Broadway. "C'mon," he said, going south.

I hustled to catch up. "You mean you worked on these skyscrapers?"

He nodded as we headed south. "Back before I started woodworking, I was an ironworker right down here."

I'd seen enough red girder skeletons framing the sky, seen enough guys in yellow hard hats walking the beams to know how cool that must've been. "How'd you get to do that?"

"Well, a few months after I got back from 'Nam, a guy offered me the job. Paid about five times what I'd been making in Jersey driving a delivery van, so I moved to Greenwich Village and hired on."

"How'd you know what to do?"

"I didn't. I signed on as an apprentice with a surveyor's crew, joined the Operating Engineers Union, and on the first day, the guy who hired me pointed to a beam on the sidewalk and said, 'Close your eyes and walk on it.' I did. Slipped off the first time, but then I did okay, kept my balance, and that was good enough for him. Ten minutes later, I was two hundred feet in the air standing on a six-inch girder."

"Wow! That is so cool."

He gave me a small laugh. "Cool," he said, "if you got a death wish."

I let that go. "What were you surveying? I mean, up there?"

He darted across Exchange Place against the red, just ahead of a taxi. I waited, since traffic was light, then followed to get my answer.

"Well, you gotta make sure the buildings go up straight, don't you? That's what we did all day long. Clamped the transit on the very farthest outside column and took our readings. No net, no harness, no guide wires. Nothing below but street."

"Wow," I said again, my eyes skipping from building top to building top. "You were—"

"I was crazy. Had to be to work like that. Wind blowing, rain pouring, snow coming down. Didn't matter. At least, I sure didn't care. I just loved being up there. Above it all. Those days—this was about 1970—the mess this country was in, I didn't mind being above all that one bit."

"What mess? What do you mean?"

Coach walked along slower now, still a half step ahead, but like he was wandering through some remembering dream, shifting his eyes from the storefronts to the sidewalk up ahead, studying stuff. Like he was looking for something.

"I grew up in a small, blue-collar town in Jersey, outside Trenton," he said. "And I was taught, when the government puts a gun in your hand and tells you to shoot somebody, you don't ask why. You shoot. That was your duty. You did what you were told."

"That's how I was raised, too," I said, meaning, of course, doing what I was told. In my house, nobody ever mentioned the government.

"Well, you probably know something about Vietnam, don't you?"

"A little bit."

"People don't talk about it much, but in this country, it was the closest thing we ever had to a civil war since the Civil War. It tore families apart, turned brother against brother, father against son. The anger in this country during the sixties and seventies was so hot and thick, it was like lava."

My meager knowledge of those times gurgled up in my brain. Anger? "You mean the war protesters?" I asked.

"I mean everybody. Protesters, soldiers, World War Two vets, politicians. And guys like me. Guys who'd been taught and brought up a certain way, then realized later on we'd trusted people who'd lied to us."

An unfamiliar edge worked into his voice. "But in a way you could say it saved my life. The anger, I mean."

"What? But I thought you said anger was—"

"What I mean is, it kept me moving. Kept me alive. Kept me from giving up during a rough and ugly time." I noticed he checked my reaction after he said that. I had no reaction. I kept my face blank as a subway rider's.

Block after block we walked until we reached a place called Battery Park. Passing a tourist bus filling up with people, Coach went on.

"I lost two close friends in 'Nam," he said, almost as if addressing the red-and-white bus. "One by small arms fire not ten feet from me. My second week in country." He paused, shaking his head. "The other one—was by accident. Near the end of my tour. A good man. But he'd seen enough, knew too much, and one day he started circulating a petition against the war. A couple of days later, he was dead. By 'friendly fire,' they called it. Accidental."

"I'm sorry," I said, hoping it didn't sound too lame. I wanted to know more, but I figured Coach would tell me when he was ready.

"You're gonna see that memorial wall next weekend, right?" he asked.

"Yeah."

"Well, when you look at all those names, try and remember one little-known fact. That war took a bigger toll than most people realize. The fact is, more Vietnam vets have died by suicide since that war ended than actually died in it. I'm talking, over a hundred thousand guys."

And then I realized what he'd meant about his life being saved. That he could've been one of those guys.

"But there's no wall for them," he said. "People don't even wanna think about stuff like that. What they made those guys go through."

By then, we'd reached a small plaza where rows of people sat on varnished wood benches, reading the Sunday paper, sipping coffee from paper cups.

Next to a lamppost, I saw a woman with a sunburned face, her gray hair pinned up in clumps. She sat on the sidewalk, dressed in a long T-shirt pulled over grimy jeans, and held a crumpled coffee cup in her lap.

I'd never given money to a beggar before. I didn't actually know how. I mean, did you wait for them to ask or did you just walk by and plop some coins in?

She didn't look at us. Maybe she was off duty. Her eyes scanned the Peter Minuit Plaza across the street, as if looking for somebody over there among the cranes and girders and construction debris.

That's when I saw the sign. "Vietnam Veterans Plaza." An arrow pointed east. "That where we're going?" I asked.

Coach shook his head. "No, this way." He pointed, then cut through the State Street Plaza. "Here's the building I wanted to show you."

As we reached the foot of Whitehall Street, we looked up. "You helped build that?" I asked.

"Nineteen seventy," he said. "The old J. C. Pierpont headquarters. Fifty-one stories tall. And from up there you could see forever. I still remember topping it off."

"Topping it off? What's that?"

"It's an old tradition. You see, when carpenters finish framing a house, they'll put up a Christmas tree. But when you finish the structural steel part of a skyscraper, the tradition is, you take an American flag and plant it at the highest point. To top it off."

"You did that?"

"I helped. I'd been out of the army less than a year by then. And on that particular day, there was an antiwar march scheduled for the old U.S. Capitol building on Wall Street. From where we were you could see it perfectly."

I followed Coach across the street so we could get a better look at the top of his black-glassed building.

"For days those demonstrations had been going on. I knew some guys from the Village who were protesters. They'd march and chant antiwar slogans, maybe burn a few draft cards. Then go home. But on that particular day, they did something that was, back then, unthinkable. They burned an American flag."

I'd seen pictures of that. In fact, our social studies class had debated flag burning last year. Whether it should be legal or not. One side said it showed total disrespect for our veterans and our country and should be outlawed. But the other side argued that America calls itself a free country. And if you couldn't burn a flag in a free country, then you'd better call it something else. Me, I didn't know for sure.

Coach went on. "Well, most guys got so infuriated when they saw that, that our foreman jumped on the horn and called a bunch of other job sites all over lower Manhattan and told them, 'We're going down. We're taking our flag down there and we're gonna bust up that rally. You coming with us?' "

"Really? Everybody stopped working because of that?"

"Yep. We rolled right down this street, then took Stone over to Broad." Coach led the way, like some historic tour guide. "Someone grabbed the flag off the building and, man, it was something to see. Hundreds and hundreds of guys, hard hats spun backwards, flag decals shining, flag patches on their work shirts, all pouring off the job sites and marching toward Wall Street. More guys coming all the time."

As we walked farther along, I could really picture it.

"And by the time we reached the protest rally right up there, the cops were grinning from ear to ear. They just stepped back and let us in."

"They didn't think there'd be a fight?" I asked.

"They knew there'd be a fight. And they knew who'd win. But hey, most of those cops hated all these long-haired peace-and-love freaks, so why should they care? Plus, the cops saw what the ironworkers carried in their garrison belts. Solid steel spud wrenches about twenty inches long and about ten pounds each."

"Whoa, that could cause some damage."

Coach answered with a quiet look. Then he led me to Wall Street again, a few blocks from where we'd been before. I saw the white marble columns of the old U.S. Capitol building, the statue of George Washington in front with his hands stretched out, welcoming us.

"So when the sparks started flying," said Coach, "man, those kids were no match. I mean, those wrenches—they didn't just break bones, they splintered them. And skulls, too. I'm talking blood splattered everywhere."

"And you—" I said. "You saw it all happen?" My real question went unasked, but I did wonder if—in all of his anger—if he'd crushed any skulls, too.

"Saw enough. But I stood back a ways. What'd I care? I mean, I'd seen enough fighting. But that wasn't a fight down here, kid. It was a massacre."

I finally got a small sense of what he'd meant by a civil war. The blood in the streets. Americans against Americans. Then he said something that really hit home with me.

"People act like those days are way in the past, that thirty years has healed those wounds. But, man, I'll guarantee you, it still festers in a lot of people."

Yeah, I thought. I know about wounds that never seem to heal.

"And," he said, "that's the whole reason I dragged you down here today."

"It is?" I scanned the plaza, eyed the New York Stock Exchange across the street. "What is?"

He backed away from the building, his hands in his pockets, looking up at the Capitol steps, but seeing people who weren't there anymore. Then he turned and started down the sidewalk. Back toward the subway.

"What?" I asked again, still a half step behind him. Still no answer.

We crossed over Broadway in silence. Back to the old, brown church.

"Tyler, I had buddies on both sides that day. And when I got home that night, I found out that one of the best clockmakers in New York—a good friend from my hometown named Rafael, who was an art student at NYU—was lying in a coma downtown. He'd been at the rally. And all of a sudden a wave hit me."

We walked along a red-and-black stone wall in silence. Then he started again. But now in a whisper. "I couldn't even go to the hospital and see him. I walked the streets all night long. And finally, I curled up on a gravestone right here in this cemetery and I just cried."

Those words took me way, way out of my territory. I gave him a quick glance, trying to see his eyes—trying to see how I should take what he was telling me—but he'd turned, showing me only the back of his head.

I looked off past him, surprised to see an old graveyard behind the stone wall. I was more surprised to read the name "Alexander Hamilton," the American patriot, on the tombstone where Coach had finished his long night.

"Something hit me," said Coach, as he leaned on the cemetery wall. "Something I know now I must've carried back with me from 'Nam and just never realized it. But that night it hit me."

I kept quiet, eyes searching, my brain working. I glanced up at the sharp points on the wrought iron fence that rimmed the top of the cemetery wall and wondered how Coach had made it over.

"Every day I ate lunch with one bunch of guys up on the iron girders. And I ate dinner with the others down in the Village. I knew their hearts, their dreams. Both groups. Guys like The Pope and Red Dot and Rafael down on Charles Street. Woodworkers, good craftsmen. Artistic guys. And Randall LeBlanc, the Nova Scotia Indian, and Little Joe Sanchez and Fritz Newton on the construction site. Real salt-of-the-earth guys. Philosophers, all of them."

He slapped the stone wall. "And in normal times, I knew they could've all sat down around some table at Bianca Margherita's and worked out the whole stinking Bill of Rights if you would've poured them enough red wine. But that war—that stupid war—had everybody's guts churning. The whole country was at each other's throats. From those who wanted to pull out and quit the fight to those who wanted to 'nuke the gooks' and burn down their whole blessed country. Nothing was normal those days. Nothing."

This was the first time anybody had explained the sixties like that to me. I mean, the protest marches, the war—it always seemed so dry. So old. But now, I could see the people. And Coach could, too. And I saw that it still meant something to him.

That something still festered. Hadn't healed.

As we crossed Trinity Street, I noticed a quick wash of embarrassment cloud his face. He brought a hand up to his forehead.

"That was the day, kid, I decided that if I was gonna stay alive, I needed to let the anger go. All of it. At the government, the flag burners, the head smashers—all of 'em. Because it was tearing up my gut. And it was gonna kill me. I was so tired of living like some scared and wounded animal all the time. I could see myself just giving up, walking off a beam or something." He gave a shrug. "So the very next day, I quit that job and about a week later I took up cabinetry. Figured it was something I needed. Something graceful." Now he grinned. "Like I got any grace."

I did not have the ability, the proper words, to tell him right then what I knew was true. That, yeah, he had grace. Tons of it.

I just nodded like a dumb guy. My throat tight, my eyes blinking.

Coach spoke louder now. Too loud, but I understood why. "So all I'm telling you, you little rat dog—" He grabbed a clump of my shirt and shook. "Lots of ways to solve a problem. But fighting's the worst. It's the easiest. It takes the least courage. And as far as I'm concerned, it's like giving up."

He let go, nodding toward the station. "C'mon," he said. "Let's go get some lunch."

I had nothing to say, nothing to offer. Like stragglers in a strange land, we clumped along the sidewalk with heavy feet, two guys drawn too close, now looking for distance. Looking for food and shelter. I had taken no pictures, but I was leaving with images I would never forget.

At the subway entrance, Coach set his hand on my neck. "Look," he said, "this whole deal—coming down here today—it's just that your aunt asked me if I'd talk to you. Before your trip down to D.C. Me being a vet and all."

"Did she happen to know what you were gonna say?"

His face exploded with a big grin. "Not a clue. But she asked the right guy, far as I'm concerned. That town—D.C.—has always been a rough damn place for me. I can't go there anymore. All those war monuments. All that good ol' boy backslapping and flag waving. All those gravestones."

He wagged his head. "I've seen where a bunch of that leads."

As we dropped down into the subway, he shook my shoulder again. "But you'll like it there, Tyler. I'm sure you will. All boys do."

WHEN YOU COME FROM A HOME WHERE YOUR DAD walks around like a zoned-out zombie half the time and your mother lives in a dreamy Garden of Eden, you don't necessarily believe everything someone tells you.

But I believed Coach. And one thing he'd said the day before at the ball field kept rattling around in my brain.

That somehow I had to get down to the *root* of my anger. And that it usually had to do with pride. That was tough to see because, man, my pride was my identity, and you *have* to defend that. But I listened.

I listened because of one thing. Out of all the counselors and teachers and ministers I'd ever had to sit around and listen to, he was the first one who'd shown me a part of himself. I mean, that at one time, he'd been like me.

So I let it in.

And that next Friday morning, Aunt Chrissy, Breena, Louie, and I trudged up the walk at Penn Station heading toward the train to D.C.

"What are you lugging in that backpack?" Louie asked me.

I lowered my overstuffed bag before entering the car.

"Just some clothes," I said, "and a bag of tortilla chips, a few candy bars, and that pita bread, tuna-mush deal your mom made. Plus my camera and that book about Vietnam."

Louie opened his khaki vest showing lots of inside pockets. "I got everything I need right in here. My tunes, my toothbrush. And my Game Boy."

"Yeah, well, I thought I might wanna change my underwear or something, since we're staying overnight."

He backhanded my chest. "That's what you get for wearing underwear." He stood and grinned like he'd made a great joke. "And why the book, Mr. Studious Maximus? Why're you so interested in Vietnam all of a sudden?"

I shrugged. "No reason." I didn't feel like telling him what Coach'd told me. Or that I was looking for the reasons why people in a certain country would turn against each other and make a civil war—in Vietnam or here or anywhere.

As we followed a bunch of businessmen into the air-conditioned coach, a conductor in a blue uniform called out to Aunt Chrissy.

"We have a seat just for you, ma'am." With a little wave and a smile, he directed us to two bench seats facing each other. "These are especially for families."

Oh, great, I thought. I gotta look at Louie the overgrown Pokémon trainer the whole way there. Then Breena slipped in, like a breeze, into the window seat facing opposite mine and saved me.

And since the train had lots of open seats, Louie plopped down in another part of the car, and when Aunt Chrissy decided to spread out across the aisle, things didn't seem too bad at all.

I bounced my pack into the cushion next to me. "All right," I said. "A nice, big window. Best part of riding on a train." I unzipped my camera pocket.

"It's okay," said Breena. "The light's better." She opened up the book resting on her lap.

"Kelly doing all right?" I asked.

She nodded. "For now. She's at her grandmother's." With a flick of the pages, she began to read.

Tapping my feet to nothing special, I reached down and pulled out my war book, but didn't open it. Maybe later.

Train rides did that to me, got me excited, all hyper. I loved to roll along like an old-time stagecoach rider and look down the littered, broken-glass alleyways, into grimy warehouses full of massive machines spinning huge iron gears, or scan along the spray-painted windows and pipe-crossed walls that towered above this skinny, ancient ribbon of track as it cut through the ravines of the back city.

At least that's how it looked from San Diego to L.A.

Weed lots full of busted-up cars, house by ramshackle, add-on house, with backyards like junkyards, only better. Every few moments, another snapshot. Upside-down washing machines filled with stones, toolsheds tilting with windows long gone, bedsprings rusting, wet clothes hanging, kids hiding-and-seeking, peeking at trains, calculating time and speed while fingering hot, jagged rocks in hand-grenade hands.

But the land around New York City—hey, I did not have that figured at all. I couldn't believe it. Within five minutes of rolling out of Penn Station, I was staring at ponds and lakes and fields all filled with cattails and reeds and tons of trees. Open country, just like back home. Sycamore trees, their mid-June leaves much smaller than the ones I'd left behind, encircled small ponds where little brown ducklings floated in a straight line behind their black-headed mama. I spotted herons and sleek white cranes standing stock still, gazing out like one-legged guardsmen over the marsh.

Then, bang. Before I knew it, the train had blasted into Newark, and once again tall, burned-brown buildings and blaring billboards shot up all around.

Farther down the line, I saw a perfect set of baseball diamonds, with mowed grass and smooth dirt baselines. California-style fields. A pang of homesickness mixed with a butterfly tingle flickered through me. Then I saw a small, bright green graveyard dotted with a scattering of tiny American flags and I remembered why we were making the trip.

Before long, we'd settled into the rocking rhythm of the ride. Breena buried in her book, Aunt Chrissy lick-thumbing her *Vogue* magazine. Louie hunched over his Pocket Rocket fighting game or running to the dining car, bringing back french fries and plastic-wrapped pastries.

And I had my Minolta, eye-level ready, snapping random shots.

Sometimes, when Breena seemed to be reading intently, I studied her. Hardly even turning my head, I'd move my eyes from the window scene to where she sat crooked and cocooned into her seat across from me. One hand held her book, the other a clump of honey-colored hair, precision cut, flaring out from her fist like spray from a garden hose. Or I'd glance down at her thin white ankles, crossed one over the other, the top one decorated with silver-and-blue speckled bracelets that jangled with the train ride and sparkled in the light.

From time to time the conductor barged through, announcing the towns. "Ta-REN-ton!" for Trenton. "PHILLAY!" for Philadelphia. And "WEEL-ming-ton!"

And before I knew it, two and a half hours had passed like a fast-action jungle safari on the Discovery Channel.

I'd shot nearly two rolls of film, and now I sat back hoping to finish up the last few shots on Breena.

Bravely, with the cool eyes of an explorer, I studied her face, noticing how the window lit her smooth, light-pink skin, noticing now for the first time a finger-sized patch of delicate freckles across her nose, and noticing the train-track tremble of her lips as she read.

And I wondered. Is it okay to kiss your cousin?

But I kept the camera on my lap. Some images you just have to memorize. Still, I wondered if maybe she had any of these feelings for me. And if she did, how would I ever find out?

She looked up at me. A grin rose on her face. "What?" she asked.

I pushed my shoulders up to my ears. "Nothing. Just thinking." I pointed to her lap. "That book any good?"

"I love it." She squinched the glittery, romance paperback against her, then turned to the outside scenery. Up raced a big billboard showing a scared little guy in a crowded jail cell, with the words, "Commit Insurance Fraud. Make New Friends."

"What about the one you're reading?" she asked.

I thrust out my bottom lip. "It's okay. Lots of pictures and stuff." One in particular, I wanted to say, but I didn't want to have to show it to her.

I kicked my legs out, sending them under her as she sat curled in her seat, and drummed my fingers on the book cover next to me. Thinking about pictures that come from war.

What if Grandad, I thought, had dropped a bomb, had dropped napalm on a little girl like the one in the picture?

Breena closed her novel and looked at me. "Stuff like what?"

I picked the book up and flipped it over in my hands. "Oh, facts and figures. The whole history of Vietnam and stuff. How they'd fought the Chinese for over a thousand years. How in the 1800s, the French invaded their land and set up colonies because they wanted their gold and coal."

"They've been fighting for hundreds of years?"

"Pretty much. Off and on. Mostly trying to keep invaders out."

"Why did we fight them?"

"Well, see, it's all weird. Before World War Two, Japan invaded Vietnam and took it from the French. So when the Japanese lost the war, the French decided they wanted Vietnam back. But the Vietnamese people fought and fought and finally kicked the French out. And so, for like the first time ever—this was like in the 1950s— the people in Vietnam finally got a chance to hold elections and actually get to pick a *Vietnamese* leader."

"That was good. What happened?"

"What happened was—and this part's kind of hard to understand—but, all the big world powers, the U.S. and Britain and everybody, came in and decided to split Vietnam in half. Then we made sure they wouldn't hold their election because it looked like a communist was going to win."

"So what? Why should we care?"

"Well, we cared because we were afraid that if the communists took over Vietnam, they'd be controlled by the Russians or the Chinese."

"So?"

"So then they'd go on to control the whole region. All the countries. One by one, like dominoes falling. But the Americans never understood how different the Vietnamese were from the Russians. Or how much they hated the Chinese. That all of their cultures were so totally different."

"Why didn't they just say so?"

"They tried. Way before the war with us. It was like, nobody listened. Americans, you know, just figured we knew what was best. But the Vietnamese, most of them just wanted to be one country. To elect their own independent government and be left alone. But we wouldn't let them. We figured communism was communism. And back in those days, Americans were totally scared of communism. So we basically put in our own people to rule South Vietnam and fought against anybody— the communists in the North *and* the rebels in the South—who tried to get rid of them."

"We'll be arriving in D.C. in half an hour," Aunt Chrissy called out.

"Yeah, okay," I said, rising. "Breena, want a Coke or something?"

She shrugged, like she was lost in a thought.

Fifteen minutes later, I returned with a couple of Cokes plus a cup of french fries dunked in chili. "Want some?"

She looked up at me with eyes that seemed tight with pain.

"I think war is so stupid," she said.

I swung down into my seat, unfolded a little table from under the window, and set the box of drinks and fries on it.

"Yeah," I agreed. "It's pretty wacko." That's when I realized she'd been looking at the pictures in my book.

In her hand, she bounced a straw endwise on the

table and popped it out of its wrapper, then popped it through the plastic lid of her drink.

After a big sip, she said, "I say, all the people who believe in war should live over in one part of the world. And all the rest of us should live in the other."

I considered the idea. "But that would be, like, almost our whole country living on the war side."

"Fine, I don't care. If anyone believes that war is *ever* okay, then they should just go off someplace and have their little wars and leave the rest of us alone."

I didn't get into it with her. Not because it was Breena, or that she was upset, but because I suddenly wondered, if that happened—if we split the world in two—which side would I live on?

I was a fighter, I knew that. I believed there were times you just had to fight and even kill. I mean, you couldn't let everyone walk all over you, right? Still, the longer I thought about it, the more I realized I'd rather live with Breena and people like her, than with people like me who figured war was okay. I mean, having peace was obviously better. It's just that, for me, fighting was so automatic.

Facing into the window now, she asked, "Do you know how many Americans died in Vietnam?"

"Yeah, I guess. Doesn't it say that the Vietnam War Memorial has, like, over fifty-eight thousand names on it?"

She tossed the book back across to the empty seat, like it was all the book's fault. "Yes, well," she said, "I just read something else. Do you know how many Vietnamese died?"

I stared at her, clueless.

"Over three million," she said. "And that's men, women, and children."

"Whoa, that many?"

"How can people do that to each other? Human *beings*."

"I don't know," I said.

Of course, I did know. I knew about fighting and how easy it could happen. And I doubted that I'd ever qualify to live on the peace side of the world no matter how hard I tried.

"Do you know what that means?" she asked, but didn't wait for my answer. "Think about it. We've got that one massive wall that lists all those names, right?"

"Yeah, right."

"Okay. But if we were really gonna list *all* the names of *all* the people who died during that war, we'd have to build *fifty more walls*."

chapter 19

"THIS WAY, EVERYBODY," AUNT CHRISSY SAID AS she pushed us along, charging through the crowd at D.C.'s Union Station. I could tell she was pumped.

At the far wall near the depot exit, we bought our Metro cards from the vending machine and were on our way.

Boarding the sleek underground Metro train, Aunt Chrissy called out, "We want the Smithsonian station, kids. Pay attention. It's not far."

Before long, the train had dumped us and a few hundred others at the clean, white-tiled stop. Up the stairs we tramped into a sticky ocean of hot, humid air, bright sun, and my first glimpse of the Washington Monument.

I could barely suck in a breath. "This weather's worse than New York's," I said.

"Who *you* tellin'?" said Louie as he pulled out the neck of his T-shirt and fanned his chest.

"Oh, but look," chirped Aunt Chrissy. "Way down there's the Capitol Building." Then she turned. "And way over there's the Washington Monument. You're in the middle of a lot of history, Tyler."

I glanced across the grassy midway in both directions.

The dollhouse-sized Capitol looked like every other old white building I'd ever seen, only with a dome. And the thin graystone monument to our first president, I'm sorry to say, was a disappointment, too. I mean, even at 555 feet high, after coming from New York and its 100-story skyscrapers, seeing this puny thing sitting all by itself in the middle of a green field was a letdown.

"Mom," said Louie, "it's too hot. Let's go to the Air and Space Museum. Someplace air-conditioned."

"No," said Breena. "That's so boring. I wanna see the National Art Gallery."

"Breena, we're here for Tyler," Louie said, not meaning that at all. Just thinking that I'd vote with him. "You wanna see the fighter jets, don't you, Tyler?"

"I guess." I watched Breena's shoulders slump, and I noticed once again how I hated to separate myself from her. But an art museum? Hey—she had to realize, love had its limits.

"Okay, boys, we'll go there first," Aunt Chrissy decided. "After all, we are an Air Force family. But I also hoped we could visit the American History Museum. For Tyler. Then, when it's a touch cooler, we can see the outdoor sights."

We all agreed, just to get out of the heat, if nothing else.

But the Air and Space Museum was awesome. In the lobby they had real airplanes hung in midair from the tall ceiling, including the exact plane the Wright brothers flew. They also had actual space capsules where real astronauts had lived—like in some high-tech cave—as they circled the earth.

"Grandad would've been in that," said Louie, pointing to the Apollo 11 command module. "If he didn't go to 'Nam."

"What do you mean?" I asked.

"Your grandad Waltern," Aunt Chrissy answered, "joined the Air Force to be a test pilot, hoping that eventually he could enter the space program and become an astronaut. That was long before the war heated up."

"Really?" I asked.

She nodded. "It was his big dream. He used to tell us kids that he wanted to 'shoot for the moon.' "

"Yeah," said Louie. "He could've been Neil Armstrong or John Glenn."

"But, Daddy had a sense of duty," said Aunt Chrissy. "And he went where they needed him most." She looked like she wanted to say more, but swallowed instead.

"Hey, whoa," said Louie, pointing behind me. "Check it out. Missiles."

On the far wall, a U.S. Pershing II nuclear warhead stood side by side next to a Soviet SS 20 missile, and a sign told how they'd both been disarmed in the 1980s.

"Look. Our rockets were a lot bigger than theirs," said Louie. "We could've kicked some serious tush with those bad boys."

I could tell Breena was hating this war stuff. She kept studying the hot-air balloons, Lindbergh's *Spirit of St.*

Louis—which, like me, was actually from San Diego!— and the human-powered glider. And of course, she didn't follow us into the war exhibits upstairs.

But just as we were on our way out, she pointed to the coolest thing.

"Tyler," she said, taking my arm. "Let's fly to the moon!" Then she showed me a sign that read: Touch a Piece of the Moon.

"Oh, yeah, I forgot," said Louie. "C'mon! It's cool."

We walked around to the front of the display. Sure enough, there was a little black, sparkly moon rock sitting in a small open case. You could just walk by and touch it.

I let Breena and Louie go first.

See, I had to wait. The pull of the moon meant something special to me. Back home, it was the moon that I'd look up to on certain hot summer nights, walking out of my house and down the horse corral path to find Dad.

And I'd let that baseball moon pull me up. Let it take me high above the sadness, the guilt, the heat, the dust. Must've been the Air Force in my blood, but it was like I could look up and just fly off with it.

On earth you could put up fences and build borders. But the sky had no limits. No barbed wire. No border patrols. No walls to keep you from going anywhere you wanted to go.

No wonder, I thought, that Heaven was in the sky.

And in that instant, as I stepped up and stuck my fingertip on that four-billion-year-old chip of the moon, I remembered all this. And I felt lifted.

The feeling stayed with me long after we left and marched across a huge grassy field, toward the Smithsonian American History Museum.

In the distance, I could hear military-style drumming. Not continuous. More like a band setting up, getting ready for a parade or something.

Be fun to see a parade, I thought. All right.

But once we'd crossed Constitution Avenue to the museum, I saw that the drummer was just some tall, skinny kid in a T-shirt and shorts, beating the bottoms of three plastic buckets and using the metal sides of a shopping cart for cymbals.

Even with that equipment, though, he sounded pretty good.

Farther down the sidewalk stood a gold-faced mime juggling with five silver-colored bowling pins. Putting on quite a show. Up and down the street rolled these goofy-looking red, open-air motor carts, cruising by full of camera-to-the-eye tourists capturing the carnival-like scene.

All around us, groups of day-camp kids ran past with sodas and hot dogs. It all reminded me an awful lot of a crowded day in Disneyland.

Near the American History Museum entrance, some old, bearded guy dressed in a ripped ball cap, a white cotton shirt, and army fatigue pants slowly made his way up the crowded sidewalk, pushing a tall cart stuffed with cardboard boxes and ringed with plastic shopping bags.

His face had that creased, scuffed-leather look a guy

gets from too many days of cold wind, burning sun, and hard stares.

Wired to the front of his cart was a hand-lettered sign that read: BeWare of the CuLTure Whose HEroes Are SoLDiers. Under that was a paper cup.

Even in the home of our nation, I thought, they've got homeless.

Of course, why would I expect D.C. to be any different from anyplace else? We paused while Breena plunked coins into the old guy's empty cup.

"Bless you, darlin'," said the old man. "Bless you."

Watching her nod with such an air of confidence and understanding made me feel like the selfish, unsophisticated country boy I was, who'd never given coins to a beggar before. Gawky. Ignorant. Unblessed.

Then something strange happened. Not thirty feet away, another guy stepped through some bushes that bordered the museum side lawn.

He crossed the grass and hopped up on a little wall along the sidewalk.

Dressed in dark pants and the stained smithereens of a suit coat buttoned over a white shirt, he carried a black leather book that I guessed was a Bible.

Through a gray-and-black speckled goatee, he grinned, showing nicotined teeth that matched his light brown skin.

"I'm a government man," he announced to no one in particular.

Breena and I stopped in our tracks as Louie and Aunt

Chrissy walked ahead a few more feet. Then the guy said, "And I got a bomb in here."

He tapped his chest. As he did, a chunk of gray hair flopped down over his forehead. "And I'm gonna *blow your minds!*" Now he was shouting.

"Every month," he said, "I get a check from the U.S. government. And I'm here to earn it." He pointed at Aunt Chrissy. "Why are you here?"

I thought she'd turn and huff away. Instead, she answered, "To show these children our national heritage."

The man nodded, eyeballing the three of us.

"Yes," he said. "The national heritage. Which is what? To destroy all the godless heathens who lived here all along and replace them with God-fearing Christians. Go inside the museum, lady, and see for yourself. That's how this country was formed. Are you a Christian?"

Aunt Chrissy took a step away. "Yes, I am," she said, and kept walking. "Come on, kids."

Louie followed, but Breena and I waited a moment longer.

"A good Christian woman," the man called after her. "Good, good, good." He waved his Bible in the air. "You're not afraid of me are you? Jesus said, 'Fear thou not.' But this country is full of fear. Ain't that a fact?" He laughed, doing a quick dance-shuffle on the top of the small white wall, then hack-coughed twice, sounding like a barking dog, and turned his attention to the small crowd of onlookers gathered near us.

"Look here, folks, lookit!" He shouted again as Aunt Chrissy stood in the museum plaza, urgently waving us toward her. "If Sad-*dam* Hussein was lying in the street, beaten and bloody, how many of y'all would pick him up? Carry him to shelter? Pay for his needs? Jesus said, do it. Said, don't walk by. Said, you don't walk by and you don't shoot him. He don't care if it was Bill Clinton! He don't care if it was Adolf Hitler or Slow-Me-Down Milosevic. You don't walk by! You step up and help the man. You carry him to shelter. You reach in your pocket and pull out money for room and board. That's what Jesus taught, y'all." He shook his head. "I ain't making this up. Fear not."

He barked once more, then jumped backwards off the stucco wall to the grass behind him. I saw his wide eyes glance quickly at a park policeman riding his bicycle along the street, approaching us.

As the man retreated, he shook a finger at the crowd. "This country's full of fear, people. Y'all know what I mean."

He fell to his hands and knees, catching himself, scanning back and forth like a trapped dog, ready to bolt, before rising to a low crouch and scampering, straight forward, over the wall and onto the sidewalk in front of us.

Without breaking stride, he bounded down the walk, right toward the policeman who stood curbside, waiting, straddling his mountain bike.

"Good afternoon, officer," said the dog man. "May I treat you to an ice cream bar? I'm having one myself."

The park policeman sent a frozen stare, then slowly grinned. "No, thanks, buddy."

Dog-man never slowed, but pranced on past, arms pumping like a drum major, wild and fast. A one-man parade.

Fearless.

"What a lunatic," said a guy behind me.

I held my camera to my eye.

"C'mon, Tyler," said Breena. "Let's go."

"I am, I am," I answered as I clicked away, freeze-framing forever a dog man on the government payroll disappearing down a street called Constitution.

chapter 20

NONE OF WHAT THAT LOONY DOG MAN SAID would've stuck with me at all, except that when we entered the American History Museum, the first place I went—well, after the bathroom—was a little video theater in one of the exhibits.

In the lobby, Aunt Chrissy had told us, "Meet me here at four, kids. That'll give you an hour and a half."

Louie knew right where he was going—some classic car exhibit on the second floor. That sounded fun, but I liked to do stuff in order, so I said I'd catch up with him later.

And while Breena and Aunt Chrissy went off to the gift shop, I headed toward the first exhibit.

It was a full-on re-creation of an American Indian pueblo village in New Mexico. On the video monitor, a woman spoke about her Native American ancestors, how they'd been treated by the Europeans.

The pictures were great, mostly because they reminded me of the open land and sagebrush hills where I grew up.

"When the American settlers came out west," the woman in the video said, "they carried this idea of 'either/or.' It's either you or me, but both of us can't stay here together."

The screen showed vast stretches of mountainsides, dotted with trees and red-iron boulders all the way to the tops of jagged ridges. Hollow, wooden flute music rippled in the wind.

"And to them," she continued, "the idea of land was the same. It's either mine or yours, but it can't just be left alone."

Yeah, that's it, I thought. That's just what's been gnawing at me since Breena talked about splitting up people into two sides. Her solution seemed the safest— to stick with people who thought like you. I mean, I agreed with her.

But now this New Mexican woman was saying there's another way to look at it. That maybe both sides could share this land. That there was room. They *could* live together. But what would it take for that to happen?

I mean, weren't the two sides enemies? The settlers and the Indians? Weren't their cultures totally different? Their values totally opposite?

As I thought about how that could possibly work, the dog man scampered into my brain.

Yeah, I decided, that'd be like sharing your home with a homeless man. I mean, it would take that kind of fearlessness. But who would ever do that?

When the show was over, I wandered out into the main exhibit room and saw Breena looking at an Indian display.

"What are you doing here?" I asked.

"Thought I'd pop in, take a quick look," she said. "Then go see the other exhibits. But this is really interesting." Her eyes settled on these old, turn-of-the-century pictures of Native American fertility dancers.

"It's weird to think that this is America," said Breena. "I feel like I'm walking through a foreign country."

"I feel like I'm in my own backyard," I said.

And it wasn't just the short video—which I watched again with Breena—but the rock art, the willow baskets, the pottery bowls. All stuff I was fully familiar with and that Breena had never seen before.

"White sage," I told her, pointing at the herbal medicine display. "Tea from that will cure colds and fight infections."

"How do you know?"

"I've used it before. A Mexican woman showed my mom. There's all kinds of secret stuff out where I live that only a few people know about."

"Tyler," she said. "You know what? I wanna go to California someday. I wanna see all your secret stuff."

"Okay," I said. And I froze my face, not smiling or anything, being all cool. But, man, I had a zillion neat thoughts to think after that.

At a minute past four o'clock, Breena and I trooped back into the lobby as planned, though I wished we could've stayed away forever.

That whole time, it'd been like having Breena alone with me at home on my mountain, looking around, exploring the trails, touching the granite grinding stones the Kumeyaay Indians had used before their land was invaded.

"I liked being in there," she said.

"Me, too," I told her, feeling a twinge of sadness.

A few minutes later, Aunt Chrissy arrived.

"Where is Louis?" she asked.

"Probably still drooling over cars," Breena answered.

But he wasn't. Within moments, he'd come out of the gift shop with this tinplate military dog tag he'd bought that read, "Louie Ka-blooie. Stay outta my face."

I nodded and grunted, but fully wished I'd bought one, too.

Then he pulled out some miniature American flags. "Gotta have some of these," he announced. "For Grandad." He handed me one.

"What do you mean?" I asked.

"You can stick them in the ground in front of the wall."

"It's okay? You can just leave stuff there?"

"Sure. You'll see. There's flowers and flags and notes and all kinds of stuff all over the place. You do it to re-member somebody."

I grunted again and stuck the flag in my backpack pocket.

Once we left the air-conditioned museum and hit the moist wall of heat again, I noticed a greasy, french-fried, pukey feeling rising from my stomach.

"How far is it?" I asked.

"Close," said Louie. "Just a few blocks." He pointed west, down a street lined with trees. Tons of people hiked and biked along the walkway next to it, lugging packs and cameras and pushing strollers along.

Our route took us west down Madison Drive, then straight past the Washington Monument, that still looked strange standing on a knoll all by itself in the middle of that field.

Number one, I thought when I looked at it. He was our first president, so of course his monument looks like a big number one.

Tall trees filled the National Mall, which was more like a park than anything, with ponds and pools and flowers. Along the walkway dotted with low-back benches, squirrels zigged and darted, gathering fat, green walnuts.

Even so, the mood was zombie. Seemed like the heat and damp, heavy air was crushing everyone, especially poor Aunt Chrissy. She dragged along behind us, arms crossed, her sunglasses aimed downward just ahead of her feet.

"It's on the other side of that grass mound," Louie said, after we'd circled a small pond. "You can't really see it from here. It's sunk down. It's, like, in this little depression."

He was right. I couldn't see any sign of it, but I did see bunches of people filing in and out of a sunken walkway. And in a few moments, we were standing at the beginning of that asphalt pathway ourselves.

No one spoke. I heard Aunt Chrissy sniffle.

Breena came close and took my arm.

"Tyler, come on," she whispered. "I'll take you down and show you where his name is."

I didn't answer. I mean, what was the big deal? I'd seen pictures of the thing before.

I sloughed off my backpack and retrieved the tiny flag. With a flick, I shook it open and all four of us started toward the gray stone path that ran along the Vietnam Veterans Memorial wall.

Suddenly I found I couldn't lift my eyes from that monument. I mean, all the pictures in the world couldn't have prepared me for this.

Moving along, I saw how the wall starts off small— you hardly notice—as it grows right out of the ground, then builds and builds the farther down the path you go, chiseled name next to name, row after row, white names carved into black rock, white names separated by small dots like multiplication signs, line after line, panel after panel, it just sucks you in and seems to go on forever. Down that rocky path you go as the black wall wells up huge, looming over you, higher and higher, and step by step, before you know it, you're in over your head.

"There," said Breena. "This panel."

My eyes scanned dozens and dozens of names. Where? I wondered.

Breena hunched forward, slowly sliding her finger down the stone. "Oh, yeah. Right there. See it?"

"Yeah," I whispered. "I see it."

Ba-bang. Chiseled in stone. *John Tyler Waltern.*

I knelt down, heart banging my chest, and looked at my grandfather, as if he were right there. Looked through the wall, right through his name, and imagined him, stern-faced, staring back at me.

I imagined him flying, his F-100 Super Saber in a thirty-five degree dive, five hundred, six hundred knots, swooping down, two thousand feet above the jungle, napalm bomb ready to drop. Then shot.

I imagined him shot. Diving, dying, looking through shattered glass, seeing the treetops of the jungle rushing up to catch the plane.

More shots. Shots from the ground. Shots from the trees. Fired in anger.

And I wondered, did he die in anger? Was he angry at the man who'd shot him? Was he angry at losing, at dying, at feeling so out of control of his life?

Was he afraid of what people would say? That he'd lost the plane? Lost his crew? That he'd let his country down? And did that make him even more angry?

Did he feel what I feel when things go wrong?

Breena touched my shoulder. I heard Aunt Chrissy sniffle again and whisper nearby. I wondered how long I'd been kneeling there.

"Here's your flag," said Breena, placing into my hand the skinny dowel that I'd somehow dropped.

I took it. But I didn't plant it. For some reason, it seemed so useless.

I just stood there, like an island in a stream of people, holding that little flag. Aunt Chrissy leaned forward against the wall, resting on her upraised arms, and kissed her father's name.

And I choked up the same way I did every year at Lissie's gravestone watching Mom set her fresh cut flowers into the little tin cup. I'd always choke up. Not for Lissie, but for Mom.

But it wasn't until I stood a ways back that I realized I couldn't see this wall the way everyone else did. Not now. Not after what Coach had told me. About the civil war that roared in our streets. And about all the guys who'd died by suicide. Where was the wall for them?

And especially not after what Breena had said about the millions of Vietnamese who had died. About the fifty more walls it would take to remember them.

I mean, I could still see what everyone else saw. All the loss of life. All the human destruction. The sacrifice. But now I could see so much more.

Or maybe, it was that I didn't see enough.

That something was missing.

chapter 21

THE REST OF THE WASHINGTON TRIP SHOT BY. The Capitol tour was boring, but I liked seeing the White House, the museum with the dinosaurs, and the Bureau of Engraving where they make all the big sheets of money.

But you know what I liked best of all? The Lincoln Memorial. I'm serious.

Sure, I'd seen pictures of it, lots of times. But in real life, that huge white marble statue of Lincoln sitting in a chair blew me away.

The memorial building was as big as a two-story barn. Much more humongous than I'd thought. Every-thing was. The statue, all the stone pillars, and the giant walls surrounding it.

I climbed the tall set of steps that led way up to the top where President Lincoln sat gazing out. At what? I turned around and saw a long, narrow reflecting pool, which carried the mirror image of the distant Wash-ington Monument in it.

That image—the tall, gray, dagger-shaped tower mir-rored in the blue-sky waters of the pool—made me ap-preciate the Washington Monument for the first time.

I spun three-sixty, taking in the whole scene.

And that's when something caught my eye.

Chiseled into the brown stone wall inside the Lincoln Memorial was the Gettysburg Address. Now, I'd read that speech before, had even memorized part of it in fifth grade. But this was the first time it seemed like President Lincoln was talking to me.

With one word.

Don't ask me why it stood out, but one word just grabbed me and wouldn't let go. And it helped me make one of the biggest decisions of my life.

"We have come," the speech read, "to dedicate a portion of that field as a final resting place for those who here gave their lives . . ."

That's where I stopped.

I knew about the Civil War. How the North had fought the South. The U.S. government regulars against the Confederate rebels who had split off and started up their own country.

And what word did Mr. Lincoln use when he wanted to come and honor the soldiers killed at Gettysburg?

Those.

". . . for *those* who here gave their lives . . ."

Not just the Union soldiers. Not only the Confederate side. But *all* of them. Including, I realized, Colonel Henry Jacob Waltern.

Lincoln made no distinction between armies or the governments behind them.

For me, that was huge. All the way back to New York I thought about it. That Lincoln was saying almost the same thing Coach had told me about guys on other teams. That people are people. And someday I'd see.

Well, even though I never considered myself a guy who went around making weird connections, this one was easy. And today was the day.

From that moment on, I began to see what was missing.

Later that night, I went to sleep trying to imagine a fifty-story war memorial. The best I could do was to imagine one as tall as the building Coach had worked on.

I saw fifty black-granite memorial wings climbing high into the sky, and chiseled on all that rock was every single name of every man, woman, and child killed in the Vietnam War. *Over three million people.*

Talk about huge. That would be humongous.

The next morning, as I came to breakfast, I heard Uncle Phil's voice and immediately remembered that he was back in town again. I quickly geared myself up for his little chat.

"How's the season going, Champ?" he asked as I plopped down.

"Fine." I dumped a bunch of cereal into a blue-and-yellow bowl.

"Just fine?" He grinned, scanning Louie and Breena. His arm muscles bulged and twitched like some weird energy was spurting through his body, keeping him in constant flutter. "Tearing it up out there, aren't you?" Even his words came out in quick, sharp, rapid-fire bursts.

"I don't know." I hated those kinds of questions. I splashed milk off my spoon as I drenched my bowl of Hunee-Pooffs.

"Well, what's your batting average?"

"Four hundred something," I said, not exactly sure, since one of my last hits might've been scored an error.

"Whoa, that's adequate," he said, still grinning, head bobbing, eyes searching. "Adequate, for certain. How many home runs?"

I answered softly, "None." What's he think? I wondered. I'm Super Dwarf? Home runs are hard. Then I added, "Yet. Lots of doubles, though."

The toaster popped, and Louie jumped up to get his bagel, slightly burned, it smelled like.

Uncle Phil sliced down into his sausage, clinking his knife against the flower-petaled china, then stabbed the chunk and dunked it into goopy yolk. "When's All-Stars?" he asked.

"Latte, Phil?" Aunt Chrissy called, from over by the espresso machine. "Or a mocha this morning? I've got a new syrup."

Uncle Phil chomped down on his sausage and pointed at me with his fork. "That's a given, right, Champ? All-Stars?"

I shrugged. I was still waiting for him to answer Aunt Chrissy. "Hope so," I said. "Still a couple more weeks to go."

"Dad," said Breena. "I found these cute ceramic birds down in Soho that look just like they're paper origami. With the folds and everything."

He looked at her with a clinched eyebrow, like she was a girl he didn't even know.

"That's nice, angel," he said. "It's still soccer and birds for you, huh? Someday you might decide you've outgrown your toy birds, don't you think?"

Breena hunched over her muffin, lips pressed together, her thumbnail picking at the paper wrap. She lifted one shoulder in a tired shrug. That was weird to see. I mean, she could be shy around strangers, but I'd never seen her act shy at home. Softly, she added, "I'm going to arrange them in river pebble nests."

"Phil?" Aunt Chrissy asked again.

Uncle Phil jerked back to speak over his shoulder. "Just one single cup of normal coffee, Christine. I don't want any *syrup* in it." He turned back to me. "Well, I'll be at your game today, count on that. Noontime, right? And I'll put a bug in Trioli's ear, too. My gosh, a kid with your speed, hitting four hundred plus. Forget about it. They oughtta be *paying* you to play All-Stars."

"Him?" Louie said, smacking down on his blueberry bagel. "Yeah, right. When Mike Tyson gets a tryout with the Yankees."

I jabbed him under the table. "Like you know anything," I said, wondering why he'd want to say something like that for no reason.

He scooted his chair back, laughing. "I know baseball ain't supposed to be tag-team wrestling." Then he turned to his dad. "I got two RBIs last game. Both with two outs."

"Good for you," said Uncle Phil, who spoke as if

some distant thought was squeezing his brain. "By the way, Louie, did you get that packet from the Air Force Academy? I had them send you a packet."

Louie lowered his eyes. "Yeah, but I didn't need it. I already got that stuff online. I'm already taking all the right prep classes and everything."

"Well," said Uncle Phil. "Stay on top of that situation for me, will you? Don't want anything getting all fouled up. And why don't you get in touch with the academy's New York liaison officer? Let him know your intentions."

"Dad, I'm only gonna be a sophomore. I got plenty of time—"

"Never too early to introduce yourself, start them thinking about you. Set yourself up as someone special in their eyes."

Uncle Phil turned toward me.

"So, Tyler. All-Stars is when? I don't wanna miss that."

I dunked my spoon, loaded it with yellow Pooff balls, and held it ready. "Um, I don't know."

"In about three weeks," said Louie. "The coaches are supposed to get together at Mr. Trioli's on the last day of the season. Then the next day is Sunday, the Fourth of July, which'll be the league picnic. That's when they'll announce the All-Star team. Games start the end of that week."

Nodding with an urgent bob, Uncle Phil dragged a slice of rye toast across his plate, bit down on it, licked a finger, and talked out of the side of his mouth. "Well, they'll call your name, Tyler. Whata ya, kidding me? That's a no-brainer." He rapped his knuckles on the table. "Christine? We got coffee? Thought you were getting coffee."

"Phillip, I am not some waitress at your beck and call." Then she spoke more calmly, slowly. "It's drip-ping."

I shoveled the cereal into my mouth.

Louie talked into a Matterhorn of cream cheese he'd plopped on top of his bagel. "Last year, my English teacher said that people who use the term 'no-brainer' usually are."

Uncle Phil glared at him. "What's that supposed to mean?"

Breena, gliding like a quiet ghost, got up and left, her carrot muffin showing one bite gone.

"Nothing," said Louie, chewing hard, cream cheese caking both corners of his mouth. "Just an observation."

Closing his eyes, Uncle Phil swiveled back to me. "So the games start in about three weeks, huh, Champ?"

"Yeah, I guess."

Aunt Chrissy tiptoed in, placing coffee at his elbow.

"Okay." Uncle Phil tapped my arm. "It's my busiest time of year, but I'll make sure I'm in town for that. Forget about it." He cut down hard again, *clink-clanking* the whole kitchen. "Those tournaments can be something else, believe me. Some good, tough ball-players in that mix."

What could I say? Louie sat crushed. I mean, okay, we all knew he was no great athlete, but two-out RBIs don't come every day. Uncle Phil should've said more than just, "Good for you."

The whole thing was weird to watch. I mean, my dad ignored me, sure. But watching how Uncle Phil changed the subject or got distracted by other stuff or answered—but never really answered—a question made me see I was closer to Louie and Breena than I'd ever realized. In a weird way, our dads were a lot alike.

And, besides, it wasn't a "no-brainer" that I'd make the team. I thought I would. By rights, I should. But they'd already warned me they weren't judging just on stats and skills.

They'd hung that "attitude" thing out there in front of me. How I had to stop being such a "loose cannon." And so far I thought I was buckled down. But, man, I couldn't promise anything about the future.

One bad shake, and I could break loose again, no doubt.

And all those thoughts followed me to the ballpark that morning. While Louie and I were tossing the ball around before the game, I took another look at him and realized I understood Louie better than I ever had. That now I could see why he hunkered down with his head-phones and sunglasses and spent hour after hour blasting little black jets out of the cyber sky. In that world, he was in charge.

Funny thing about making connections. Seemed like, once you started, you couldn't stop. They were everywhere. And I wondered if Louie could see them, too. One in particular I thought I'd try on him.

"Hey, Louie," I said as I caught his toss. "Did you know that in the Vietnam War we lost, like, fifty-eight thousand guys? But that the Vietnamese lost over three million?"

"What?" He stepped closer to me. "What are you talking about? What brought that up?"

I shook my head. "Nothing. Just been thinking about something since we got back from D.C." Then I repeated the numbers and threw.

"All right!" he said, grinning as he snagged my throw in the web of his glove. "Fifty-eight thou to three million? Yo, cuz. Who says we lost that war? We kicked their butts!"

He fired the ball back at me.

So much for sharing connections, I thought. "No, man," I said. "It's not like a video game. You don't just keep score. Besides, a lot of those Vietnamese fought on our side."

"Yeah, well, so what? See, we had the firepower. We had *da bombs!* That's what happens when you blast away, baby. You take charge. You get results."

Da bombs. For a moment I flashed back to the little girl in the black-and-white photo running down the dirt road, trying to shake the burning napalm jelly off her flesh.

Results.

And as I caught the ball again, I saw the other team break out of their dugout and swarm onto the field.

Running full speed, screaming their war hoots, banging their fists into oiled gloves. Cleats thundering, leather snapping, a chorus of cheers from distant fans.

The song of baseball. Of hope. Of getting one more chance.

And I loved it.

Give me the clean page of an unmarked score book, scratch my name in the number three slot, dust the dirt off home plate, and say, "Play ball!" For me, that's enough to keep my blood pumping.

For me, every game was a new beginning. A brand-new chance to make up for yesterday's errors, for home run fastballs tipped or missed or popped straight up.

Another chance to connect.

And always another chance to scan the stands, hoping to see a quiet, stone-faced man in gardener bibs sitting on the bleacher boards, callused palms on bent knees, watching his son play ball.

Or the chance to spot a pretty girl who watched the game, who cared less about the score or the count, but vowed to come watch to keep her cousin from self-destruction.

But today, I saw neither. Saw only red hats pitted against the green. Boy army against boy army. Saw my name in a string of names on a scorecard. And then I made another connection and realized Louie was right.

That's what it all came down to. Keeping score. That's what counts. In baseball. In life. And in war.

Except that I knew a baseball game always comes to an end. Life does, too. But what about a war?

What does it take to end a war?

Yeah, I decided, that was it. That's what I'd really seen in D.C. as I stood back from that wall.

A war that never ended.

And I wondered. Did the Vietnamese ever build a monument, a big, long wall someplace, listing every single name of everyone who died?

Or is our side the only one that counts?

chapter 22

BASES LOADED, ONE OUT. THEIR CLEANUP HITTER stood at the plate, huge shoulders rolling, thick neck loosening, a sly smirk signaling how happy he was to be in this spot.

With their side down by a run in the sixth inning, I was sure he was dreaming of a game-winning hit right here.

From shortstop I yelled to Tony at second, "Turn two!" even though we'd never turned a double play all season.

"No way," said Tony. "Throw home. We gotta cut off the run."

"Infield in a step," Coach shouted. "You gotta make the play at home."

I turned to the outfielders. "Hit your cutoff man!"

First pitch, the guy pulled it deep down the left-field line, but it curved foul.

I squeezed my eyes shut. That shot was two feet from a grand slam.

I ran up to Benny on the mound. "Keep the ball low. Low and away on this guy. We need a grounder."

"Man, I tried," said Benny. "He went down and got it."

"Well, try again."

He did. And talk about a grounder. The next pitch shot off the bat, a screaming, one-hop laser blast to my right that I stepped and lunged for. I felt the ball goat-butt against the palm of my glove as I stumbled backwards and skidded on my hipbone in the dirt.

Sitting on my butt, both feet in the air, I whipped a side-arm toss to Tony. With one foot on second, he gloved it, turned, and fired to first.

In time by a step! Out at second, out at first. Double play.

Nobody scored. Inning over.

Cheers rang out from everywhere. I rolled to my side, grabbed my hat, and breathed in that wonderful baseline dust, knowing that that was one of the greatest plays I'd ever made.

Slowly I rose and jogged to the dugout, head bent low, taking it all in.

My palm burned, my hip stung and bled, and as I put on my cap, dirt rained down on my head and face.

It was the greatest feeling in the world.

I was alive. I was in charge. *That* was baseball.

And though I'd already had a good day, that last play seemed to get the whole team fired up. The next inning we scored four more runs and walked away with the game.

But afterwards, it was almost embarrassing listening to Uncle Phil rave on about me to Coach Trioli.

"He put on quite a show out there, eh, Coach?

Four-for-five. Two doubles. Four RBIs. Stole third twice. And he handled shortstop like the next Derek Jeter."

"Tyler's certainly made some progress since he first arrived," Coach told him, knowing full well I was sitting nearby changing out of my cleats. Of course, Coach was using his social tone, the voice he always used with parents. "He's taking charge out there. He's contributing."

Uncle Phil turned to me, so I'd be sure to hear. "Taking charge? He's a regular Napoleon. The Little General."

Oh, great, I thought. He would have to pick a guy who was only five feet tall. Why not Colin Powell or somebody?

"By the way," Uncle Phil added. "Does the league have everything it needs? Enough equipment and so forth?" He slapped Coach's back. "Let me know, my friend."

Whoa, I thought. He's laying it on a little thick.

I wasn't sure what those two had talked about during the game, and I didn't ask. But I could tell, Uncle Phil had kept his promise. Coach got an earful.

But what I really hoped was that Coach would see how hard I was trying. How I didn't mumble cuss words at the umpire even once, didn't yell at their hot dog shortstop, and tried all game long to see that showoff as an All-Star teammate. Which was *not* easy.

Even so, I had a feeling, as Uncle Phil and Louie hustled over to a pushcart to pick up some sodas and dogs, that I should hang back and double-check things with Coach Trioli.

Just to be sure.

"Um, Coach," I started as he clipped the buckle on his equipment bag. "I know we only got a few games left. And so, I was wondering if—you know—if I'm on track for All-Stars."

He paused a moment, reading me for something, I thought. Then he nodded. "You're on track." He hoisted the equipment bag over his shoulder and added, "For next year."

My heart plunged into my gut. All of a sudden, I felt lightweight, floaty. I didn't know what to say. *"Next year?"*

Coach started walking off, then paused, as if waiting for me to catch up. But I was too shell-shocked to move.

"Like I said," he called back, "you're making some progress. But it's fairly unusual for a thirteen-year-old to make the All-Star team. The pressure of an All-Star game is intense. And I think you'd be better off taking it easy this year. Worry about All-Stars next year."

"Coach, wait. Didn't you see what I did today?"

"Yeah, I saw. And you had a good game. But there's a few things I saw that I didn't appreciate. For example, you sending your uncle down here to campaign for you. This ain't politics. This is baseball."

"I didn't tell him to come! He did that on his own."

"Okay, well, that could be even worse. Because that

tells me other people are putting pressure on you, too, besides what you put on yourself."

He turned away.

I could hardly believe my ears. "Coach, wait!" I called again.

He didn't stop walking, didn't slow down, didn't miss a stride. Just called back, "My advice to you, Tyler, is to just go out there and enjoy the last two weeks of the season. Have some fun. Then come back next year, and we'll see how it goes."

"Next *year?* Coach, no." I started to run after him, then I stopped. Dead. What was I gonna do? I wondered. Try to talk my way onto the team? That'd just make me look like Uncle Phil.

Forget about it. I drop-kicked my sports bag into the chain-link fence, then spun in the dirt, looking for something to throw.

I spotted Uncle Phil and Louie charging back and I turned away, wishing those two guys weren't rushing up right now, laughing, ready to go over the whole game play-by-play.

In fact, I wished I wasn't even alive. I mean, why do I even try? It's not worth it. I just had the greatest day of my life. And it wasn't enough. Maybe I should just die at the top of my game. I sure felt like it.

Stooping down, I snatched up my bag from the dirt, tucked it under my arm like a football, and tore out of there.

"Tyler!" Louie yelled. "Where're you going?"

I shouted over my shoulder. "I'm going home." And I hoped he didn't know what I really meant.

I cut across the outfield and ran through another ball diamond, right in the middle of a game. I didn't care.

Up a rocky slope I ran, clopping over sunken bedrock boulders, through a bunch of weeds, and into a cluster of trees. Deep into the woods I ran, scraping my arms on low branches, and I ran deeper still.

If I could've run to California, I would've. What was I doing here? I wondered. In this stupid, noisy town where no one cares who you are or how hard you try. Who was I kidding? Shouldn't I be back home helping out?

Or maybe it didn't matter. They're probably doing fine without me. Maybe nothing I do matters. How would I know?

I slumped against the trunk of a white-barked tree and fell into a nest of leaf litter and forest mulch. And I felt useless. Cast aside like a broken bat.

Listening to little gray and white birds chirp in the branches above me, I realized I had lost it. The magic of baseball just wasn't there for me anymore.

Where once I had the pure joy of playing ball, playing catch over the wildflowers with my dad, hitting the long bombs into the chaparral—even the diving double play I'd made today—now it was all gone. All lost in that horrible phrase, "Next year. Come back *next year*."

Yeah, right. What am I gonna do now? I wondered. Who cares? I got a better phrase—"I give up."

I give up.

I mean, why'd I think it was up to me to bring back the spark in Dad, anyway? I knew I could never be Carl Yastrzemski or Roberto Clemente in his eyes. Maybe I'm just one of those kids, like Louie, who'll play ball a few years, then give it up and go on to other stuff.

Is that such a disaster?

Above my head, one bird chirped louder than ever. I looked up in time to see a bigger bird swoop down and feed it. Beak to beak. Then fly off again.

For a moment the woods fell quiet.

With barely another thought, I zipped open my bag, dug out my cell phone, and began clicking numbers.

On the other end, I heard my mother's voice.

chapter 23

"OH, TYLER. WHAT A SURPRISE. I'M GLAD YOU called, though. Listen to this—those white flies I told you that were taking over the tomato plants, smothering the leaves? You know how they can get. Well, I discovered a pure, organic vegetable spray that seems to—"

"Mom?"

"Yes?"

I squeezed shut my eyes. "Can I talk to Dad?"

"Oh." Mom's voice sounded distant and distracted. "Your father? Well, Tyler, I'm not sure it's the best time to talk to Dad right now. He's out back. Down by the horse corral."

I knew what that meant. Having a bad day. Well, so was I.

"Mom, I just wanna ask him something."

"No, Tyler, you don't understand. He's been like this all week. We—we started these counseling sessions, and it just opened up so much—"

"Okay, wait. Mom, listen. Are you on the cordless phone?"

"Yes."

"Okay. Could you please walk outside and give the phone to Dad? This is really important."

"Well, I suppose, honey, but—what is it? How can I help?"

"The best way to help is just let me talk to Dad." I paused as a sneak attack of tears began to well. "Please, Mom."

"Okay, honey," she whispered. "Hold on."

I could hear the screen door squeak and slam. Could hear her tiny white tennis shoes skid on the decomposed granite as she wound her way down the path to the empty corral. Could hear her talk to Dad, pleading, saying it was important. Finally, Dad's voice came on, soft and shaky.

"Hello?"

"Hi, Dad, it's me. Tyler."

Silence. Then he said, "Yeah, yeah. I was just thinking about you."

"You were?"

He gave a small laugh. "Got a little mockingbird up here, Tyler. Lives in that old eucalyptus on the edge of our land."

I knew the tree. Tallest one on our property. It was also our left-field foul pole.

"Anyhow," Dad continued, "that mocker won't leave this old crow alone. Pesters him all the time, flapping and jabbering. They fly around each other in circles. Cawing and squawking. Go off one way, then turn around and go the other. Can't quite figure it out."

"Why'd that make you think about me?" I asked.

"Well, I don't know. You're on the edge of the land over there, aren't you? In the middle of a bunch of squawking and squabbling yourself, I bet, the way cities can get. Somehow started me thinking about you."

Whoa, I thought. That's pure Dad. Even on a good day, he had the weirdest way of seeing things. But these days, Mom must be going crazy. I should just hop the next plane west.

"Look, Dad. I'm thinking about coming home."

He hummed a grunt. "Season over already?"

"No, not yet. It's—it's just not turning out like I wanted it to."

"Tyler," he said, almost laughing my name. "Listen, you be sure to tell me if it ever does." He laughed again.

"No, I know. But—"

He cut me off. "Remember when we used to come out here to the field and play catch, and I'd throw you a little batting practice?"

Clear as a minute ago. "Yeah, sure."

"Boy, we had some times didn't we? Talking baseball. All those old ballplayers. I really miss that."

Tell me about it, I thought.

"I've been thinking about those times a lot recently. You know, the past and all."

Sure, I thought—the counseling Mom mentioned.

"But I think about the future, too," he continued. "Like how much better you must be getting, playing all that ball. And that someday you're gonna come up to bat in some big game and hit one of those long shots, and—" his voice turned huffy, breathy—"and I won't be there to see it, since I don't, you know, do so well in crowds these days."

What? I wondered. Did I hear him right? *That's* why he never came to my games? Because of the people?

He's afraid of crowds.

"Oh, well, that's okay, Dad. Doesn't matter."

"No, it matters a lot. I know it does. Because someday, Tyler, you're gonna be the best there is. It's what I see when I come out here and sit and look down at that field. Another Clemente. Won't be long . . ."

Wow, I thought. I had no idea what to say. What *could* I say? All this time, my dad's been wishing he could see me play.

I rubbed my face hard and slow. Then I stood, brushing the crushed leaves off my uniform.

"Guess I better be going, Dad. Just wanted to call and say hi."

"Yeah, sure," he said. "Good to hear from you, Tyler. Let me know how it goes. If you decide to come home, or if things start turning around for you."

"Okay, I will." But by then I already knew. Things had already turned. Like those birds circling the sky.

And that image caused me to ask one last question. "Hey, Dad. Those birds you were watching? I was just curious. Which one am I? The old crow or that jabbering little mockingbird?"

He laughed big and loud. "Neither one," he said, like he was surprised I had even asked. "You're the tree."

chapter **24**

AFTER I CLICKED THE PHONE OFF, I SQUINTED into the woods, into the image of what Dad had just said. The tree? I was that huge eucalyptus? That's how he saw me? Man, he had a weird way of looking at things.

But maybe that ran in the family. Because now I knew I couldn't fly home. Not after what he'd said. Mom and Dad had their work to do back there, and I had mine to do here. And I had two weeks to do it in.

I mean, Coach didn't exactly say no, did he? Just that I needed to show a little more maturity. That I could handle pressure. And enjoy myself.

Well, I could do better than that. I had two weeks to show him I could be Roberto Clemente.

But I knew my real test would come in a week and a half. That's when we'd face Dumbo's team again.

I had to be ready for that game. It came only a few days before the All-Star vote. Somehow in that game, I'd have to do something that would prove myself to every coach in the league.

Back home, I straightened everything out with Louie and Uncle Phil, who was leaving town the next morning anyway.

Told them that I needed the workout, that I had to run off the energy of that great game. Uncle Phil nodded, bought the whole story, then they both headed out to an electronics store.

I peeled my uniform off and took a long shower. Tried to let the whole long day just wash off me and down the drain.

Afterwards, I wandered into the kitchen. Not hungry. Still thinking.

Breena stood at the counter cutting up a green apple.

"How'd the game go?" she asked. "Sorry I missed it. Any good fights?"

"Oh, not really." I hooked a chair leg with my foot, pulled it out, and sat.

"Wanna go for a walk?" she asked.

I gave her a quick glance. "Oh, man, I don't know." I was dead-dog tired, but it was hard to say no.

Breena wrapped the apple quarters into a napkin, then dropped them into her backpack. She spun toward the kitchen table, picked up a thin white sweater off the top of a pile of clean clothes, and pulled it on over her head.

I watched her body take shape within it, like food through a snake. Her shiny brown hair popped out the top, followed by her face. She smiled and gave her head a shake.

"Come on," she said. "I'd really like you to."

Well, at that point—hey. "Where to?" I asked.

"I have to pick up some pictures at the One Hour Quikphoto on Broadway."

"Oh, cool," I said. "I got some rolls to drop off."

"Then I thought we could Rollerblade around Central Park. Maybe get some ice cream or something. Okay?"

I bounced right up, and we were off.

On the sidewalk outside the photo store, Breena flipped through her pictures. All dumb shots of her soccer team—boring to me since Breena took them, which meant she wasn't in any of them.

"I wanna give these away to everybody tomorrow," she said. "It's our last game." She thumbed through a few more. "These are so *cute.* I can't stand it."

I looked, but I didn't see cute. I saw dorky. But I was polite. "Oh, yeah," I said, "she looks like fun."

"She is total fun. That's Rosa. She's not really cross-eyed. Oh, she's gonna die."

Breena flipped through a few more, then stopped. "Oh, speaking of dying. Isn't this death warmed over?"

She held up a picture of Aunt Chrissy, looking fierce.

"How come she hardly ever smiles?" I asked.

Breena laughed. "I don't know. She probably thinks it causes wrinkles."

"Oh, yeah, right. Beauty hint number 109. Give up laughing to keep your face smooth."

Breena tucked the picture behind the others. "Well, she hates going to my games, anyway. She'd rather be out with her friends than watching soccer."

I almost said, "Who wouldn't?" and normally, I would have, but this time I didn't. That was a first for me.

As Breena stuck the photos in her backpack, she paused a second, then looked at me with this lightbulb glow in her eye.

"Hey," she said. "I was just wondering. Our game tomorrow? Why don't you come and watch?"

Yow, I thought. Soccer? Watch what? The grass grow? To me, soccer was a big waste of a nice lawn.

"Man, I don't know." I scanned my brain for some excuse. "See, I got this little idea I'm working on. I might be cybernating all day tomorrow."

She tisked her tongue against the roof of her mouth. "Ty-lerrr. C'mon. I want you to. It's our last game." She grabbed my elbow with both hands, pulling me down Broadway. "I know I missed your game today after I promised I'd go, but—today was weird. My dad and everything."

"Oh, yeah. He's, um—" I looked for the perfect word.

"A jerk," she concluded.

"No, no," I protested. "He's, you know—"

"Hey, I *do* know. He is. You saw how he treats us. And it's getting worse. His whole life's all about how important he is. Or how important you are, if he decides you can do something great that reflects on him. So, naturally, he never pays any attention to us at all."

I nodded. "Yeah, well, maybe our family isn't that big in the 'paying attention' department. My dad, you know—he can be a lot like that, too."

Outside a pharmacy, I watched a crusty old guy in a purple cloth poncho pull open a door for a woman shopper.

"Uncle Lyle's like that?" Breena asked. "No, no, Daddy's worse. He used to wrestle us and hold us and everything, but, like, lately, he might pat me on the head if he touches me at all."

The purple poncho guy stood at attention, like a freelance doorman, as the woman dropped coins into his hand.

"Well, look," I said. "Once you visit California, I don't think you're gonna complain anymore. My dad—my dad's really out there." Right away I wanted to change the subject. But I couldn't think fast enough.

"You know," she said, "Mom used to tell us stories about your dad all the time. He was her big brother. When they lost Grandad in Vietnam, she said the whole family cried for a solid month. All except your dad."

That got my attention. We stepped under some construction scaffolding set over the sidewalk, then dodged a steady drip of water coming from above our heads.

"Of the three kids, your dad was the oldest. Fourteen. And he never cried. All he did, Mom said, was get angry. He started arguing all the time, growing his hair long, running with some wild hippie kids and stuff."

"He did? Dad?"

She nodded. "She said he was just so full of rage."

I tried to imagine that. "At what?"

"At everything, I guess. The government, for one. She said he blamed them for killing Grandad. He knew Grandad wanted to be an astronaut, that that was the big reason he joined the Air Force. And so, Uncle Lyle—your father—thought he got cheated. Big time."

"So that's why Dad never joined the Air Force."

She nodded. "He broke the chain. And that's why you were brought up so antimilitary."

"I was? News to me." I brushed against a support pole as some people came our way.

"Well, you weren't ever, like, expected to join the Air Force or to prepare for the academy, were you?"

"No, but they never talked against it, either." Escaping the scaffolding, we turned down 90th toward the park.

"Your dad used to march in all the antiwar demonstrations, too."

"He did? How come no one ever told me that?"

She shrugged. "Maybe because of what happened to your sister."

"What do you mean? Why would that have anything—"

"Because when he was in high school, he got into this big, huge argument with Mom and Grandma about the war and how unfair it was, how immoral it was—" She stopped, hesitating. "You don't know any of this, do you?"

I wagged my head, lips tight.

"Well, Mom said that just before he slammed out of the house that day, your dad turned and shouted out that he'd rather die himself than ever take another person's life."

Oh.

Oh, wow, I thought.

I stopped in front of a junk pile of construction

boards, wires, and concrete chunks to look at her. "He really said that?"

Breena gave a small shrug. "I thought you knew. Mom used to bring it up all the time."

I lifted my eyes away from hers and shook my head. Shook like one of those people on the news when they stand looking at the broken-up, fallen-down walls of their house after a hurricane or a tornado. Or an earthquake.

All the way down 90th toward the park, I kept thinking how cousins, separated by a continent, probably grew up hearing all kinds of stories about each other's parents without realizing the other cousin didn't know those stories at all.

Except in my case, Dad never talked about Aunt Chrissy. Or anyone.

As we approached Central Park, Breena added, "I think that was one reason Mom wanted you to go see the Vietnam Memorial before you left."

"Why?"

"Because your dad—you know—he's never been."

Another shock. "I figured he must've gone before I was born. I always thought that had something to do with—you know—the way he is."

She cocked her head. "Well, I don't know. But he told Mom that he refuses to go. That he didn't ever want to see it."

"Did he tell her why?"

"He said it wasn't fair. Your dad was always concerned with being fair."

I nodded with a grunt. "Well, we all see things differently, don't we?"

"Tell me about it," she said. "But, hey, how about you seeing our game tomorrow? That's different. It's our last one. It'll be fun."

Right then I had too much stuff flying around my head to put up an argument. "Yeah, sure, I'll come," I said. "No prob."

"Yay!" Breena jumped in place, all kidlike. "No one ever comes. And now you can meet all my friends. You'll love Rosa."

I lifted my closest shoulder and gave a short hum.

"And," she continued, "I'll come to the rest of your games, too. They're not that bad, really, when you know someone who's playing."

I nodded agreement, happy to hear it, actually. "Okay, sure," I said. But then I thought it through. "Wait, wait. Not next Wednesday's game. All right? You can skip that one."

"How come?" She stepped even closer, banging her shoulder into mine. "Will I make you nervous?"

The answer was, no doubt—but that wasn't the problem.

"No, it's just—that game—that's the team that hates me."

"Yeah, so? All the more reason I should be there."

"No, no. That's the guy who jumped me in the park and everything. Really, I'd rather you didn't show up at that one."

"Too bad. Now I *have* to come," she said.

We crossed Central Park West and sat down on some benches to change into our blades.

I was shoving my shoes into my pack when Breena asked, "What's his name, anyway?"

"Whose name?"

"The guy who hassled you. Your big enemy."

"I don't know his name. I just call him 'Dumbo.' Some big, goofy-looking guy with a fat nose and stuck-out ears. Barks all the time."

I double-checked my blade shoe for spiders, then stuck my foot inside.

"*Barks?*" she asked.

"Yeah, sounds like a little chihuahua. It's so annoying." I pulled the ankle laces too tight and they broke. "Ugh, I *hate* when I do that."

"Wait a minute. The yellow team? They wear yellow hats?"

"Yeah." I started undoing the lace, hoping I could use the remains.

"I *know* that guy. I swear I do." She reached over and grabbed her pack. "That's Carmine DeLucca. His sister Tina plays on my soccer team."

"No way! Why do you think it's him?"

"Because you described him perfectly." She unzipped a compartment and pulled out her photo pack. "I've been over at Tina's, and he's always wearing his yellow baseball cap. Plus, I've heard that bark. He does it when something good happens. It cracks us up."

"Oh, it's so pathetic." I tried to imitate it, but sounded more like a hiccuping cow.

Then a thought hit me. A pathetic thought.

"Cracks who up?" I said.

"Our team."

She fingered through the pictures. Then she grinned, giggled, reached out, and flicked my cheek, just like I always did to Louie.

"Look," she said. "Tina *and* Carmine."

I looked. It was.

"Isn't he cute?" she said, beaming her cool blue eyes at me. "And he's *so* funny."

I glanced down. "Funny looking! Check out those clothes. He's the typical dweeb from New Dork City."

"He *is* not. He's totally sweet. But, hey," she said with a giant grin. "Now you'll get to see for yourself He comes to all of our games."

chapter 25

"WHAT ARE YOU DOING, DRESSED LIKE THAT?" Breena asked me.

We'd just hurried out to catch the elevator on our way to her game. She was in rumpled blue designer sweats over her soccer uniform.

I was incognito.

"Like what?" I asked, removing my blue-blade sunglasses, folding down my shirt collar, and folding up the knitted wool skullcap from my forehead. "Looked windy out there today. Could rain. I figured, if I'm gonna be bored to death, I don't wanna freeze to death first."

"Freeze?" she said. "It's eighty degrees and muggy as a swamp."

I winked. "That's why I'm wearing these shorts, baby. I'm prepared for anything."

"Oh, yeah, *baby*," she said, snarling the word. "Takes a whole lot of preparation to change from a boy into an idiot."

I slid the glasses back on and clutched at my heart. "Oh, that hurts, girl cousin. That's cold."

She giggled as I swaggered on past, slipping like a

sneaky base runner into the role I'd really prepared for. James Bond, secret agent, double-oh dude.

Not only did I have my wide sunglasses and blue wool cap to hide my face and hair, but I also wore the dorkiest, New Yorkiest clothes I could find—or rather, steal—from Louie's closet. Beat-up, high-top Nikes two sizes too big, a designer-labeled, floppy-collared, black pullover shirt with a maroon swipe across it, and blimpo, black shorts with foot-long pockets and a logo up the leg.

Almost no one in California wore this stuff anymore. Out there we'd mostly dress down, keep the low pro, and not go out and be some walking billboard for some clothing company.

The whole way to the park, Breena kept looking at me, laughing into her hand, and stomping away.

"What?" I'd say, then jump up on some little iron fence around a tree or something, balance there, play a few riffs on an air guitar, then flop back to the sidewalk, losing a shoe.

She'd scream, run ahead, and pretend she didn't know me.

But, of course, I wasn't fooling her. She knew what I was up to. As we reached Central Park's North Meadow, she finally said, "You know, you don't have to hide from him."

"Hide? Who's hiding?"

But she didn't press the point. Too busy shaking her head and laughing.

Up at the field, though, once her soccer game got underway, the comedy show was over. I got serious.

With double-oh cool, I slithered my way into the mob of mothers and fathers and little kids crab-walking up and down the sidelines following the black-and-white ball.

Dumbo was there all right, but he didn't recognize me. And it wasn't that I was scared of the guy or anything. It's just that I'd come here to watch Breena, not to get into it with him.

I soon realized, I didn't need to have been so camouflaged up. Dumbo was too preoccupied arguing with his mom.

"Why do I always have to watch them?" he asked. "I wanna see the game, too."

"You can see the flippin' game and still watch your baby brother and sister," said his mother, whose XXL-sized Yankees T-shirt fell halfway down her tight black shorts. "One hour, Carmine. So I can watch Tina in peace. I mean, geez. It's not gonna kill you." She waved a hand and turned away.

"It could," he mumbled, mostly to himself, as he leaned down to untangle his little sister's death grip from around his knees. "I could die from baby snot gluing my legs together, then get trampled to death by a runaway gang of screaming parents."

"Hush! Right now! Or I'll smack you." His mom pointed off behind him, snapped her fingers, and Carmine hobbled away.

What a dork, I thought. Serves him right. Besides, his

baby-sitting problems left me free to relax and scope out Breena. Who was amazing.

Man, if I would've known she'd look so cool—her thick, powerful legs digging against the turf, her hair, lit now almost the color of honey, flying back like a battle flag, sweat pouring down her face and neck—forget about it. I would've come out here a long time ago.

And she took charge on the field, too. Like a real Waltern. Shouting directions and encouragement to everyone on her team.

Every once in a while, I'd see Dumbo step up to the sideline, clapping and shouting and yipping like a junkyard coyote. For our side.

And I have to admit, it cracked me up, too.

Then, after only fifteen minutes into the game, Breena did it.

Sprinting from the far sideline, away from the ball, she took a pass and without even adjusting her stride, she drilled the ball into the corner of the net.

"Yeah, *Breena!*" I yelled, jumping up and out of a shoe, waving my fist, as everyone around me clapped and cheered. "Go, cuz! Yo, baby!"

I even waited to hear Dumbo's bark, to mark the moment of triumph, but it never came.

Seemed like the little kids had wandered off, bored or something, and I spied the poor guy about fifty yards away, holding his baby sister on his hip, talking to her, bouncing her. Then he squatted down, pulled a tissue from his pocket, and wiped his little brother's nose.

Not exactly your typical tough guy, I noted. Yeah, but he deserves it.

Meanwhile, Breena was at it again. Dogging the other team, darting after them, squirting her lightning feet at the ball, rolling on the grass, making steal after steal.

And even when the ball was clear down field, she kept moving, bouncing, her eyes on the action, hands clapping, feet dancing.

And I saw how the teamwork of soccer was like the teamwork of baseball. Everybody with a job to do, one person at a time, but all contributing something. Like one big family, really. Or the way a family should be.

"Hey, dude," came a deep voice aimed my way. "How'd they score?"

His accent was stronger than I'd expected. "Score" sounded like "sco-wah." But I knew without looking who it was. Dumbo the Elephant Boy. Sliding right up next to me.

I kept my eyes on Breena and pointed. "Um, that real fast girl with the brown hair. She got a pass from the tall girl over there and kicked it in."

"A high kick? Or a skimmer on the ground?"

"Low and sharp," I said. Then I caught his accent—I couldn't help it—and added, "A one-hoppah."

He stepped in front of me—I should say, the three of them did, his brother on one hand and baby sister on the other—and he nodded.

"Dude," he said. "She smokes. That Breena. She's on fi-yah."

I didn't respond, drifting back into the crowd.

No—I drifted farther than that. I drifted clear back to Coach Trioli at his softball game. Back to the time he said these other guys were just like me.

The whole game long, I watched Dumbo skirt the sidelines, taking snacks from his mother's bag to feed the kids, keeping them out of her hair, yipping it up, one play after another.

And I hated it. Every time he tossed his kid sister in the air, swooping her around like an airplane, every time he tied his brother's shoe, every good-time yip, yip, yip.

Hated everything I saw. Because right there, in the muggy heat of New York City, a prickly, acid rain of realization washed over me. That not only wasn't this guy, this Carmine DeLucca—with his hard dude attitude—some big, dumb jerk, but he was really a pretty nice guy.

After the game, Breena ran up, her uniform soaked, her cheeks blotched pink. "How'd you like it?"

"Was great! I'm impressed." We bopped fists in midair, and I made a smile. "Pretty incredible. We should go celebrate." I started backing away. "I mean, celebrate anyplace but here."

"Wait, Tyler, wait. What's your hurry? I gotta talk to everyone and say good-bye and stuff."

"Oh. Okay, then I'll meet you later." I backed up some more.

"What? Get back here. You can't go yet."

"Breena—" I drew in a big breath and blew it out toward the trees. "I wanna get going."

She glanced around, spotted Dumbo encircled by several of her teammates, reliving the game. Then she looked at me again.

She seemed to be reading me like I read Mom and her farm report.

"Okay," she said. "I guess I'll see them at the team party, anyway. Let me get my stuff."

We left the North Meadow and stopped at the first market we came to.

"My treat," she said. "I owe you one." She grinned and ducked inside to get some ice cream sandwiches. I followed as Breena went on and on about how she really wanted to play on a soccer club team and hoped she'd get asked, and how cool it'd be to travel all over the place to all kinds of tournaments.

"That team we just beat had the best goalie in the league, and Ms. Hamilton thinks I might get invited. I'd do it, too, but only if they asked Rosa."

I listened, nodding, but didn't say anything.

"What's the matter with you?" she finally asked as she took change from the clerk and handed me the frozen sandwich. "Why aren't you talking?"

"Nothing to say," I said, and I didn't even feel like saying that.

Sure, she was higher than the Empire State Building. Some traveling team wanted her to join. And today she was the big hero. The goal she scored turned out to be the only one of the game.

But I was dragging. I'd already stashed the sunglasses and skullcap, and as we strolled along, I ditched my double-oh swagger. Just kept my eyes on the gritty, scum-covered sidewalk.

When I slowed down to peel back the wrapper on my chocolate sandwich, Breena stopped and waited for me to catch up. Last thing I wanted was to spoil her mood, so I forced another smile, though I couldn't think of a single thing to say.

But I didn't have to. I'll never forget it. She stepped up and put her arm around me. Pulled me so close, the dry strands of her sweaty hair tickled my cheek.

And she didn't say anything either.

Just steered me down Amsterdam Avenue—not the usual way we went home—but nothing was very usual about that day, so I let her.

But her touch was enough. Enough to give me the courage to start talking about something that'd been going round and round my head ever since her game today. Something I was trying to figure out.

"Breena, can I ask you a question?"

"I don't care."

"Promise you won't laugh."

I felt her squeeze. "How can I promise that?"

"Okay, laugh if you want. But, I mean, it's really important to me."

"Go ahead."

chapter **26**

BREENA ONLY HELD ME NEXT TO HER FOR A FEW
more steps. Which was all I'd expected, but I wished
she would've held on a little longer.

"Okay," I said. "First, tell me, who's your worst
enemy?"

She looked straight ahead. "That's a funny question.
My worst enemy? I don't have one."

"Ever? In your whole life?"

"No, I don't think so." Then she held up her hand.
"Okay, maybe one. Janna Kranauer in the sixth grade,
who spit gobs of her chocolate birthday cake on me
when she found out I kissed Jason Briggs at her party."

"Yuck."

"Sorry, best I can do," she said. "I don't really have
that many friends, much less enemies. I have one good,
close friend, Kelly, and all my other ones are, basically,
casual, because, see, at school, people think I'm too
quiet. I guess because I read so much. I got this rep of
being sort of a weirdo."

"No, you don't. You're joking."

"I'm not. That's what people say. Ask Louie."

I laughed. "I *know* what he'd say. But you're not
weird to me."

That caused her to give me the biggest smile. No words. She just hunched up her shoulders and smiled.

After a moment, she asked, "Okay, so what's your real question?"

"My real question has to do with how people should treat their enemies. That's what—I mean—okay, now you're gonna see how my brain works—"

"It works?"

"Shut up. This ain't easy."

I waited while she squeaked out a laugh, then waved her hand, pretending to get serious. "Okay," she said.

"Okay. You know that girl, Janna, who spit on you?"

"Yeah."

"What if, one day, you found her lying on the ground, all beaten up and bloody? Would you, you know, pick her up and help her?"

"You mean, do the Good Samaritan thing?"

"You know that story?" I tried not to sound too surprised, but I was.

"I'm not a complete heathen," she said. "I used to go to Sunday school, too, you know."

"No, I didn't. I mean, I thought maybe you guys didn't—"

"Well, we don't. We're not churchy. But that doesn't make us bad people."

"No, no, I didn't mean that. It's just—I mean, look, here's what I'm getting at. If I really try and do what I was taught in confirmation class—"

"In what class?"

"Oh, that's like this two-year church class you go to.

In the Lutheran Church. When you're in seventh and eighth grade, you take it to become a member."

"You're a member of your church?"

"Next year, I will be. Anyway, the pastor gives you all these rules and stuff, and you're supposed to memorize them. Like how you should live and treat other people. And you get to ask him questions. And so when he told us that Jesus said you gotta love your enemies, how if someone's a jerk to you at school, for example, you're just supposed to show them love, I asked him, what about guys like Slobodan Milosevic? What about ethnic cleansing? What about war?"

"Good questions. What'd he say?"

"He said that Jesus just meant, you love them as people, that we're all God's children, so you love them. But that you can still go to war with them, if you have to. You know, like if you get attacked. Because you love your family more. And your country more. And you have to defend yourself."

She started shaking her head immediately. "He is so wrong. That's what's so dumb about church. Oh, I can't believe he said that. No, I can. I totally can. Church people are so phony."

"No, they're not!" I mean, call me anything, but don't call me a phony. "Especially not my minister. He was just trying to explain—"

"I don't care, Tyler. Okay, you asked me about Janna. Yes, I would help her. I don't care if she *was* Slobodan Milosevic. I still would. I'd stop and help. I'd help anyone. Even during war. And that's why I could never go to war. I'd never last a minute. I'd get shot by my own side for helping the enemy. But you don't have to go to church to learn about being good to people. It's just human decency."

"But church people go to war all the time. There's nothing against it."

"Nothing against it? Look, I know what they're supposed to believe. And I know what they teach kids like us. And that's why I quit going. They are so phony! I mean, get real. Could you ever imagine Jesus in an army uniform, standing up and spraying the enemy with bullets? Is that what he taught?"

"Well, no, but, you gotta protect yourself. I mean, come on. You either fight back or—or—"

"Or what? They'll hang you on a cross?"

"No, Breena, that's dumb. But—well, actually, yeah! Yeah, they will. If they think you're weak, they'll crucify you. People're like that. People are—"

"Phony!" she answered. With a twist, she spun away, gazing west down 93rd. "I feel like going to Riverside Park," she said. "Can we go to the park?"

"Yeah, fine. I don't care. But I still wanna—you're not mad at me are you?"

"No, no, I'm okay." She kept looking away. "I just get frustrated when people can't see my side. It's so clear to me." She turned and gave me a quick smile.

I tilted my head, unable to hold her glance, while I sorted through a jumble of thoughts. I mean, she had some good points. Stuff I didn't really want to hear. Besides, I needed to think this through. I mean, what *did* I believe, anyway?

Finally, I said, "Well, don't get too frustrated. People have a hard time seeing my side of things sometimes, too."

That got another smile out of her.

Then I got a great idea. "Oh, wait," I said. "Wait a minute! Oh, man, this fits right in. Look, I know the perfect place to go."

"What? What are you talking about?"

"Come on, I wanna show you something."

We headed west, and in a little while we'd crossed Riverside Drive and hit the huge park that ran along the Hudson River, with its playgrounds and flower gardens, asphalt walks and scattered benches.

As we joined the small stream of evening joggers and dog walkers moving south along the Riverside Park walkway, I took a big breath.

An orange-breasted robin triple-hopped across our path, down into some tall, seedy grass. I took that as a good sign.

"Okay," I said, "it's not that far away. C'mon." I slipped my hand into Breena's and started to run.

She ran right along with me, without complaining, just ran along like she trusted me. It was the coolest feeling. We dodged people and traffic, crossing 92nd, crossing 91st, all the way to the Soldiers and Sailors Monument and up to the flagstone plaza.

And there, I gave her the grand tour. Had her read

the battle town names on the marble stones and the dedication plaque—which she'd never read before—and she even listened as I pointed out how unfair it was.

Unlike Louie, she saw exactly what I saw. And unlike what I'd ever do with Louie, I showed her even more.

I led her around to the side of the tower and showed her my own little monument. The one to Col. Henry Jacob Waltern.

"Oh, wow," she said softly. "What made you decide to do this? What gave you the idea?"

"Nothing. Nobody. I just thought someone should do something. That, you know, everyone deserves to be recognized."

She dropped my hand and stepped closer. "To be fair?" she asked.

"Yeah." And then it hit me. Like the finger of a ghost up my spine—a gray ghost, an odd-jobbing, tree-trimming, weed-whacker of a ghost—up my spine. It hit me that I'd done something exactly like Dad would've done.

When he was my age.

chapter 27

"AUNT CHRISSY?" I TAPPED ON HER BEDROOM door.

She answered my knock wearing her fluffy blue bathrobe. "Yes, Tyler, hi." A loose strand of hair dropped to her nose. "Dinner's coming shortly. Sorry, I just called it in." Her face flashed into a quick "problem-solved" smile. She began to shut the door.

"No," I said, protesting. "I—I mean, good, thanks. But I wondered, Aunt Chrissy, if I could, um, talk to you?"

Now she gave me an eyebrow-pinched glare. "I'm really in a hurry, honey. I'm chairing an organizational meeting for the Summer Daze Fund-raiser for Louis and Sabrina's Brookside Academy. Can't this keep?"

Well, why not? I wondered. It's only been keeping for nine years. But so much depended upon her answer that I pushed ahead.

"Just take a minute," I said.

She opened the door wide, glanced at the digital clock on her dresser, and forced another smile. "Sure, of course," she said in a tone that told me my minute was running.

She backed up and sat on her black velvet vanity bench.

I stood. "Can you tell me what my dad was like before—" I wiggled my hand in front of me. "I mean, when he was a kid?"

"In one minute? Goodness, I—"

"What I mean is, was he ever normal?"

Her mouth plopped open with a startled laugh. "Normal? Well, of course, he was normal. Typical all-American boy. What makes you ask?"

"Well, the other day I found out he was, like, a hippie, antiwar demonstrator and everything, and I know how he is now, so I wondered if, you know, he was always kind of weird."

Her eyes flickered, darting about for a place to land, while her lips puffed apart. Finally, she motioned to a low white chair with a high back. "Tyler, have a seat." She glanced again at the clock. "I'll give you the short version. It's all I have time for."

She moved to the edge of her bench, opposite me. Through the French doors behind her, I could see Babe, the dove, bobbing in the planter for seeds.

"Lyle—" she started, "my brother—was the kindest, most considerate boy. Very sensitive. Artistic, too. And active. Boy Scouts, baseball, he volunteered at the animal shelter. But being the oldest of us kids, he knew Daddy better than we did. And his death hit him really hard."

"But you told Breena that he didn't even cry. Doesn't sound like—"

"Lyle's pain, I really believe, was so enormous, it overwhelmed him, honey. Some people react like that.

With rage. And with blame. And I don't think that was weird. Your father had to blame someone. And he blamed the Air Force, the government. And today we would say he acted that out."

"So it was all an act?"

"No, no, he was sincere." She rose, stepping to her closet. "It's just—that's the way he expressed his grief."

"So was he over it by the time my sister—and what happened to her?"

"Oh, yes, by then he was, I'm sure. Meeting your mother was a big help. She was so supportive. She helped him set up his landscaping business. And, of course, his art studio."

"His what? *Art* studio?"

She acted surprised. "Your father is quite an artist. Or at least he was. When your parents moved out to California, way out into the boonies, he wrote me that the first thing he did was to scrounge up enough lumber to build an art studio right behind the old ranch house."

I thought a moment. "The toolshed?"

"That's what it is now. But before you were born, Lyle was one of the first eco-political artists. Had lots of expressionistic, scavenger-art sculptures in parks and even galleries when hardly anyone was working in that medium. Got some terrific notices in the reviews, too. We all thought he was on his way."

She came out of her closet holding a black sequined dress and hung it on the door. "He doesn't sculpt anymore, does he?"

"Aunt Chrissy, I never knew he did."

"Oh, Lyle was so creative. And he was always draw-ing connections between things that seemed totally un-connected. I still remember when he came home with a combat boot, a toilet bowl, and a manhole cover. Used them to make some sort of statement about war. Cov-ered it all with motor oil. For a fifteen-year-old boy, he had a vivid imagination."

I sat with my mouth open. So, I thought, that's why our house had so much junk around it. Dad's not a weirdo. He's an artist. "No one ever told me any of this stuff."

Aunt Chrissy reached out, pulling me up off the chair, then hugging me against her robe. Her hand squeezed my arm, adding to the hug.

Then she stepped back. "I really must finish dressing now. Maybe later, we can—"

I was already ahead of her. I needed to leave. I backed away, startling the dove outside. It flew up and hovered as I made my way to the door.

But before I left, I had one more thing to ask, and I had no easy way to do it, so I just fired away.

"Aunt Chrissy," I started. "Do you think that, in the Vietnam War, Grandad ever dropped napalm?"

Her head rocked back.

"No," she said, but said it with such slack-jaw quiver, such apology, that I knew the real answer was, "Yes." The real answer was, "Of course he did. That was his job."

As I walked to my room, my first impulse was to get on the Internet and follow up on a question that'd been growing in my brain ever since Louie'd said that—by the numbers—we'd won the Vietnam War.

But in my room, I found Ryan and Louie hyper-thumbing their video joysticks like dueling hamsters, blasting each other to smithereens on that Blood Hawk Bomber game.

Only Ryan—with his scruffy, whitish yellow hair and black eyebrows—had ever rescued the empress in distress or whatever the goal was. I tried it once, but got so bored I just dive-bombed the 3-D Starjet and put myself out of my alien-bashing misery.

But Louie claimed the game—like practically every one he owned—was perfect training for the military. First-person-shooter games that tested your reflexes and treated the enemy like targets instead of like people.

"Target fixation," he called it. And at the moment, he and Ryan looked "target fixated" all right. Like a couple of slobbery dogs riding in the back of a pickup truck with their lips blown open.

"Yeah!" Ryan shouted. "Dude, you are dust." He stood, tossed the controls on the bed, and grabbed a bag of chips. "Cosmic dust!"

"Lucky shot," said Louie. "C'mon. One more."

Ryan munched away, bouncing on the bed, finally noticing me. "Yo, Tyler, I was screaming. I got the touch! Your cuz never had a chance."

Louie responded with a dirty sweat sock flung into Ryan's face, which escalated into a wrestling match on the floor between the beds.

I backed up and out the door to Louie's strained cries of, "C'mon, you little Blood Hawk wimpboy. One more game, chicken."

Across the hall, I tapped on Breena's half-opened door.

"Can I use your computer?"

"Yeah, sure," she said. "Just a minute." With her back to me, she dashed about gathering up little pieces of clothing.

I stood in the hall, noticing how I couldn't get over how different I felt with her now. Like we had this invisible connection.

"I'm going down to Kelly's," she said, giving her room one last look. Then she started out the door, passing me. "It's all yours."

But before she was gone, I had to say something. "Breena?"

She glanced back, then smiled into my tongue-tied silence. "What?"

"Um, I just wanted to say thanks for—" Suddenly the whole afternoon clicked through my mind. Carmine at the game, Breena's big goal, her hug, her squeeze, her patience. "Thanks for, you know, the ice cream sandwich."

"Oh, sure. Anytime." She hurried off.

And for the next couple of hours, I surfed the Net for all the Vietnam stuff I could find. I lurked in chat rooms with borderline psycho guys who I pictured jamming on their keyboards, still dressed up in their camouflage fatigues and black face, as well as regular old war vets from both countries, the U.S. and Vietnam, which was totally cool.

Also ran into plenty of college students and professors at universities around the world.

One site had testimony from something called the "Winter Soldier Investigation," which looked dense but interesting, so I bookmarked it.

Another site had grumpy old vets arguing with grumpy old antiwar protesters, as if the points they were making still really mattered.

But the strangest—and probably the strongest—stuff came when I stumbled into a site full of poetry written by soldiers from both sides.

I just wasn't expecting anything like this one from an American vet:

> But still the branches are wire
> And thunder is the pounding mortar,
> Still I close my eyes and see the girl
> Running from her village, napalm
> Stuck to her dress like jelly,
> Her hands reaching for the no one
> Who waits in waves of heat before her.

Like the thunder of that "pounding mortar," this poem, which eerily echoed the picture I'd seen, left me shaking.

I printed it out, plus a bunch of others I found. Not

sure why, but somehow I knew I wanted to hold these poems, to know them, to use them for something.

But after all that surfing, I never found what I was looking for.

A list.

All I really wanted was a list of names—of *all* the names—of the people who died in that war. Over three million Vietnamese had died, but was there a book or a wall or a monument somewhere listing their names?

If there was, I couldn't find it.

Well, of course not, I decided. I mean, when a whole village is bombed out, like these guys described it, and the aircraft come in and strafe every square inch with bullets, who's going to come back later and check IDs?

You could get a printout of all the Americans who died, how they died, when and where. But no one had anything like that for the enemy. Even the enemy.

The next day I was lying on my bed balancing my two broken bats over my head when Breena walked past the door.

"Hey," she said, "what're you doing? Don't you have practice?"

I was so lost in thought, I barely heard her.

"That's it!" I said.

"That's what?" She stepped into the room.

I bounced up off the bed, set down the black bat, then took the other one and split it over my knee. Just the way I once saw Ken Caminiti do it after he'd struck out. Only his bat wasn't already fractured like this one was.

"Why'd you do that?" Breena asked. "Thought you wanted to glue it up and use it."

"I will use it. But now I got a better idea." I tossed the two pieces on the bed and dug out the Tony Gwynn bat, which had already been split.

"Look," I said, plopping myself back onto the bed. I held the two splintered bats—half bats, really—in front of me, crisscrossed at the barrels like a big X. "Fifty bats. Just like these. Stuck in the ground like this. In pairs of two. And each bat will have one name on it that'll represent fifty-eight thousand people."

"What are you talking about? Fifty-eight thousand people?"

"Because, remember what you said on the train? That's how many names are on the Vietnam War Memorial, right? But to represent *all* the people who died, it'd take at least fifty more of those monuments. And what I wanna do is build a memorial that'll do just that."

For a moment she just looked at me, her eyes shifting back and forth between the bats and my face.

Finally, she said, "You wanna do what?"

chapter 28

I WALKED TO THE CLOSET AND PULLED MY SWISS Army knife out of my backpack. Gripping the blade edge and opening the knife, I began.

"I saw that guy, Carmine, at your game, right?"

"Yeah, no kidding."

"Okay, so"—I picked up the black bat and began shaving at the signature part of the barrel—"it took a while for it to sink in, but I finally started seeing people like him in a different way."

I sliced off a slender strip of wood, surprised to see the whiteness of the new wood underneath. "I mean anyone who's against me. My enemy, right? It's like those video games Louie plays. The enemy is always some nonhuman nobody. You know, with no family, no friends, no home, no memories. So it's easy to smart bomb those guys to smithereens. And I realized this is what I have to do. To make this, like, remembrance. So people will never forget."

"Forget what?"

"I don't know. That Carmine is somebody. Has a mother and a brother and a baby sister. Stuff you wouldn't wanna think about if you were gonna smash his face in."

"Smash his face?"

Her tone sent prickles of embarrassment. "Well, I felt like it once. I could've. But now . . ." I shrugged. "I remember—when we went to that wall in D.C.—I remember thinking something was missing. It all felt so selfish. So—like we only cared about ourselves. The enemy was nobody."

I sliced again, and the wood strip fell to the floor. "So talking to you the other day, about church people and everything, it all kind of gave me this idea. And I decided I wanted to set this thing up somewhere."

"Whew," she said. "Sometimes you amaze me."

I shrugged again. "Can't help it. Sometimes I'm amazing."

She laughed. "Yeah, right. Too bad you're also wrong. Tyler, when I look at that wall, I see a grandfather I'll never know. I see the sadness in Mom's heart. That's what's missing. I see the sacrifices those men made. There's nothing self-centered about sacrifice."

"So? I wasn't talking about sacrifice. I was talking about recognition. And why we always put some people on top of others, and some just get ignored."

I could sense her pausing to think about that.

"But *fifty* bats?" she asked. "Where're you gonna get fifty broken baseball bats?"

"I don't know. Same place I got these. I'll ask around."

I turned the bat, slicing back the other way to smooth out the new signature spot. "It just seems like we never know that much about people from other places. And, so"—I paused—"that just makes it easier to throw baseballs at them or to drop the bombs on them when the time comes."

I bounced back onto the bed and scooted against the wall.

Before Breena could say anything else, we heard Louie slam shut the front door and come tromping down the hall.

Like some clueless invader, he appeared at our door.

"What're you guys doing?" he asked.

"Talking," said Breena as she backed up and sat on Louie's desk.

"She's talking," I said. "I'm working."

He eyed my knife and shavings. "What're you doing that for?"

I smiled. "An art project."

"Art project?" He spun his cap around backwards and fired up the computer. "Why do you wanna make an *art* project? School's out, bro."

Breena answered. "He's gonna make a monument."

I gave her a quick, pleading glance, crimping my mouth, shaking my head, as if to say, "Not now."

"What?" said Breena. "Why not? I think it's an interesting idea. You mean, you don't want anyone to know?"

She had me. Obviously, you don't keep something like this secret. "No," I said, "it's okay. I just haven't thought it all through yet, that's all."

Well, within two minutes Breena had blurted out the whole idea and even my reasons why.

But as I listened, the thing sounded better and better. Hearing someone else describe it made me think I could actually build it. Besides, Louie'd have to find out sooner or later. I could even use his help.

"Tyler," said Louie. "You can't be serious about this. Don't even think about it."

"I'm dead serious."

"But it's so stupid. I mean, first of all, where you gonna stick it? Out in the park or something? This ain't the Wild West, like where you come from. I happen to know that a display like this is totally illegal. Defacing public property or illegal dumping or something."

"Oh, yeah? Why couldn't it be like that community service thing you did with your school last year? Putting name tags on those trees."

"Yeah, right, and to do that we had to pay for inspections and get tons of permits before we could do anything. And besides, if you're so hot about recognizing dead guys, then I'm thinking you should just go back to Washington and visit the real wall again. Because, man, I'm saying you did *not* get the true sense of it. I'm telling you, bro. Those guys sacrificed themselves for *America*."

"I got the sense of it, don't worry."

"Oh, yeah? Well, if you did, then you'd see that doing something like this is pure, felony stupid."

I hacked away. "Well, you're the expert on that."

"I'm the expert on something. Because I've got a mom whose dad's name is on that wall."

"That's my dad's dad, too, remember?"

"Yeah? Well, I've seen her face, reading it."

I stopped hacking, leaving the blade stuck in the blond wood. "Maybe so. But I say that wall only helps one side feel better. That if people really wanted healing, they'd help everyone to heal."

"No, no, Tyler," said Louie. "You got it all wrong. Look, it's not up to us to put up shrines or whatever to the Vietnamese. That's their problem."

"Tyler," said Breena in a quiet voice. "I agree. I'm sorry, but I've heard Mom talk about the power of that wall. So I'm thinking it'd be better if you let the Vietnamese do their own thing. Put up their own memorial. In their own country."

"But, you see, that's my point." I slammed the bat to the bed. "If you just divide everything up, then it's still one side against the other. Just like our Civil War. It's like it's still going on."

I yanked the knife blade out of the bat and folded it up. "I'm not saying I should do this because what anybody did was so great or anything. I'm saying it's important for people to see the damage *we* did, too. Not just the damage that was done to our side. Or else, it's like all those millions of dead people don't mean anything to us at all."

"But that ain't how it's done," said Louie. "Yo, all through history, each side honors its own, okay? That's just how human beings do it. It's not our place to build monuments to the enemy."

"Yeah, well, I don't think that's how Abraham Lincoln would see it. Or Jesus."

"How do you know how they'd see it? What, you're speaking for Jesus now?"

"No!" I looked to Breena for support. "I thought you saw what I meant. Especially after what you said at the tower."

"Well, yeah," said Breena. "I know what you're saying, Tyler. But I know what Louie means, too. They were the enemy. You have to understand how people think. They fought against our country. They killed Americans. They killed our grandfather."

"And we killed their grandfathers, too! And grandmothers. And little brothers and sisters. Man, I can't believe this! I mean, you tell me to go shake hands with the other side after I'm in a fight, okay? To treat them with respect, right? But it's like, that only counts when it's just kids playing a game. That in real life people hold grudges forever. They never get over it. I mean, this is dumb. Listen, I'm gonna do this. I'm serious. If you can't see why, then it's your problem, not mine!"

I pushed up off the bed sending the bat and knife flying onto the floor. I flung the door open, banging the knob against the wall.

"Tyler, wait," said Breena. She rushed up behind me. "We're not saying you're wrong."

"I am!" Louie called. "Let him go. And, hey, Tyler! If you go out and do something like this, man, someone's gonna kick your butt, big time. And I'm just gonna laugh about it."

I kept walking. Near the alcove, Breena caught my arm and yanked me back.

"Wait, wait, wait," she said. "He doesn't mean that. He's just—"

"I know, whatever. But he should be on my side. You should be, too."

"Well, I am, Tyler, I am. But, look, there's probably lots of other ways for you to make your point besides this. I mean, you have some good points. Really. Let's think about it. Like, what if you wrote a letter to *The New York Times* and explained how you felt?"

"Oh, yeah, sure. They'd really wanna print a letter from me."

"Or you could contact your congressional representatives. Listen, what if we did go back to D.C.? We could even knock on their doors. Let them know you wanna make this big point for the Fourth of July or something. I'll go with you. I mean, there's lots of ways for you to get this idea across—to get attention."

"Attention? You think that's why I wanna do this? To get attention?"

"Well, isn't it? Aren't you really doing this so Coach Trioli will notice? That this is your big demonstration of how mature you are?"

I stared in sheer disbelief. "No way! I don't care if he sees it or not. I don't care who sees it. I just wanna do it. Forget about it."

I spun around heading back into the bedroom.

Man, I thought, I didn't wanna get all upset like this. Especially in front of Breena. I'd been doing so well.

As I walked in, Louie said, "This is like something your dad would do." He rolled his chair over to his keyboard.

"What?" I picked up the black bat. "You don't even know my dad!"

"I know he was a hippie, antiwar protester. He was a traitor. Everyone knows that." He tapped a few keys.

I propped the bat on my shoulder. "He was not! You don't know what you're talking about!"

"Yeah, well, how come he just sits at home all the time? Never goes to work?"

"He *has* a job. He has a business." I gripped the bat as tight as I could. "I work with him sometimes, so you can just shut up about my dad!"

I stepped up to Louie's F-16 model jet, brought the bat back, and swung. But at the last instant, I let go, and flung the barrel between him and Breena. Smashing the plaster wall. Cracking it like an eggshell.

"Tyler!" screamed Breena.

"You lunatic!" said Louie, jumping up. "Whata ya, *nuts?* You could've killed somebody!"

"Shut up!" I said. "You guys know *nothing*."

I ran to the window, unfocused. White light filling my brain. With one motion, I threw it open.

"Tyler, stop!" said Breena.

I leaned halfway out, eyeing the fire escape, trying to focus, trying to calm down. But I couldn't.

I hopped onto the sill, leaned forward into the light, and jumped.

"Tyler!" said Breena. "*No!*"

Somehow I missed the top rail, slashing my hands against the skinny vertical side bars of the fire escape balcony. I managed to grip one bar, but slid down to the bottom of it, scraping my hands and wrists even more, while my legs dangled in midair, a hundred feet above nothing.

Tight as I could, I held on and closed my eyes, forcing out all the light, focusing on the black, trying to come back, to get back into control.

"Hey," Louie called. "You okay? You need help?"

"Oh, God, *Tyler!*" screamed Breena. "Louie, help him!"

I squeezed harder, slowly pulling myself up, hand over hand.

"I'm okay," I shouted. "Leave me alone."

Last thing I wanted was for Louie to run into Aunt Chrissy's room, come out onto the fire escape, and rescue me. I'd never live that down.

Finally I crawled up and over the iron rail. I brushed myself off, ignoring the scraped shreds of skin on my palms. Easy, cool, under control.

When I glanced back at the window, I saw Breena, her arms folded against her stomach, eyes brimming, glaring at me.

Then she turned and ran away.

All I could do was hunch down toward the Hudson River and whisper long, compound cusswords.

Just great, I thought. I blew it big time. And I'm on my own, now.

I picked up a handful of birdseed and realized even the doves had deserted me. What next?

Trickling the seed over the side of the rail, I decided one thing. I wasn't going to quit. If I really believed in this thing, I couldn't give it up now.

That was something Dad would do.

chapter 29

FOR THE REST OF THE WEEK, I SHUT EVERYTHING out except putting my "art project" plan into action by the Fourth of July.

It was funny, but something about having this new goal took the pressure off my other one—of building my stats for All-Stars—and made it easier to relax and do just that. In two games, I got six hits in eight at bats.

But at home, the war was still on. Louie gave me the silent treatment—with the help of his headphones—while Breena just disappeared every time I came around.

That part hurt. But being shunned by Louie and Ryan was almost a welcome deal. Part of my thanks, I guessed, for sparing his model plane.

I did have to buy a can of spackle, though, and patch the major divot I'd made in the wall and all the cracks spoking out from it. Kind of looked cool, actually. Like rays from a rising sun.

But having Breena ignore me—that cut into my stomach.

All I could really do, though, was just try to keep busy with things like filling up an old notepad with design sketches for the memorial or heading off to the park to look for bats.

By Sunday afternoon, Louie still thought I was a virtual traitor—certain I was going to be executed one day by some super patriots—but Breena had softened. No, that's the wrong word. Because what she did was actually pretty tough.

At least it would've been tough for me. She apologized.

She found me sketching out a few designs on a checkerboard-top table down at the monument in Riverside Park.

I'd noticed her coming about a block away, and you don't know how worried I was that she would just walk on by. Still, I kept working. Hoping.

Finally, she shuffled up close and sat down next to me on the bench.

"Tyler, I hate this. I'm sorry I said what I said."

"Me, too," I told her, which was as close as I could get to apologizing.

"In school," she continued, "they teach us to resolve conflicts by looking at both sides. Even if one side is obviously right." She paused to let me think about that. "So I'm willing to take another look at your side."

Turning the pad to shade in the barrel of a bat, I kept on working.

"So," I said, "you think I'm all wrong about this?" Slowly, I began lettering in a name on the sketched bat. On the signature spot.

She made a big sigh. "Well, I don't know. But I do

know that you're my cousin, and I love you, okay? It should never've gotten this far."

I completely messed up the lettering while that word "love" sledgehammered my chest. Was I blind? I wondered. She *loved* me?

But I kept cool. "Well, tell that to Louie. He started it."

"Tyler, it doesn't even matter. The thing is, you've got to know some people may take this thing the wrong way. They're not all going to be as understanding as I am."

"That's their problem."

"Don't be like that. I wanna be friends, okay? And Louie does, too. Really. And to be honest, the more I think about what you're doing, the more I like it. Besides, I miss your games. I want things to be normal again."

I finally looked up at her. I should've done that the whole time, but I was too scared. Now, seeing her face so near, so close, the only thing I wondered was, is this the time when I get to kiss her?

She leaned in even closer. My heart was going to burst my ears.

Her hand touched mine, sliding it off the page.

"Let me see," she said, completely unaware of the out-of-breath idiot I'd become. "Whose name is that? Whose name are you writing down?"

I glanced at the sheet. "Oh, this?" I had to breathe a moment. "Oh, it's a guy named Ho Chi Minh."

"Never heard of him."

"Me neither, before I started reading all this stuff. But I'm putting his name on first because a long time ago he was, like, this big leader in Vietnam. And he gave a speech to the Vietnamese on how their country's freedom should be based on America's Declaration of Independence. That all people on earth are born equal."

"He did? You mean after the Vietnam War was over?"

"No, no, this was, like, in the 1940s. After World War II. And then he wrote a letter to President Truman asking for help to set up a new, independent government based on those principles. To help Vietnam do something like what he'd seen the U.S. do for the Philippines."

"Well, that was cool. So what happened? I mean, why'd they turn against us?"

"I don't know. I mean, it was weird. See, Truman never even answered his letter. Ignored it completely— like he'd done with a few others—because he was afraid if he helped the Vietnamese be independent, he'd insult the French who wanted to take over Vietnam again and put back in all of their colonies."

"How do you know all of this? We haven't studied this at all."

"Us either. Got it from your mom's books, mostly." I shook my head, laughing. "All those cool pictures, I guess. I just started getting interested in, like, *why?* Then I found some more stuff on the Net and just got into it."

Breena leaned back against the bench slats. "Grandad died because of that? Because the president didn't even bother to answer those letters? To see if maybe our countries could come to some kind of understanding?"

I shrugged, knowing full well that her Peace Patrol brain was kicking in. "Well, you know," I said, "he had a lot of pressure on him. He figured he had to support the French, and they wanted Vietnam."

"Yeah, right. Support the French stealing a country. I mean, that whole war. It was all because of politics and greed."

"Maybe so, but it's what most Americans wanted, too. Especially in the fifties. I mean, you don't know. I read a whole chapter on it. There was like a total witch hunt going on against communists. People were building bomb shelters, stocking up on food. They were really scared."

"But our countries could've been friends!" she said. "We could've worked something out." She stood up. "That's what I mean! War is so stupid. Oh, you just wanna shake people."

I finished the name and held out the drawing so we both could see.

"Or shake them up," I said.

She took a long look. "Wow, fifty bats? With fifty names?"

"Hope so. But I don't know. I don't have that much time."

"When do you need them by?"

"A week from Friday. Exactly eleven days."

She looked up at the trees. "You got a lot of work to do!"

"I know. I don't mind working. Besides, I hired some kids at the ball park to help, and they were so good at getting the word out, a couple coaches said they'd bring them a bunch of old bats from home. I'm paying them three bucks for each cracked bat."

"With whose money?"

"I got the money. I dig ditches for my dad, remember?"

She glanced back down at my drawing, then pushed up off the bench. "I hope you know what you're doing, Tyler."

"Don't worry. I'm an artist. I know everything."

"Well, what about your own coach? Did you ask him?"

I tapped my pencil a few times. "Hey, that's not a bad idea. He's an old guy. He might have some wooden bats laying around."

"You still remember where he lives?"

I nodded. "Yeah, sure. Near Columbus. Over on eighty-eighth. We could be there in five minutes."

I stood up wondering why I hadn't thought of this before. But as I stashed everything into my pack, a big, huge doubt flooded over me.

What if he doesn't see this thing the way I do? What if he's totally offended?

"Um, you know, Breena. Maybe we shouldn't. He might not like it."

"Yes, he will. The way you described it to me, he will."

"Yeah, but, also—if I tell Coach about it, that kind of makes it official. Like, now I *have* to do it."

She pushed my shoulder. "Tyler, you always do stuff on impulse and look at the trouble you get into. Now for once, you've got a plan. You've thought it out. You gotta do it."

chapter 30

COACH WASN'T EXACTLY HOME WHEN WE GOT there. But we spotted him coming up the street clutching a paper bag of groceries with a long stick of bread poking out the top.

Right off, I asked him if he had any old, wooden bats lying around that he might want to donate to "a worthy cause."

"You kidding me? I'm the worst pack rat in the world. I probably got a whole bin of old bats down in my shop. But, I don't know. How worthy is your cause?"

I sent Breena a quick glance. She raised her eyebrows and nodded.

"Well," I said. "It sort of ties into what you and Mr. Steinmetz asked me to do. That 'honest-to-goodness demonstration' thing he was talking about. You know, to the other side?"

"What?" That made him laugh. "What do you mean?"

I felt my ears heat up. "Um, I don't wanna say too much about it. It's kind of a surprise. But you'll see it when I'm done. I mean, I hope you will."

He waved his hand at me. "Ah, what do I care what happens to them? Always thought I'd turn them on a lathe some day and use them for staircase spindles or something. Good, solid ash. But if you wanna haul them off, be my guest."

"Really? We can?"

"Take them right now if you want. Here, follow me. Shop's right below my apartment."

And we did. Lugged home twelve old bats, most of them cracked. And by that next Tuesday, I had over thirty. Still short, but I was getting there.

Pedro let me stash them in an old, dusty hole by the utility room, instead of having to lug them up to the apartment. That worked out great because it also gave me a good place to set them up and paint them.

See, I'd decided to spray them all shiny black. Except for the space where I sliced off the name and wrote in the new one with a black marker. That way, the names stood out.

I'd set Friday, July 3, as my deadline. By then, I wanted to get the whole thing all set up. Besides, working on this took my mind off something else that was looming over me like a big, black storm cloud.

Carmine DeLucca.

The game with that jerky yellow team was coming right up. Tomorrow afternoon, to be exact.

And when I rolled out of bed that Wednesday morning, it felt like two hands were gripping my gut like they were squeezing a bat handle. I hadn't been this nervous in a long time. I just hoped I could make it through the day without losing *my* grip. Hoped that the game would actually be another chance to show Coach I was All-Star material.

After lunch Louie finally broke his silence. "You scared?" he asked.

"No."

"Should be. Everybody's gonna be watching how you take care of him."

"Yeah?" I stepped close and flicked Louie on the cheek. "He comes after me, and I'll send in the Air Force."

He just shook his head and grinned. "Just don't be stupid, okay?"

And that was the end of that. Two cousins, two warriors, back on the same team.

But as we left for the field that day, I knew two things. I wasn't going to fight the guy. That would ruin everything. But I wasn't going to walk over and apologize, either. I mean, I knew how that would go over with Tony and Eugene and everybody. I didn't need that.

No, I'd deal with Carmine later. Just between him and me.

Walking out of the dugout, Tony slapped my shoulder. "Hey, you gonna jump that guy, or what? Lemme know, man. I'll watch your back." He grabbed a weighted bat and started swinging.

From our bench, I watched Carmine as he took a few warm-up grounders at third base. Cat-quick, but muscular, he stabbed a sharp grounder near the line, turning his body, shuffling his feet to make the throw, pretty as a dancer. An ugly dancer.

Not bad, I figured, for a baby-sitter.

He spit into the palm of his glove, whammed it with a fist, then squared his shoulders, set his feet, and bent forward, waiting for the next dance.

And for the first time, I saw that his arrogant, aggressive style was as much a part of his approach to baseball as it was to mine.

It was a necessary attitude, a take-charge attitude, that simply said, "I'll play the ball. The ball will not play me. This is my turf, and I'll defend it."

Watching him glove another hard shot, I began to feel a sense of kinship for the guy. Seeing how he charged his coach's bunt and made the quick sidearm flip to first, I started to imagine how great we'd be working together, anchoring down the left side of the infield during the All-Star games.

From then on, I noticed it really didn't bother me when his team started dishing the diss as I took my position, picking up where they'd left off the game before.

The sting was gone. I could finally see the game behind the game.

Even the "yip, yip" chihuahua bark sounded almost friendly to me. Standing at shortstop, I spit over my shoulder, glanced off to the side and saw a grinning Breena sitting on the grass, her arms wrapped around her knees. Now that she was back, everything seemed perfect.

"I feel a good day coming!" I shouted to Tony on the mound. And I remembered that the last time I felt like this, I went four for four. I spit again. "I feel good!"

I spun around to the outfielders, pounding my glove. "Tight D, you turkeys! Let's go, talk it up!"

They answered like chattering chimps at the San Diego Zoo.

Everything felt right, alive, in balance. The sun, the sky, the faint whiff of pushcart hot dog water in the breeze. Even this ball field with its rickety, redwood-slatted fence winding along like a snake seemed perfect.

The umpire dusted the plate, then rose.

"Play ball!" he said, yanking on his mask.

And we started off playing perfect ball. In the first two innings, Tony brought the heat, with a change of speeds mixed in, and recorded three strikeouts, two ground outs, and a pop-up to first.

In my first at bat, I was locked in like I was looking through a rifle scope. First pitch, I laced a two-out single to left center. But I died at second when Louie sent a line drive to right for the third out.

No sweat, I thought. We were in charge. Felt like we were going to get to this pitcher. Just a matter of time.

And I was in charge, too. In charge of me. That's what felt so good.

In charge, in fact, all the way to the bottom of the fourth, when I came up to bat with a runner on third base, one out.

One sure RBI for me, I thought. Then I thought again.

The season was almost over. Why not two RBIs right here? Why not hit one over that rickety fence?

Especially, I thought, with Breena watching.

Trouble was, I got anxious and fouled off the first two pitches, which were both borderline.

"Tyler, back out," Coach called from the third base coach's box. "Take your time. Don't forget to focus. Wait for something you can handle."

He was right. I stepped out, waggled my shoulders, and tightened the strap on my batting glove.

Then Carmine DeLucca gave a suggestion, too. "Don't forget to wave bye-bye after this one, Curly," he called from third. "Because you're going down. Yip, yip, yip!"

The other boys hooted along with him. And that did it.

Yeah, I thought, I'm going down, all right. Downtown.

But the next pitch was outside, so I laid off, resting the bat on my shoulder.

"Stee-rike three!" the umpire called.

I froze. I could not believe the call. Oh, no, I thought. No, man, don't do this to me.

"Yip, yip, yip, yip, yip! See ya, Stump! Two outs, everybody!"

This was absurd. I felt all my sense of fairness, all the good I saw in baseball, just shatter around me like a ceramic bird crushed by a boot.

And you know what I did? Nothing.

Just spun around and headed back to the dugout.

Didn't toss my bat. Didn't say a word. But I vowed right then, I'd show that arrogant jerk something before this game was over.

"Tough call," Coach Trioli said as he and Louie met me near the on-deck circle. "Looked outside."

I hung my helmet on the wire hook, walked off, and sat down. Coach slapped Louie on the butt and said, "Up to you, big guy."

"That's what you get," Carmine yelled, "for sending up a midget to do a man's job. Yip, yip!"

Silently, head bowed, I peeled my red leather batting glove off my left hand, smelling the animal stink of old sweat mixed with musty pine tar. I yanked it off inside out, shifted on the bench, and jammed the whole mess into my back pocket.

That was it. That's all I did.

Biding my time. I stayed in control.

By the bottom of the last inning, I realized how important that strikeout was. We were losing, 2–1, when I came up to bat. One out, tying run on second.

Okay, no problem, I thought. Just like in some old-time baseball movie, I've got my second chance. Only this time, I'll do it. Drive a two-run homer out of the park and score the winning run myself.

I stepped into the batter's box. Please, God, I prayed. You know how long I've waited and how hard I've tried. How about now? Let me hit one over the wall.

First pitch, fastball, inside corner. I swung late and fouled it straight back off my handle.

"Be set," Coach called. "Little sooner, now." He clapped.

I dug in, setting my feet in place earlier, and watched the next pitch go wide. Ball one.

I knew I needed a pitch I could drive to the outfield, to at least advance the runner to third. And the next one looked close enough. I swung, but immediately cussed into the cheers from the other side as I fouled the ball down the right-field line. Still behind it, still too slow! I needed to adjust.

But now, I had to be careful. Two strikes, and the umpire had a wide zone. Anything close, I had to swing.

I opened my stance a little, facing the pitcher more, hoping that if he came inside with the heat again, I could catch up to it this time.

And, whoa—soon as I saw it, I knew. Inside fastball, maybe not even a strike, but I turned on it and boy, did I *connect*.

The sweetest dream feeling in the world. To launch that little white ball off your bat like a missile through the air.

The left fielder turned his back and ran. The ball shot high into the puffy clouds of the New York sky. I rounded first base feeling like the hero in that old-time movie. I mean, I knew how this flick would end. It was pure feel-good. And I was ready to feel real good.

Thank you, I prayed again. Thank you!

I watched the ball sail. High and deep. And I watched it fall. Hit the ground.

And bounce over the wall.

"Ground rule double!" the umpire yelled, and I jumped straight up, groaning, smashed my fist into my palm, then walked into second base.

Well, I'd tied the game, at least. How could I complain? No one else was. Breena was cheering like crazy. But I told myself one thing. The next time I pray about something, I'm gonna have to be more specific.

Louie stepped up to the plate. He'd made contact all game long, but he hadn't gotten any hits. With only one down, I needed to steal third, I decided. Then if Louie hit it anywhere, I could score the winning run.

I watched Coach run through the signs, and he must've been thinking the same thing. Skin, shirt, skin. The *steal* sign.

All right, I thought. Stealing third was no sure thing. He must really trust me.

"Louie!" I yelled. "Hey, Louie! Good solid contact now, huh?"

But that's not what I meant. I just wanted him to look at me while I tapped the side of my helmet.

That was our signal, telling him I saw the sign, that he better not swing, because I was running on the pitch.

He barely looked, tapped his bat on the plate, then adjusted the bill on his helmet. That was his answer back, our team signal.

The play was on.

"Hit it someplace hard, Louie," Coach yelled, as another decoy.

I took a casual lead, reading the shadow of the short-stop behind me to judge how close he was. I glanced at second. No prob there.

And you know what I thought about? I stood there, crouched like a thief, taking my lead, and all I thought about was how impressed Carmine would be after I stole the game right from under his nose. How later, when we're on All-Stars, he'd remember this play, shake his head, then maybe talk about my perfect slide.

I realized it was just what Coach'd been talking about. And now I was doing it. Seeing Carmine not as the enemy, but as a future teammate.

All right, I thought. All right.

The pitcher came set, looked at me, looked home, looked back at me.

As soon as his head drifted forward once more, I was off.

And forget about it.

Hc had me dead.

The pitcher hadn't gone home with the pitch at all. Instead, I spotted him giving me one more glance, and he saw me break for third. He shot the ball to second.

I wasn't even halfway. All the second baseman had to do was flip it to third, and I was a dead midget.

The next two seconds passed like a bad dream.

The only chance I had was to keep running, running for all I was worth, to see if I could beat the throw.

But I could see it was worthless.

Why'd I been so stupid, so anxious? I thought. The

game on the line, Louie at the plate, ready to be the hero. Breena on the grass, waving her giant pretzel, screaming for me.

How could this be happening?

As I came closer to third, Carmine stepped in front of the bag, knelt down blocking my path, holding his glove chest high to catch the toss.

But where was the ball? I wondered. Should've been there by now. Maybe the guy booted it! Maybe I can make it!

I read Carmine's eyes.

No, I thought, here it comes. By his eyes, I could tell the ball was going to the inside of the base. High. He'd have to straighten up and stretch across his body to catch it.

The ball beat me there. Carmine stepped toward home plate to snag it, keeping his back knee hovering over the bag.

And in that instant, I realized I couldn't let this happen. I was not going to be humiliated in front of everybody.

I had one chance. If I could slide in so hard I could jar the ball loose—knock him over if I had to—I could make it. That was my only shot. But it had to be more than just a good, hard slide. I'd have to bend my knee, then lash out with my foot at the last instant. Blast my cleats straight out with all my might.

The play was bang-bang.

The throw, his tag, my shoe, his knee.

His tag got me, dead. But on contact, I'd given my

foot a huge, driving thrust, like afterburners kicking in to let a jet pilot turbo his way out of danger.

And it worked. From the tangled, mangled mess we'd become, I saw the ball trickle out of his glove. Saw it bounce and roll in the dirt. Yes!

I was safe. I was still alive.

Then I heard something.

And even though I'm sure everyone at the field was screaming and yelling all at once, I heard none of it. My focus was too tight.

I only heard one small voice. A tiny squeal.

Like from a chihuahua.

chapter 31

IT WAS CARMINE.

He rolled away, onto his back, gripping his knee.

He sucked in big batches of air, one after another. His face was a twisted pretzel of agony.

Coach was all over him. Other guys, too. But no one could stop his pain.

"Ice!" Coach yelled. "Someone bring some ice."

"What happened?" Carmine's coach wanted to know.

"My knee, my knee, my knee," Carmine squeaked out, his teeth grinding, his eyes shut tight.

I left. I deserted. Kneeling there, only three feet away, I climbed into the mountains of my mind, hid behind a boulder somewhere far away, and watched.

At least, that's what it felt like. Floating there. Watching.

Carmine was a good, tough, defensive player. He'd taken his position, had planted his foot and dug in. But his reach for the ball had extended him, leaving his back knee open and awkward as he brought down his glove.

And I'd launched myself like a missile right at that

glove. In front of his knee. I'd aimed and fired and cut him down.

I could barely think. I killed him, was all I knew. I gotta leave. I blew his knee apart. I know I did.

But I couldn't move. On the field, I knelt on hands and knees in the middle of a big huddle of guys swarming around third. Somehow, a long, red ice chest had appeared, parked next to Coach, where he knelt over Carmine.

"Well, you got him," Tony whispered to me. "Good slide, 'mano. You got him good." He elbowed me and grinned, then added, "Hey, you're bleeding. You all right?"

"What?" It was only then that I could taste the salty blood, could feel it on my bottom lip. "I'm okay, I'm okay," I said, holding the crook of my elbow to my mouth.

All I wanted to do was hide, to have no one look at me.

"Cool slide," said Louie. "You *wasted* him."

I should just quit, I thought. I can't control myself out here.

"Man," I mumbled, pushing myself to my feet. "I wasn't trying to—"

"Course not," said Louie, his eyes glued on Carmine. "That was a clean play. You came in hard. That was an accident."

I heard my breath roar in and out of me, and I didn't answer.

But I knew, that was no accident.

The whole reason I crashed into him, the whole reason I uncoiled my foot for that extra hard pump, was not so I'd be safe.

I did it to save my life. I did it because everyone was watching and I knew what they'd think if I didn't.

In a little while, my breath fell into its natural rhythm. I felt the burning of the cut to my mouth. Suddenly, I was back. I hawked up a stream of red spit.

Well, all right, I thought. This was just a game of good ol' country hardball, right? That slide was just part of the game. One of those things.

"That's ligaments," I heard one kid say as I crept closer. "He's out for good, man. That's surgery."

"Shouldn't of been blocking the base," said Tony. "That's what you get."

"Shut up," said another guy. But no one really argued.

We all stood, wobbly, watching. A silent boy army. Scratching jaws, adjusting our cups, spitting. But I could tell that each kid was thanking whatever God he believed in that it wasn't him gripping his knee. That the missile had landed someplace else.

I squatted down next to Coach, who held a towel full of ice on Carmine's bare leg.

"Feels okay, now," said Carmine. "Think I can walk."

"No," said Coach. "Don't even try it. We'll lift you up."

For a moment, I froze. Watching. Seeing two guys who'd jumped me in the park creep forward.

And I shouldered my way in between them. Feeling Tony's eyes lasering into me, I stuck one hand under Carmine's thigh, one under his calf.

As we lifted him up and turned, I looked right into Tony's glare.

"Oh, dude," he said, shaking his head. "Let them other guys do that!"

I kept moving, as we carried Carmine to his dugout bench, keeping his leg straight, his knee supported.

"Where's your mom, Carmine?" his coach asked. "She here?"

"Nah. My little sister's sick."

"Okay, hang tight. We'll call 911, then we'll get ahold of your mom."

In the dugout, I scraped the back of my hand on the rough wood bench as I lowered down his leg.

I straightened up, wanting to leave. Wanting to run all the way back to yesterday. But I couldn't.

I had to know.

And at that moment, it was harder to find my voice, to find the words, than it was to talk to Steinmetz a month ago.

But I did. Somehow, I did.

"Hey," my voice squeaked out. I cleared my throat. "Sorry, man. I came in too hard. I'm—I'm really sorry."

His eyes found mine and narrowed. Seemed like it was only at that moment that he finally recognized me.

"What, too hard?" said Carmine, the last word coming out long and stretched, like, "hawwed."

He forced out a blast of air. "Fuh-get about it. Part of the game. One of those things."

I gave one more look at his red, puffy knee. All around it wet, black hairs dripped from the melting ice.

With a shaky hand, I reached out and jostled his shoulder, saying nothing more. But knowing. Knowing Louie and Tony and Carmine were right. That it wasn't my fault.

That no one blamed me. And no one hated me.

Except me.

chapter 32

I WALKED HOME THAT NIGHT. THE LONG WAY.

All I wanted to do was to walk and keep on walking.

And the farther I walked, the more I could see that the whole monument thing was a stupid idea. I wished I'd never mentioned it to Coach.

I headed down Central Park West, under the umbrella of elm trees that hung over the sidewalk, jumped a downtown train about an hour later at 59th, and rode it all the way to Battery Park.

Then I really started walking.

Who in the world am I, I wondered, to build a monument to anything, much less to some dead soldiers from another country?

Who am I to suggest that people treat other people different, when I can't even bear to have anyone see me screw up in a baseball game? That I'd rather maim a guy than to let that happen.

Don't ask me why I decided to head all the way down to the tip of Manhattan, but once I stepped up out of the subway hole and hit Rector Street, I just followed my feet and found myself retracing the path I'd taken weeks ago with Coach.

To Trinity, to the end of State, up South Street along the East River piers. Only this time, I kept on going.

The closer I got, though, the clearer my destination became.

As soon as a cluster of sycamore trees came into view, I left the sidewalk, climbed up a few steps, then down into a battered, brown brick plaza, set up like an arena with a semicircle of tiered brick benches facing a glass-block wall.

The New York Vietnam Veterans Memorial.

Etched into the glass wall were a bunch of personal letters from American soldiers writing about what it was like to be in the war.

In my sports bag, my phone started ringing. I realized it'd been two hours since I'd left the ball field. I reached in and shut it off.

Please tell me, I prayed, what I need to know. Amen.

My shoes crunched against the grit and the loose concrete patches that held the broken bricks together. I walked through an opening in the wall and found a bronze dedication plaque buried in the plaza floor. And I studied the words.

To those who served and those who sacrificed,
to those who wept and those who waited,
because of the Vietnam War.

Man, I thought. This is it. Here's New York's answer to the Gettysburg Address. Here's a monument that includes all the people on earth. Aunt Chrissy, Coach. Dad. Even Ho Chi Minh.

I don't have to build my stupid shrine after all.

I clicked open my phone, called Louie, and told him I'd be right home.

Then I headed back to the subway. I crossed right under the building Coach had shown me, remembering once again the violent scenes he'd described, the fights that had taken place down there.

Gazing at the rooftops as I passed by, I almost stumbled over the legs of the very same homeless woman we'd seen before, now sitting on a cement-block tree planter.

Without hesitation, I zipped open my bag, dug down into a side pocket, and pulled up all the coins I could find. Carefully, I trickled them into her paper cup.

She glanced down, said nothing, staring blankly. Same as Dad sometimes did. And I took off running.

I ran all the way back to the uptown train station. Ran like I was being chased by ghosts.

And even though I'd abandoned my artsy plan, nothing felt settled, nothing felt right all that night and into Thursday. I tried to concentrate on baseball, our final game on Saturday. Tried to think about normal stuff. Our team was out of the play-offs, but I still thought I had a chance for All-Stars. I just wanted to get the season over with to find out where I stood.

But mostly I tried not to think at all.

Thursday afternoon, while Louie was out with Ryan somewhere, I lay on my bed flipping up a tennis ball, playing home run derby with the ceiling fan. Anything so I wouldn't have to think.

And it helped. The game was really cool. What you do is, first, turn on the fan. Then lie underneath it with a few tennis balls.

And one by one, you toss them up. *Whap!*

You should see them fly off the fan blades. And if they make it all the way across the room and over the plant shelf—home run!

But after a few hard shots against the window, Breena poked her head in to investigate.

"What's all that noise?"

I didn't answer. I demonstrated.

Whap!

That one almost hit Breena. "Hey," she said, dodging it with a twist. "Would you watch it!"

"Sorry. It's not as easy as it looks."

"It looks ridiculous." She tossed me the attack ball.

That one had hit the bottom of the blades and shot downward, which is what usually happens. That's an out. In fact, anything that's not a home run is an out. But if you can angle your toss to the very edge of the fan—*blammo!* That's what you want.

"How's your memorial thing coming?" she asked.

"It's not," I said. "I bailed on it."

"You did? How come?"

"Ah, it was stupid."

"Tyler, it was not. Besides, that's never stopped you before."

"Shut up." This time I flung the ball at her, but not hard, just enough to annoy her.

She whacked it away. "Stop that. And don't try and

change the subject. I thought you were in here carving bats. What happened?"

"Nothing. Just what you and Louie wanted me to do from the beginning. I changed my mind."

"I never said that. I just had to get used to the idea."

"Well, now you can get used to this. I'm done. It's over. I just—I ran out of time."

That seemed like the easiest thing to tell her. "This is Thursday already. The Fourth of July weekend starts tomorrow. And it's not ready. Don't have enough bats, they're not all painted. Plus I wanted to get a little plaque made."

Those, of course, were my official reasons. The real reason was too embarrassing to mention.

"Why tomorrow?" she asked. "Why not later?"

"Because, you know, Independence Day. Stands for freedom, right? The impact of doing something like this in, say, Central Park on that particular holiday weekend, I mean, we'd find out how free this country was, right?"

"So, how many bats do you have?"

"Thirty-four."

"Really?" She seemed impressed. "Well, hey, that's almost enough. You could go down and buy the rest."

"What, new? Yeah, right. At twenty-five bucks each or something?"

"Well, I don't know. Maybe they'd give you a quantity discount. Daddy might know somebody. Why don't we ask Mom?"

"Forget it. You kidding? She's the last person I'd want

to know. Besides, wouldn't change anything. I'm not doing it."

Breena stepped closer and picked up a few of the sketches sitting out on my nightstand. "These are nice," she said. "You really put a lot of thought into this idea, didn't you?"

"Some."

She leafed through the pile, stopping at the bottom sheet.

"What's this?"

I gave a quick glance at the computer printout. "That's the list of names I was using. The fifty Vietnamese names I wanted to put on the bats. But I could only dig up about ten. I guess there's no official list."

"Hmm," she said. "Ten names out of three million." With a light tap on the table, she neatly restacked the whole pile, then set it on my bed.

"Tyler, why are you giving up?"

"I told you. Time ran out."

"I don't believe you. Tell me why, really." She knelt down on the bed, picked up the last ball, then flopped over on her back next to me.

Holding the ball high, she flipped it toward the fan. *Whap!* Home run. "Hey, that's fun."

"That was pure beginner's luck."

She punched my thigh, then said, "Just tell me why you gave up on it."

"Breee-na." I shifted onto my elbow. "Look, it was a dumb idea. You guys were right. And besides"—and here came the real reason—"I'm not the guy for it."

I hoped that would settle it, that I wouldn't have to explain that, yeah, deep, deep down, I knew now that I wasn't the kind of guy who was qualified to stand up and tell people, "Hey, why don't you think about this?" That I was a phony jerk who would rather take a guy out—maybe ruin his future—than be humiliated in front of everybody.

"You're the perfect guy for it," said Breena.

"What are you talking about?"

She lay there quiet for a moment, staring at the fan, the breeze lifting her bangs like a curved brown feather.

It seemed like she must've sensed how horrible I felt. That somehow, Breena, my kid cousin, this wonder girl, who could look and act five years older than me, knew I was hiding out in the underbrush of the chaparral, a little, scared coyote. Maybe that's why she didn't answer the way I thought she would.

"Tyler," she said, "did you ever stop and think how in the world you'd get fifty baseball bats to Central Park?"

I fell back down and looked at the fan. "Yeah, I don't know. Put 'em in a taxi, I guess."

"Oh, right. And then what? Hire a horse carriage to haul you to the exact spot?"

"No, I figured—you know—I'd carry them somehow."

"They must weigh tons."

"Not that much. Pound and a half each. But so what?"

"So, what if you used something else besides bats?"

"Breena, didn't you hear me? I'm not doing it." I sat up, putting my face right in front of hers. "Look, if I told you what really happened in that baseball game, would you just drop this? Because then you'd see me like I really am. Because I'm not some art guy. I'm not some baseball hero. I'm a big poser who can't live up to what I believe in at all."

She looked at my face for a long time. I mean, too long. And I knew I was about to ruin her image of me forever.

But I had to. I had to tell someone.

"Why would I see you like that?" she asked.

"Because I cheated. I didn't just try and slide in hard to knock the ball out of Carmine's glove. I kicked his glove. And I kicked his knee really hard on purpose. I tried to hurt him. So he'd fall over and drop the ball."

She answered slowly, as if imagining the whole scene. "It looked okay to me."

"Sure, I covered it up. Made it look like a good, hard All-American baseball slide. But it was more than that. They'd picked me off second, and I was gonna look like a complete idiot. And I couldn't stand to let"—I paused, realizing what I was actually saying—"to let you see me like that."

I dropped back down, turning my head toward the fire escape, which, at that moment, seemed a good place to be.

"But, Tyler, I've seen you look like an idiot lots of times."

"That's not what I mean. This time—this time, it

was real important not to . . ." I whapped the bedspread and sat up.

"Oh, man, this is so backwards. You're *supposed* to take guys out in baseball. Slide hard, sacrifice your body, and knock them out of the play if you can. But, what I'm saying is, this time I did it *dirty*. That's all. Pure bush league. I did it because I was picked off—and that is so humiliating. I couldn't stand it. And I wish it never even happened. But it did. And I don't care if you hate me forever and ever, amen. Because I do, too."

Those words were the hardest ones I'd ever said. My throat was dry as an old, shriveled batting glove.

She didn't say a word.

Breena got up, and I figured she was ready to leave. I knew I was ready to have her leave.

I parked myself back against the headboard of my bed and tossed up a few more balls at the fan.

Out. Out. Out.

The last one, Breena retrieved from under the dresser. But she didn't toss it to me. She brought it back, covering it with her hands, and sat next to me on the bed.

"Remember," she asked, "that afternoon—your first week here—when I was walking to the kitchen? After my shower? And I didn't think anyone else was home?"

My heart skipped like a wild pitch. I couldn't believe she was bringing that up. I pushed out my bottom lip, then said, "Yeah, I guess so."

"I saw your head turn," she said. "I know you saw me."

I froze. I couldn't even look up at her. For the first

time that summer, I felt fully awkward, fully uncomfortable being with her.

But in a strange way, I was glad she'd told me.

She waved her hand. "I'm not saying anything about it, okay? So don't get all weird. I'm not, like, mad at you for looking at me or anything. It wasn't—I mean, how could you help it?"

I wobbled my head, my mouth dry as a cracker.

"So," she continued, "you saw me then, and"—she picked up my drawing of the circle of bats—"I see you now."

She joggled the ball in her hand while she studied the picture. "Tyler, you're a human being. You're like Weetzie Bat's Secret Agent Lover Man."

"What?"

"You're a crazy, silly, imperfect human being. And I say, you need to do this for all the crazy and silly and imperfect people like you on earth. That's what qualifies you to put this thing up. Because if you don't, who will?"

She let the memorial design flutter down on top of me like a leaf to a pile. "And I'll help," she said.

I looked up. "Serious?"

She shrugged. "What, you need to paint a few more bats? Make a little plaque?" She shook her head. "Not a problem. I'll help you get all that stuff ready by tomorrow." She bounced the tennis ball from hand to hand, smiling. "And you need what, sixteen more bats, right?"

"Right."

"Well, what about this? What about using sixteen finely painted, miniature ceramic birds instead? It's symbolic, right? That'd work, wouldn't it?"

"You're not serious."

"Tyler! Stop it." She shook the ball at me. "I am if you are. But you gotta commit to it, okay? I mean, do you believe in it or not?"

"Yeah, I do. I really do."

"Okay, good. But you gotta promise me one thing. We won't put it up in Central Park."

My image of the project shrunk a little. "Well, where, then? In your room or something? I mean, what's the use, if people don't see it?"

"Oh, I agree. I'm just thinking that tons more people would have a much better chance of seeing it if you set it up somewhere special. Like, say"—she lifted her shoulders—"on the National Mall. You know, in Washington, D.C."

Without looking, she tossed the ball straight up.

Whap! Home run.

chapter 33

"ARE YOU READY?" I WHISPERED INTO BREENA'S doorway on Friday afternoon.

She tugged on her backpack strap, tightening it up for a snug fit. "Almost. How'd it go?"

"Mission accomplished."

My mission of the day was to whittle away on nearly twenty bat barrels, then apply names to each one using a black marker.

"You go to the trophy shop?" I asked.

She nodded. "Yeah, it's in my pack. And I like the verse you picked. I think that's all that needs to be said."

"Yeah, thanks. That's why I picked it. Okay, we gotta jam. Train leaves in about forty minutes."

She whipped a hand to her mouth. "Forty minutes? Ugh! Are the bats ready? Are they dry?"

"Dry and sliced. They're all bagged up and sitting in the lobby."

"Oh, this is too scary," she said. "Okay, what's Louie doing?"

I motioned to our bedroom with my thumb. "Playing twitch games with Ryan. They're dead to the world. What'd your mom say when I was gone all day?"

"Nothing. She's so panicky right now. She's got this ritzy dinner to go to in some mansion on the East Side. So she's out morphing-over at her beauty shop. I just told her you had some shopping to do. She understands shopping. But, look, we *have* to be back by midnight. Can we do it?"

"Yeah, more or less."

"Well, we have to. Mom's having dinner, then going off to see *Death of a Salesman*. In honor of Daddy, I suppose. Anyway, she'll be home by twelve-thirty or one."

"Yeah, no problem."

Breena sucked in a breath, then exhaled calmly. "I am so amped out. I feel like we're in this movie. Like we're launching this secret mission."

She stepped out into the hall, her cheeks flushed pink against her soccer tan.

"I'm excellent at secret missions," I told her.

She laughed. "Yeah, right, James Bond. I remember. Well, in this movie, your next mission is to get Mom's insulated picnic pack from the closet. Then empty it out. We'll need it to carry the ceramics."

I spun a one-eighty and hurried into the closet, spotted the red-and-white checkered pack by Louie's bike and reached for it.

"Ow!" I cried. I'd smacked my head on the shelf. I stood back, rubbing hard, trying to see why the shelf was sagging.

It wasn't. Slowly it dawned on me. I was taller. I eased up to the shelf again, standing as tall I could. Yes!

No doubt. Just in the last month. Probably a full inch! And suddenly, my head didn't hurt so bad.

After emptying out the Thermos and utensils, I met Breena as she emerged from her bedroom carrying a shopping bag full of little objects wrapped in tissue paper.

"Do we have to take this picnic thing? It looks a little corny."

"But it's thick and cushioned. I just hope everything'll fit."

I took her bag and looked inside. She had all of her little birds wrapped up, one by one, stacked in neat little rows. "You sure you wanna do this? I don't think you'll get these back."

She answered so quickly, I knew she wasn't that sure. "I said I would. It's okay." She placed the bag on the floor. "C'mon. We'll have to repack. But it'll work."

Before we could finish cramming everything inside the checkered pack, Louie came down the hall. He scoped us out. Backpacks and all.

"Hey," he said, "what're you guys up to?"

My mind blanked. We knelt there like burglars caught with the jewels.

Breena stood up while I finished loading and zipping things shut. "Oh, we were thinking about a movie," she said. "Thought we'd load up some snacks and go out for a movie. I was gonna leave a note."

"Well, think again, little sister," said Louie. "Mom said to stick around. And I'm in charge." He stepped into the bathroom and clacked the door shut.

"What do we do now?" I asked Breena.

"I'll handle this," she said, walking up to the bathroom door. With a slight tap, she called, "Louie, listen. Our movie starts in forty minutes. And we'll easily be back before Mom gets home. So we have to go. Ciao!"

She grabbed my arm, dragging me away from these loud, pleading shouts of, "Wait, wait! You guys! You better not go!"

"Show time!" said Breena. We raced to the front door, pulled it open, and slammed it behind us, against the sound of a flushing toilet. "The stairs!" she said. "He'd never use the stairs."

We dropped twelve flights like a couple of smart bombs, making three quick stops along the way to push the "up" and "down" elevator buttons on three different floors.

In the lobby, Pedro's assistant, Edgar, helped me load the bat bag onto one shoulder and my own backpack on the other for balance.

"Isn't that heavy?" asked Breena.

"No way," I said, knowing that she was talking to a taller, stronger guy. "Like fifty pounds. It's nothing."

"Where are you going with all of these bats?" asked Edgar. He was new to the job, and Aunt Chrissy considered him a bit too friendly.

"Um, we're finally setting up that art project," I said, trying to get my balance.

"Yeah," Breena added. She tapped her temple. "It's called, 'Bats in the Belfry.' "

"*Muy bien*," said Edgar, nodding. "Have fun." He

pulled the glass door open for us, without ever noticing all of the elevator lights lit up behind him.

"Let's jet," I yelled into the loud sidewalk outdoors. "The five o'clock train to D.C. will get us there in about three hours. That should give us just enough time to set up, shoot some pictures, and catch the 9:20 train back home."

"Wait," said Breena. "That'll be after midnight."

"But you said they'd be back by twelve-thirty or one. We'll make it."

Before she could answer, the duffel bag tipped off my shoulder and banged to the curb with a clank.

"We need a taxi," she said. "This is crazy."

She stepped over the bag and into the street, glancing up and down.

"Hey," I called. "Maybe you shouldn't go. It's all right, if you—"

"Tyler!" She aimed her glare at me. "I gave you my word. I'm going."

And she stuck to it. Once on board the train, we spent the first hour or so rehearsing the mission. We used a map I'd downloaded off the Internet to draw up an exact plan and a timetable for each operation.

"We can easily get to the Reflecting Pool in fifteen minutes," I said.

"The Reflecting Pool? Is that where you want to put it?"

"Yeah," I said. "You know." I raised my eyebrows. "Reflection?"

Breena ignored my brilliant poetic suggestion. "Seems

a little too much out in the open," she said. "But in any case, I think we ought to take the Federal Triangle Station instead of the Smithsonian stop. Less people. Then we'll take the bike path along Constitution. That'll be faster."

"Okay," I agreed. "Still, we can set the whole thing up in ten minutes. Then we can hang a while, see what people think, and easily be back at the train station by nine."

"Yeah, maybe," she said. "If nothing goes wrong."

I looked at her, wondering what she meant by that. Wondering if she was getting scared.

She caught me. And then something really scary happened. We didn't look away. For an extra moment, we just kept looking. And I remembered that thought I'd had the last time we'd rode this train.

Why not? I wondered. Why don't I just ask her?

"Breena," I said. My whole face fired up and got all tingly. Then the words just kind of snuck out by themselves. "Could I kiss you?"

Her mouth hinted at a grin. "What?"

Oh, man, did I feel totally stupid. What was I doing, asking her? I mean, you don't *ask*. People just lean close and do it. Somehow they just *know*.

Except that, me, right here, I didn't know anything.

"Nothing," I said. "Never mind." I turned away.

"Tyler!" Her voice carried a train wreck in it. "We're *cousins*."

"Yeah, I know." I fingered the armrest. "I just wondered." Oh, man, I had no defense.

"I know what you wondered," she said, stretching out the words. "And I can't believe that you'd want—I mean, you are *such a boy!*"

Well, okay, sure, I thought. What's the big shock in that?

"Sorry," I said, hoping no one else was listening. "I just, you know, I had this feeling that, here we are on this adventure, together, and all alone, and that maybe you decided to come along because you and me—well, because—"

No way could I finish that sentence. Not when practically each word brought another blazing blast of fire from her wide-open eyes and mouth.

"Tyler, that's disgusting. I hope you're not thinking anything really stupid, because—"

"No, no, no. I'm not thinking anything. Really. Just forget I even mentioned it. I'm sorry. I just thought—"

"Well, *you* can forget it." She slid back in her seat and folded her arms like she was shivering cold.

I felt totally bummed. I sank into my seat, knowing that with one stupid question I'd ruined the rest of the night. I'd ruined everything. What was I *thinking?* Normally I would never've said anything like that. Why, then, all of a sudden, did it seem okay?

After a few minutes, Breena turned my way, cleared her throat, and I knew, this was it. She hated me, despised me, and was going to kill me.

"Tyler, look."

But I didn't. I couldn't.

"Let me say this," she continued, in a slow, even

tone. "I like you, okay? I do. I even love you. So much so that I'll forget you just said what you said. As long as you never ask me anything like that again, okay?"

Whoa, that was huge. I felt like praying, saying thank you. I mean, this was huge and lucky. Slowly I turned to her, peeking out from under a blop of hair that hung above my eyes.

Her face was in full crinkle, smiling. "Come on, you idiot boy. Say something. Promise me, okay?"

"Hokay," I breathed out, squeaking the last part. My voice had never squeaked so much in my whole life. And it made me feel even dumber.

"Good," she said, craning to look around. "Now, let's get something to eat."

Nearly two hours later, full of chili fries and chocolate—and feeling like good, old best pals again—we pulled up to Washington's Union Station.

"It's 8:01," I said. "Right on time."

Breena humphed and shouldered her load. "Still have to hurry."

But once the Metro dumped us at the Federal Triangle, once I saw all the closed offices, once we'd walked out past the IRS building and I stared down that long street into the setting sun, a gigantic thunder cloud of doubt just rolled in and rained on my brain.

"Should we really do this?" I whispered.

Breena raised her eyebrows and her shoulders together.

Then she whispered back. " 'You will come to a place where the streets are not marked. Some windows are lighted. But mostly they're darked. A place you could sprain both your elbow and chin! Do you dare to stay out? Do you dare to go in?' "

I figured she was totally freaking out on me. But, no. She just nodded west and looked at me for an answer.

I started walking. She followed. Decision made.

Which was good, because if we'd waited to decide by the time we saw the red, white, and blue banners hung all over the National Mall, the crowds of people, the flags and ropes all over the place, the TV lights beaming on a woman reporter interviewing two park policemen about tomorrow's celebration—well, we probably would've turned back and gone right home.

Instead, like secret commandos, we oozed our way down the walk, silently pacing the crowd across the avenue that strolled and strollered and jostled along in the dimming light.

"I just hope our display can stay up until tomorrow," I said. "So people can really see it."

"Don't worry," said Breena. "I think people'll see it."

At about eight-thirty, the sun began to set into a gray, cloudy haze.

As we walked along, the strange, rapid rhythm of the cicadas in the trees matched our footsteps. *Wow-wow-wow-wow.* Then the racket would fade off into silence only to start up a little while later.

Around sundown, we passed the White House and the little fountain in front of it where kids ran through, laughing and splashing, as the streetlights flickered on.

"That's the lawn where they put up the national Christmas tree," said Breena, pointing.

"Yeah, okay. Let's cross at the next corner. We're getting close."

Heading down Constitution Avenue toward the towering trees and lush grass of the National Mall—and the Reflecting Pool—a warm, gentle breeze gave us a big, stinky, outhouse whiff from dozens of portable "Big John's Johns" set up side by side for the weekend's crowd.

"Whew!" said Breena.

"Biological warfare," I said as we cut in between them. Then I waved at a few fireflies that zipped nearby, seeing if I could catch one for luck.

At an empty bench above the Reflecting Pool, I dumped the bats off my shoulder, and we sat.

I followed Breena's stare across the open land toward the pool. "Plenty of places down there to put it," she said.

I didn't answer.

Two more fireflies buzzed me, then darted off, as I tried again to snatch one in my hand. I followed their flight as they headed west into the dark canopy of trees, then found myself staring right at a huge line of people dropping down the trail into the low gloom of footlights marking the Vietnam Veterans Memorial.

"What time is it?" I asked.

"Eight forty-two," said Breena.

My mind was racing a mile a heartbeat. Should we? I wondered. Could I really do what I had in mind?

Finally, I picked up the duffel and began to walk away.

"Where are you going?" she asked.

"This isn't right," I said, halting. "It's not—we can't do this here."

"Tyler!" said Breena, rising. "We came all this way."

I shook my head. "I know, I know. But all day today, I've been thinking about Carmine and what I did to him. It keeps popping up, and it's funny, but now I realize I wanted to do this because of what I did to him as much as any other reason."

"Yeah, okay. You can. We'll find the perfect spot."

"But I kept thinking about that poem on the plaque. You know."

Her mouth made a silent, "Oh."

"And that these guys—these names I put on the bats—some of them were the enemy—just like Carmine was to me. A lot of them fought and died on the same battlefields as those guys whose names are on that wall over there. Some of them right alongside."

"So what are you saying?"

"I'm saying, that's where they should be remembered. Right alongside." I pointed to the Vietnam Veterans Memorial wall. "It should be over there."

"You mean build it right in the middle of—of everything?"

Suddenly the image—the seventeen sets of crossed bats, the birds, the plaque, set right up in front of that black granite wall—filled my head.

That's where it belonged. Illegal or not. Federal offense or not. I mean, it was only fair.

"Breena, you don't have to go," I said. "This was my idea. But I think Grandad—I think he'd understand what I'm trying to do. I mean, either I follow what I believe in or I don't. But if I believe what's on the plaque, and I do, then I gotta do this for them. I gotta treat 'em right."

Without hesitation, Breena picked up the checkered pack.

"Okay, you don't have to get all sappy," she said. "Let's go. But our train leaves in, like, thirty-five minutes. We *have* to hurry!"

chapter 34

THE OVERCAST SKY SEEMED TO TURN GRAYER AS another gentle breeze blew up, cooling the humid air. And in a few moments, I saw the whole deal. The exact spacing, the pattern, everything. We'd stick the bats in a V-shape, not in front of the wall, but behind it. Well, actually, in a dark, little woodsy area above it.

I gazed over at that grassy knoll dotted with trees that hides the wall from Constitution Avenue. I remembered that spot from my first trip.

"Up there," I said. "I wanna build it all along the top of the wall."

"Up there?"

"Yeah, it's perfect. Their country was invaded, right? Their ancestors had to look down on all the destruction. On all the intruders. So now they can look down from up there."

She eyed the site.

"Oh, Tyler, no," she said. "That's too close. Don't, please, don't. I have a bad feeling about all this. Let's go find some other place. Or let's go home. Really. It'd be okay. No one'll know. I promise, I'll never say a word about it to anyone."

The tremor in her voice scared me. Until now, she'd been the strong one.

"Go home?" I forced a laugh, hoping that might break her out of her fear. Or me out of mine. Because, to be honest, at that moment going home sounded like a great idea.

But I knew I couldn't. Not after I'd come this far. And I didn't mean just to Washington. I meant all the stuff I'd been through this whole summer, all the stuff I'd seen, and the new way I was starting to look at things.

"Nothing to be scared of here." I laughed again. "This is America, right? Land of the free, home of the brave. Well, let's do something brave and free. And, man, are we gonna have some stories to tell everybody after this."

I looked away from her, sending my eyes deep into the night, hoping to show her I was full of courage.

And also hoping that courage could be like fear. That not only could you catch it from other people, but you could make it up out of nothing.

Breena stared, shook her head side to side, and puffed out a breath. But she didn't speak.

My hand slipped around her shoulder, and I pulled her close, just the way she'd done to me after the soccer game back at the park.

"It's okay," I whispered. "I can feel it. It's gonna be okay. Listen, we're on a mission, all right? We'll scope the site, fly in, drop our bombs, and leave before they know what hit 'em. Over in no time. We'll make Grandad proud."

She pressed her lips together, looking like she wanted to believe me, but I saw the muscles in her cheeks twitch.

"I don't like that word," she answered. "Proud. It's so ugly. At school, every fight I ever had to mediate was all because of someone's pride."

"Okay, then," I said. "Grandad would be real *happy*. We'll crack him up with our goofy-looking monument. Buncha baseball bats and little birds! Forget about it. He'll laugh like crazy."

"Oh, Tyler, I don't think so. Now that I'm here, it's all different. I'm not like you. I can't jump out of a window and swing on a balcony twelve floors up."

I wanted to say that that was nothing compared to this. I didn't have a sure grip on this. But I didn't want to totally discourage her. Besides, I knew the clock was ticking. It was now or never.

"I'm going," I said. "Do you want me to take the birds or not?" I grabbed my load, ready to loop the picnic bag on, too, if she said I should.

She studied her pack a moment, then started walking.

Right toward the wall.

"Let's go," she said. "I'm thinking too much." She moved out, talking more to herself than to me. "I already decided I wanted to do this. That it was a good thing. Sorry, Tyler. I lost my focus."

"All right!" I forced another laugh as we hurried to

the site. In the movies, a guy would've kissed her right then. Cousin or not. It was that kind of moment. But I didn't. This was real life. And I was too scared.

As we hiked up to the walkway that led to the east end of the wall, my heart began to pound the way it did in a ball game just before I stole a base.

At that moment of decision, when only me and the coach knew what the deal was, my heart would rock and my stomach would get all squirty. But the decision had been made. I had to perform. And like Breena'd said, the thinking had been done. It was time now to just do it.

By then, it was nearly nine. The sky, which had been cloudy and gray, was now cloudy and dark. No moon tonight. I was on my own.

Two hundred yards away, the candlelike glow of the footlights along the base of the memorial wall sent a kind of ocean spray of light up and over the heads of the people below.

We reached the east end of the wall, right where the stone walkway began, right where the redwood lath fencing rose up to keep visitors on the path. Tons of people were moving by as we slowed and stopped. But the little woods area above it was dark and deserted.

Near my feet, I spotted an open can of beer, a pack of cigarettes, and an American flag stuck in the can that someone had left in remembrance.

Farther down the walk, a ranger stood on a metal stepladder, leaning into the black granite with a pencil and paper, rubbing on a name.

As far as I could tell, no one was watching. No one paid us any attention at all. "Let's go," I whispered, and stepped up from the walkway.

And over the wall.

We quickly disappeared into the dark, away from the low glow of light below us.

As we dropped our load, I watched groups of people passing on the walkway beneath us. Some huddled, some moved slowly along, intent on reading the names, and, like subway riders on their own personal journeys, making no eye contact with others.

We stood alone, in the darkness, ten feet above their heads.

I grabbed about ten bats and trooped to the spot I'd marked in my mind. Right in the middle. I picked out the first pair of barrels and pushed the broken ends into the earth.

"Albert Pham Ngoc Thao," I whispered, reading the name off the bat, pronouncing it the best I could. Then, "Ngo Dinh Diem."

I placed all ten, and by the time I headed back to gather the second batch, Breena had set out all of the birds, arranging them in tiny rows.

We made a great team. "Looks good," I whispered.

"Thanks," she said. "I want them to represent all the little children and old people who were killed. The fragile ones." She glanced once more at the master sketch that lay on the grass, then gave it to me. "But you better hurry, Tyler. I think some people are looking." She pointed behind us, toward the street.

I stared through the trees and saw the park ranger hurrying up the asphalt walkway on the far edge of the woods. Other people were rushing along with her. But I knew no one could reach us unless they circled around the entire fence and came in here the way we did.

"Breena! I need you to take the camera and get some pictures. Okay?" As I read the stern looks on those people's faces, the pictures became more and more important.

Breena snatched up stray wads of tissue paper wrapping, then hurried to my pack on the grass.

I went back to work. "And, listen," I said. "From now on, pretend like you don't know me. All right? I mean, just in case."

"What do you mean, 'just in case'?"

"I mean, in case I don't get out of here in time." I stared into the other direction, past the top of the wall and beyond. "See that tree? After you get some close-ups, can you climb up that tree and get a shot of everything?"

"Ty-ler! That's crazy. I don't think—"

"Hey, in there!" some guy yelled from beyond the fence. "What's going on?"

"Breena, go! Look, don't freak now. I know what I'm doing. Hurry!"

I didn't wait for a response, but strode to the spot in the grass for the next pair of bats. I was placing numbers thirteen and fourteen when I heard footsteps behind me.

The ranger. A slender woman with short dark hair, about Aunt Chrissy's age.

"Quite a project you're working on, fella," she started. "But I'll have to ask you to please remove it. These types of displays aren't allowed here."

I kept working, spinning those two bats forward, mumbling the names as I did it.

"Look," she said, stepping over my master sketch. "I can see you have some kind of idea you want to get across. But we can't allow it." She knelt down next to me. "Now, I'm telling you again. Please gather all this up and remove it from the park. Do you understand?"

I had ten more sets to go. I saw the flash of Breena's camera.

And I kept moving, faster now. Two bats at a time.

"Ma'am," I said, "I know this may not seem right to you. And I sure don't mean any disrespect. But in my own little way, I'm trying to honor a lot of people who died in Vietnam, and also show that I got a sense of fair play."

I looked at the arc of nine sets of crossed barrels sheltering sixteen hand-painted ceramic birds—each bat, each bird representing over 58,000 human beings. And I took a breath. "Please let me finish."

And I set one more pair. Another flash.

For the first time she actually looked at the bat barrels. I could see her eyes read the names. Then her eyebrows seemed to clamp down on a worried thought.

"Vietnamese people?" she asked.

"Yes, ma'am."

"Who fought on our side?"

"Some of them."

She looked again at the arc. "And some who fought for the North?"

I nodded. "And some—like the kids and old people—who didn't fight at all. Just got bombed on or burned up or something."

She rose slowly, pushing herself up off the grass.

"I'm sorry, fella. But you can't do this here. You're breaking a couple of serious federal statutes. And if you persist, you have to understand, you *will* be arrested." She cast a glance around.

"Listen," she said, "why don't you take this—I don't know—take this project someplace else? Someplace where it won't tick so many people off."

"Well, that's the whole reason—I mean, it's gotta be here. Or it won't mean anything. Please?"

I turned and gathered the rest of the bats, closed my eyes, and prayed.

She said nothing, and I stepped to the top of the circle.

The ranger walked away, up toward the footpath. I heard her speak into her walkie-talkie, but I couldn't make out the words. No matter. I knew what kind of call she was putting in.

Working now at double speed, I finished the entire arc, shoving the shattered wooden tips of the last two bats into the ground. "Ho Chi Minh," I whispered. "Ho Van Trahn."

I kept busy, aware now that a small crowd had gathered at the fence behind me, watching me work. And by the direction of the flashes, I was aware that a lot of them were taking pictures.

Thirty feet away, I could hear the ranger calming people down, trying to explain me and my bats, explain that she had alerted park security, that they were en route.

Some guy yelled, "What the hell you think you're doing, pal?"

Others swore at me. Young and old voices. Others shushed them.

The ranger talked sharply to the crowd, ordering them to move away, to move along. That this was sacred ground.

I paid no attention.

I had one more thing to do.

From my backpack, I pulled out Grandad's flag and the wooden plaque. I shined the plaque's gold plate against my shirt. Then I walked to the center of the bats, dropped to my knees, and said another prayer.

This time, for the people in the crowd.

Then I read the inscription. "To *Those*," I whispered. And I silently read the words underneath. The words of Jesus.

But I say unto you, love your enemies,
bless them that curse you, do good to them
that hate you, and pray for them that
despitefully use you, and persecute you.

Then I set the tiny American flag at the center of the arc, fully believing that building this memorial was one of the most American things I could ever do. Cameras clicked like the stadium in a World Series. Or an All-Star game.

I heard people murmuring, the shuffle of feet. I heard a motorcycle roar up, coming closer.

Well, here it is, I thought. My memorial to the millions of men, women, and children who'd died in the Vietnam War.

Now *all* of their families had a place to come, where no one was left out, no one was hated, and everything was fair.

It was then that I mumbled a prayer for Carmine. For forgiveness. And a quick healing.

I did not hear the approach of the man who walked up behind me and shouted, "Freeze! Police! Drop it! Get your hands up where I can see them. Now!"

"Yeah," someone yelled. "Get 'im! Lock 'im up!"

Drop what? I wondered, but I complied with the police officer's request, raising my arms. In a split second, he yanked one arm back, twisting my elbow, and I felt the cold metal cuffs snap around my wrist. Then he cuffed the other one and shoved me chin first onto the grass.

Behind us, I heard clapping and cheering.

"What d'you got here?" the officer asked me. "What's all this mess?"

"Nothing," I squeaked out. "Just a Fourth of July thing."

"Fourth of July? Not what the ranger said." He picked up the plaque, then dropped it on the ground. "Where you from, kid? Where's your parents?"

I twisted to get my breath. "They don't live here. I ran away."

"Don't move. Stay right there. Got that?"

I lay silent, my eyes closed. Nearby, I could hear the tromping of bootsteps. And the rattle and clank of baseball bats being banged together, tossed somewhere in a pile. And the clink of broken ceramic.

"Show's over, folks!" the policeman yelled. "Everyone move back, move on. Show's over."

And he was exactly right. Whatever I was trying to do, trying to prove, was over with. I'd had my chance. And now it was history.

"Excuse me, sir." It was Breena. "I'm his cousin. I helped him."

"How old are you?"

"Thirteen," she said. "We're both thirteen. We're from New York."

"Figures," he answered. "Well, listen, princess. Just sit right here and don't move." As the man walked off, it started to rain.

I closed my eyes, feeling the wetness on my neck and arms.

Not a hard rain. It was one of those strange, East Coast rains. A summer rain. Warm. And teardrop soft.

When I thought it was safe, I whispered to Breena.

"Did you get the picture?"

"I got ten of them," she whispered back.

chapter **3 5**

"SABRINA, I AM *SO* DISAPPOINTED IN YOU," AUNT Chrissy said over and over again as she drove us back to New York. "I thought I could trust you. I thought you had more sense than to do something like this." The more she said it, the more I figured that Aunt Chrissy was implying I had no sense at all.

And maybe she was right.

As it ended up, we never got arrested. That was the good part. They just took us in and called Aunt Chrissy on her cell phone. Which was the bad part.

When she got there—after driving down in the middle of the night, still dressed for the theater—she was so overboard apologetic and full of psychobabble about me and my dad and the "accident" and Grandad being killed in Vietnam and all, that the police just seemed happy to let us go.

But letting it go was harder for Aunt Chrissy.

"Tyler, what am I going to tell your parents? That I can't control you?"

Oh, no, I thought. Don't do that. Don't tell them the truth.

"Or," she continued, "that you're a runaway?"

That made me break my silence. "You don't have to tell them anything. I will."

"Well, I have to let them know. This type of thing can't happen."

Before long, it became obvious she didn't really want to discuss "this type of thing." She just wanted to yell. So I clammed up and spread out across the backseat.

"Oh, but Sabrina," she went on, "I really thought you had more sense than to sneak out in the middle of the night! How can I trust you now?"

"Mom, we were totally safe. Security was everywhere. The whole time we were practically smothered by tourists. The only real scary, dangerous part"—she paused to look at me over the front seat and grin—"was when we got nabbed by the cops. Busted!" Then she actually giggled.

"This is *not* a joke, Sabrina! Vandalizing a public monument. Desecrating a sacred shrine!"

"Mom, it is, too. This whole thing's a total joke. We *put up* a sacred shrine. We really did. Just to the wrong people. And they tore it down. It reminds me so much of what I learned in school about pride. How everyone's so afraid that other people are dissing them. I don't care if it's American pride or white pride or what. People get their feelings hurt so easy. They're so *afraid* of what other people think or what they're gonna say about them. Including you right now."

Whoa, that little speech woke me up. Yo, Breena, I thought. You on fi-yah!

But at 4:00 A.M., my fire was burning low. The

conversation spun around a while longer, then tailed off. Or, at least, I left it. I wasn't worried about anything. Tell my parents, don't tell them. Whatever.

But there was one thing I noticed. Or actually, *didn't* notice.

My anger. Weirdest thing.

Normally, I'd be in a full-on rage at Aunt Chrissy, at the cops, at everybody—4:00 A.M. or not—for putting me down and not seeing my point. But it was like, if she punished me, fine. Called my parents, fine. Whatever.

Just knowing I'd done what I'd done—even though it didn't turn out the way I'd hoped—made me feel better somehow. Stronger. Wiser. That I'd gone out and done something. That I didn't just sit back and watch.

Somehow, knowing I was capable of that made me feel less afraid. And on the ride home, I began to see that when I'm less afraid, I'm less angry.

Weirdest thing.

I even went to bed the next night not sweating the All-Star balloting. Partly because I'd had another great game that afternoon. Tired as I was, I went three-for-four and made a couple tough plays at shortstop. Even a few guys on the other team mumbled, "Nice play. Good stop."

And partly because I just had a feeling. I knew the committee had met that evening. And, okay, I'll admit, I had carried this little thought of giving Coach those pictures Breena took of me and my shrine—they were in my sports bag fresh from the one-hour photo place—

to show him I could think of other people in a different way. But I held off.

Because sometimes you just have to go with your feelings, and I felt I'd earned the All-Star spot. So I figured I'd just go to the picnic and hang loose. Have some fun.

But when I woke up Sunday morning—or I should say, when Aunt Chrissy and Breena pounded on the door and practically woke up the whole Upper West Side—I knew that this was not going to be a normal day.

This day would be wacko.

One look at *The New York Times* told me that.

Aunt Chrissy and Breena rushed in with the paper flapping in Breena's hands. "Tyler, look!"

There, in some special photo section of all the holiday weekend picnics and softball games, was a picture of me and my plaque and the fifty more walls.

The caption was labeled: "To Those . . ." and it told all about the symbolic meaning of the bats and birds. I was kneeling, but you could still see my face, reading the plaque.

Louie took one look, then went back to bed. "How'd they get that stupid picture?" he asked.

"How should I know?" I looked at Breena, who shrugged.

Aunt Chrissy squinted for a closer look. "It says, 'Reuters.' That's a syndicated photo. Did you notice any reporters while you were there?"

"TV," said Breena. "Maybe some others, I don't know."

"But," I said, "how'd they know my name? Or that I'm from New York?"

"You're not from New York, ditz brain," said Louie. "You're just visiting, remember?"

Yeah, I thought, maybe I *am* a visitor, but I got the hometown fans on my side now.

"Oh, wait, Tyler," said Breena. "*I* know. I remember. When all those people were taking pictures, I saw a woman talking to the ranger. Then, later on, the woman came over and asked me who you were and everything. I thought she was somebody official. I mean, she was standing there in the rain writing stuff down."

As it turned out, having my picture in the paper was the best thing that could've happened to me as far as Aunt Chrissy and Louie were concerned. The little spin that the caption put on my "art project" impressed Louie. And Aunt Chrissy liked the way the picture made me look "angelic."

"You're an altar boy at home, aren't you, Tyler?"

"Yeah."

She nodded. "Now I can finally see that side of you."

That afternoon, as Louie and I headed out to the Uptown Riverside Baseball League barbecue picnic and awards ceremony, I was in a pretty good mood, believe me. Seemed like, for the first time in my life, everything was falling into place. That things were finally going my way. Couldn't wait to see Coach. I even hoped

Carmine would be there so I could find out how he was doing.

But it didn't take long for my mood to change.

Coach was there, all right, but he was distant and standoffish, all hunched up over at a table by a tree, way across the grassy clearing, working on some notes or something. And he looked so strange in "civilian" clothes—slacks and a pullover golf shirt—not his usual sweats, baseball cap, and fancy windbreaker.

Later on, when he handed out our league participation trophies and shook our hands, he glanced away on my turn. Like he didn't want to catch my eye. Instantly, I figured, bad news.

But then I thought, I could take it another way, too. That I'd made the team, but he didn't want to let on and spoil the surprise. Fine with me. Besides, I was just there to hang loose. Have some fun.

Or at least, I tried.

After all the teams had passed out their trophies, the big moment came rolling down the grassy meadow like a tank.

Mr. Steinmetz took the microphone and began naming off the All-Star team. In alphabetical order.

Being a *W*, I *hate* alphabetical order. Just meant my heart had to jackhammer my bones that much longer.

At least I found out one good thing. The third name called was Carmine DeLucca. Turns out, he was okay, that all he had was a hyper-extended knee and this big, cool-looking bruise. Mr. Steinmetz said he'd be back to normal in about a week.

"Yo, bro," Louie said to me, and we slapped hands.

As more names were called, I kept track on my fingers. Seemed like each team had one or two guys who made the squad, including Benny Navarro from our team.

Twelve spots were open. And ten had been filled by the time he called, "Seth Talbert!" Only one more left.

I was dying.

Then Mr. Steinmetz paused. He looked out at the crowd, looked us all over, and said, "And now, for our final selection. A young boy who's really come a long way—"

I closed my eyes.

"Tommy Yomada!"

And I died.

Dropping my head, squeezing my eyes, squeezing out all light, especially the white light that flared at the edges of my brain, I started to applaud like everyone else.

After a moment, I looked around, smiling, to hide my pain.

Louie watched, openmouthed, but he had no words for me.

Who did? I stood there smiling like crazy, fighting my tears.

No, no, no, I told myself. I can't get mad. What'd I expect? Coach'd warned me for weeks now. No one had made any promises.

But, man, I thought. I deserved it. I really deserved to be on that team.

Taking a big breath, I reached down, grabbed my pack, and walked off. Slumping down behind a nearby tree, blinking like a bad light, I looked way off, wishing I'd brought my sunglasses, wishing I'd never come to this stinking, noisy, no-good town, full of old, dumb jerks, wishing I'd never played in this stupid league.

Within moments, I felt a hand on my shoulder.

"Got time for a doughnut?"

chapter 36

I COULDN'T ANSWER COACH AT ALL. I NODDED AT him, though, dabbing my eyes with my T-shirt shoulders. Anything to get out of there.

On the way to his little doughnut shop, Coach filled the silence with stuff like the summer weather forecast, how backpacking in the Adirondacks would be cool right now, hiking, fishing. All sorts of stuff, but baseball.

I knew he was trying to ease my pain, and I appreciated it. Still, I was hurting so bad. I was burning. A slow, crawling burn.

Inside the shop, we pulled up chairs at a scruffy table by the window. I sat down with a doughnut and Coke. Before sitting, Coach set down his soupy brown coffee—with little white chunks floating in it—next to a giant cinnamon roll and something long and narrow that he'd brought with him, wrapped up in an old towel.

Then he reached over to an empty table and grabbed a rumpled newspaper. He leafed through until he found the picture of me kneeling on the grass at the National Mall.

He took his seat, giving me a small smile. "You're famous, kid."

I nodded, but before I could even pop the straw into the Coke, he dropped a bomb.

"You know, you made All-Stars," he said.

I looked up at him, feeling as if we were in some kind of dream. "I did?"

"Don't get your hopes up," he continued. "Steinmetz blackballed you."

The burning squeezed all through my gut. "What? What do you mean?"

"We voted you in on Saturday night. It was unanimous. Then your little sortie into D.C. caught his attention in the morning paper, and he called me up and told me to drop you from the squad."

I leaned forward, my chin nearly scraping the table. "You mean, I was actually—can he do that?"

Coach Trioli emptied a sugar pack into his coffee. "Welcome to the real world," he said.

I slumped down into my chair, folding my arms, gazing out the window at a man pushing a stroller past, talking on a phone. A brown-paper bundle of clean laundry hung from the handle by a string. The baby slept. As if the world was still normal.

"He didn't think," Coach went on, "that your actions—coming on the Fourth of July weekend and all—reflected very well on the league. There's a clause in our charter about that." He shrugged. "Steinmetz has veto power. He's the president. He wins." Between sips, Coach added, "Sorry, kid."

I could've said a million things right then, could've banged and yelled and thrown things around, could've stomped off and ran into the park. Could've cussed out New York City and the horse it rode in on. But I didn't. Felt like it, but I didn't.

He pushed the newspaper photo at me. "What's this thing supposed to mean, anyway? Why'd you do it?"

Oh, no, I thought. He hates me, too.

"I don't know." I reached down and fumbled through my bag grabbing Breena's pack of photos. Then I flipped through until I found the one she took from the treetop. The one that showed it all. I set it by Coach's cup.

"This one shows it better. I got the idea from a book on the Vietnam War Memorial. Then I found out my father used to be a sculptor and—I don't know. These ideas just started cooking." I thumb-tapped that photo sitting on the lime green Formica while I stretched my brain to come up with something more.

"It's like, it means remembering, I guess. All the killing. And all the people who died. Not just on our side, but *everyone*. The big picture. You know, so everybody knows. This is sort of like the biggest picture I've ever made."

Coach studied the photo forever. Suddenly I wished I hadn't done it. He was clearly upset. Eyebrows crimped, jaw muscles twitching.

He took another chunk of cinnamon roll, more coffee, swallowing, wiping his mouth with a shriveled napkin. Finally, he looked up.

"I wanna show you something." He picked up the

blue plaid towel and pulled off some rubber bands to unwrap what was inside. Then he opened it up and laid it all on the table.

I saw a smooth, finely crafted wooden spindle. Like the round leg of a fancy piano. Blond wood. Ridges all up and down it. The tip ended in a sharp point. "You make this?" I asked.

"Yeah." He spun it so I could see that the top part had one flat side to it. With a name.

On that section, carved, I could tell, by hand, was the name "Rafael Escalante."

"Who's that?" I asked.

"He's the NYU grad student from my hometown— the clockmaker—I told you about who was in a coma with a cracked skull. Well, what I didn't say was that he died about a week later." Coach forced an unnatural laugh, then went on. "Seeing your picture, kid, got me all worked up about that stuff all over again. And you ruined my whole Sunday morning."

"Sorry."

He wadded up his paper napkin and it disappeared into his fist. "Your little shrine down there—they cleared it all away?"

I nodded, not wanting to say much more about it.

"Well, you cleared something away for me, Tyler." He lowered his head. "Helped me to come to grips with something I tried to let go of a long time ago." A vein in his forehead bulged as he stared back down at the dark photo.

"Because, you see, in a lot of us"—he paused, rubbing

one hand over the other—"underneath the scab and scar of what we think Vietnam was or wasn't, something in there is still festering. In a lot of us."

He didn't have to tell me that. I'd lurked in the chat rooms. I'd felt the anger and the hatred swell up and ooze out.

"I just never realized how much." His nostrils flared as he took a strong breath in, then loudly exhaled. "I don't know what the answer is, kiddo. To healing that wound. I only know I'm still working on it. And that you helped."

He lifted the spindle, tracing the edges with a fingertip. "I'm just glad I had one more old bat stashed away. Because I sure had to do something."

With rough, scarred hands, Coach flipped the spindle over and over, then set it back gently on the blue cloth. After that, he restacked the photos and put them aside. "So how's your old man fit into all of this? He's a sculptor?"

I took a quick breath. "Oh, he—Dad was—well, see, my dad's dad was shot down in Vietnam."

"Yeah, your aunt told me."

"So my dad, he—well, I don't think you would've liked him much in those days. He demonstrated against the war."

Coach pursed out his lips. "I did, too. Near the end, I joined a group of Vietnam vets who all marched against it."

"You did? But you were—I mean, you punched that guy out for being against the war and everything."

"I slugged a long-haired college kid for sneering at me. He didn't say a word. Just gave me a dirty look. Cheese and rice, I hadn't even been to 'Nam yet. I was on my way and was all hopped up about it."

"But some of them spit on guys in airports who were coming home."

He shook his head. "Those stories got started long after the war was over. Mostly in the late eighties. Back when the government needed some new kids for a new war. But first, they needed someone to blame for Vietnam. So they blamed the protesters. But I'll tell you, out of everyone I could aim the blame at for my problems, I never blamed the protesters. They never wanted that war in the first place. Matter of fact, I married one. And I still love her today. But, man, I was hard to live with back then. Hard as a rock."

He drum-rolled the stack of photos and picked them up again, then spoke as he shuffled through once more.

"Tell you who I blamed. The people who treated me the worst when I got back were all the old World War Two vets and all the other people who'd told me to go in the first place. Then, when I got home and showed up back at the trucking outfit in Lakeville, they hardly said boo to me. Never asked a simple, 'How you doing?' Nothing. Treated me like a loser. Like what the heck was wrong with us, that we couldn't 'whip the butts of them little slant-eyed gooks' and all that. I'll never forget it. They didn't care what I'd been through. Didn't want to hear about it. Just wanted me to get over it and get back to work."

Boom. That was bomb number two.

Sneak attack. Never saw it coming.

My face turned hot. Not with embarrassment. But with shame.

Because how those guys'd treated Coach was exactly how I'd been treating my dad for the last nine years. Not caring at all what he'd been through. Just wanting him to get over it.

And I never asked my dad how he was doing, either. Never once. I was too afraid of the answer.

Coach rose, went over to the counter, and got another cup of coffee.

I leaned forward and broke my doughnut in half, crumbling both parts in my fists.

As he sat back down, I said, "Well, thanks for telling me about All-Stars and everything. Face to face. I appreciate it. And it's, you know, it's okay. I mean, big deal. Part of the game, right? And you guys'll still have a good team. At least you got Carmine. He'll help you a lot."

Coach shook his head. "Nope," he said. "I don't have Carmine. I don't have anyone."

"What?" I tried to read his downcast eyes.

"I resigned," said Coach. "Right after Steinmetz called, I went over to his place and turned in my equipment, my All-Star jacket, even my old, chipped clipboard with all the players' names on it."

"Why'd you do that?"

He shrugged. "I been meaning to buy a new clipboard."

"No, I mean—"

Coach laughed. "Matter of principle. And I told him so, the idiot." He pointed a pack of sugar at me. "Told him he had no guts."

He ripped open the sugar, dumped it, gave me a quick look, then stirred his coffee. "Told him that what you did down in D.C. was exactly what we asked you to do."

"Well, you didn't exactly ask me to—"

"No, no," he agreed, tapping the wet spoon on his napkin. "The fine details—that was your choice. And maybe it wasn't politically correct and all that." He sent out a sharp laugh. "But I knew what you were trying to do. Trying to show everybody what you'd learned. And in my book, that's not something you punish a kid for."

I couldn't believe what I was hearing. That he'd given up coaching the All-Star team for me. For a matter of principle. That was huge.

We sat in silence for a while, and all the time I felt more and more uneasy. I mean, baseball meant as much to him as it did to me. What if he regretted all this tomorrow?

"So," I said, grasping for something to say. "No baseball, then, for either one of us. Looks like we'll be taking the summer off."

His eyes held mine while he slowly shook his head. "Not a chance."

Oh, yeah, I thought, he likes traveling and fishing. He'll take a real vacation or something.

Coach swallowed another hunk of his roll. "You got any plans from mid-July to mid-August?"

"Plans? Me? No, not really."

He winked. "You do now."

"What? What do you mean?" Oh, no, I thought, as I imagined backpacking into some desolate wilderness with him, going fly fishing or doing some stupid, sticky, humid thing, with mosquitoes sucking my blood.

He leaned back, wiped his mouth. "I'm putting together a fifteen-and-under traveling tournament team. It'll be ballplayers from all over the city. And it's based on pure skills, not politics. Every boy on the team'll have a real potential of being drafted into pro ball some day. We'll travel from here to California, playing in four or five major tournaments. Boston. Atlanta. Vegas." He paused. "San Diego. Going from town to town, playing five, six games a week."

"Wow! Really?"

He nodded. "Got one or two sponsors in mind already. My new best friend, your uncle Phil, for one. Wait'll he hears about this."

That made us both laugh. Big time.

"He would do it!" I said. "I'm sure he would do it."

"Hey," said Coach, "I see it happening. And it's something I've always wanted to do, put together a club team and hit some of those big tournaments. Just once. But with the All-Star tourney every year, I never had the time."

"Coach, I can't believe this."

He shifted, then reached into his hip pocket and pulled out a piece of paper with a list of names. I saw mine.

"At the picnic today," he said, "I penciled in a pretty good roster. Kids I know. Players I've been watching across town and in some of the other boroughs. Hope to start practice next week. Can I count on you?"

I looked right through my name on that list.

It took only a split second for me to focus in on a distant image of my dad. Man, I thought, what would he think about this? Would he come and actually see me play? On a club team. A traveling *tournament team*.

But in that same moment, I realized it didn't matter. Whether Dad sat some place and watched birds circling the sky or me circling the bases. It didn't matter.

What mattered was that now I knew I could go home and sit down and face him. And not hate him. For anything.

I'd show him the pictures of what I'd built. Ask him about eco-political sculpture, about scavenger art.

Look him right in the eye and ask him how he was doing.

Then listen to his answer.

And then get over it.

"You said, San Diego?" I asked.

"August thirteenth. Last stop. Figured that'd work out good for you."

"Yeah, Coach, it would. Be right before school starts. And, man, I can just imagine my mom and dad up in the stands now." I studied the picture. Liking it.

"Yeah," I said. "Go ahead, count on me."

He nodded, like no big deal. Then his gaze fell back down again. On the spindle made of ash. On Rafael Escalante. He folded the towel over it, snugged the green rubber bands around the bundle, and said, "At first, I thought I was gonna give this to you. But, now I think I'll keep it."

"Yeah, well, you should," I told him. "It's a work of art."

"Not for that," he said, then took another slow breath. "But because my buddy, Rafael, was one of a bunch of kids who got killed back then, starting during the Civil Rights years, then the Vietnam War years, all standing up for what they believed in. Doing what they thought was best for this country. What they thought was right. I'm sure there'll never be a wall to any of them."

He lifted the wrapped towel and tapped it against his palm. "But now you've changed the way I look at D.C."

He scooted his chair out and stood. I did, too.

"I got two good Army buddies on that wall," he said. "Figure I'm ready now to go and pay my respects. But when I do, Tyler, I'm gonna plant this spindle right in the middle of it."

Then he reached out with his hand. I gave him mine, and we shook.

Shook like one part of this broken world had just rejoined the other.

And in that moment, as we stood eye to eye, a light came on. And that's when I knew. Time won't heal anything. No way. It could even make things worse.

Getting in there and doing something, that's what heals.

Breena holding me in the park heals. Coach standing up for me on principle heals. And picking up a battered, busted-up enemy and carrying him to shelter—no matter what anybody else is going to think—that heals.

I cleared my throat. Okay, I thought, if I really believed this stuff, then I should be able to do this.

"So, um, look," I said, forcing myself to talk. "How *are* you doing?"

He freeze-framed me for a second, reading me with his steely gaze, as he let my hand drop. Then I saw a small grin creep up.

"I'm doing okay," he said, and jutted his chin at me. "Thanks for asking."

I nodded and stepped back, scooping my pack strap with my hand. Then I turned.

And headed out into the small, friendly town of New York City.